Silent
Lies

KATHRYN CROFT

Bookouture

Published by Bookouture in 2017

An imprint of StoryFire Ltd.

Carmelite House, 50 Victoria Embankment, London EC4Y 0DZ

www.bookouture.com

ISBN: 978-1-78681-284-1

eBook ISBN: 978-1-78681-283-4

This book is a work of fiction. Names, characters, businesses,
organizations, places and events other than those clearly in the
public domain, are either the product of the author's imagination
or are used fictitiously. Any resemblance to actual persons, living or
dead, events or locales is entirely coincidental.

For Debbie and Lindsey

PROLOGUE

Five Years Ago

For better or worse. That's what marriage is meant to mean, isn't it, Zach? But not for us, not now you've gone.

The few mourners who have actually turned up are now leaving, offering me thin, but kind, smiles, no doubt trying their best to push aside all thoughts of how and why you did this, because it's impossible not to think of it, Zach.

I'm grateful that nobody has asked why there won't be a wake. It just felt wrong, given the circumstances. Impossible to do that for you, even though it's tearing me up that I can't.

Freya cries in my arms; too young, hopefully, to fully understand that we've just said goodbye to her dad. That she'll never see you again. 'It's okay,' I tell her. 'We're going home now. Everything's going to be okay, I promise you.'

'Dada…' she protests, in between her cries.

Salty tears sting my eyes as I place her in her buggy and fasten her in, but I force them back; I can't let her see how much I'm struggling with this.

'Dada, Dada, Dada…' Freya's small, yet huge, words echo in the churchyard, each one crushing me. I walk faster, heading away from the church and out onto the street, hoping the momentum of the buggy will distract her from her chant.

I need to get out of this place quickly because it's not a normal funeral, is it, Zach? Nothing about this situation is anywhere close to normal.

Out of nowhere a hand grabs me. I haven't noticed anyone approaching, but now there are two women right in front of us, both of them strangers.

Their expressions are murderous and such intense hatred seeps from every pore in their bodies that I can almost reach out and touch it.

'That man doesn't deserve a funeral,' the one clasping my arm spits. Her saliva lands on my cheek, but I'm too stunned to wipe it away.

I finally pull free of her grasp. 'Get off me!'

'Did you know?' the other one screams. 'Did you know what he was doing? It's disgusting. Despicable. And you're just as much to blame for being married to him.'

There is no point responding to this; trying to explain that I had no idea about anything, because the last few weeks have taught me that people like this don't want to listen – they need someone to bear the brunt of their anger.

I try to swerve the buggy around them but they block my path. My heart thuds violently. Another thing I've learnt is that these people aren't afraid to cause harm; to them it is justified.

One of them points at Freya, who is innocently watching the proceedings, staring wide-eyed at these two women. 'And that's his daughter. Poor kid! When are you going to let her know her father's a monster?'

'Monster,' Freya mimics, and that's when I ram the buggy straight in between them and run as fast as I can.

'You're just as bad as he is,' someone shouts after me. 'You should have known what he was doing. What kind of wife doesn't know what her husband is up to? I hope you rot in hell!'

But how could I have known, Zach? How could I possibly have comprehended what you were capable of?

ONE

Now

Mia

Someone is watching me, I'm sure of that. As Freya runs off to play on the swings, I glance around the park, but there's nobody acting out of the ordinary, only mothers like me with their young children, a few dog walkers and an elderly couple huddled together on a bench, smiling gently as they gaze at everyone, perhaps remembering when they themselves had young children. The bright sun bathes us in its warmth; this is a picture of innocence – surely nothing terrible can happen on a day like this? And there is nobody here who should pay me any attention.

'Mum!' Freya yells. 'Watch me, watch me!'

It is easy to get lost in watching Freya; she has turned into a beautiful, lively seven-year-old, despite the start she had in life, and I'm only thankful she was too young to know anything, too young to even remember her father. She is gliding through the air now, her legs swinging beneath her as she gathers momentum on the swing. Her gleeful smile brings one to my own face, but still I cannot shake the feeling of eyes being upon me.

A hand touches my shoulder, causing me to leap up.

'Sorry, Mia, didn't mean to scare you.' Will, my partner, has somehow crept up without me – or Freya – noticing.

'Don't do that! I thought… Never mind. Just don't do it again, please.'

He holds up his hands. 'Okay, I'm sorry. I really didn't mean—'

'I know, I know. I'm just a bit jumpy, that's all.'

Will scrunches his face and I can guess what he's doing. He's calculating dates to see if it's the anniversary, or Zach's birthday, perhaps. The day I married him, or the day we met. He's wondering if it could be any of these things. But it isn't, and I can't explain why I feel so on edge.

'Why?' he says, frowning. 'Can I do anything to help?'

This is Will all over. Mr Fix-It – if he can.

I shake my head and brace myself for his disappointment. 'No, it's nothing. I think I've probably just taken on too many clients this month. It's hard trying to fit them all in, in just three days.' As soon as I say this I regret it. Will already thinks I'm doing too much by setting up my own counselling business a few months ago, but I need to help people. It's the only thing I want to do.

It's Wednesday today and as it's the summer holidays I've kept my mornings free of clients so I can be with Freya until Will comes over. Sometimes I can't believe how much he does for us. He saves his annual leave for Freya's school holidays so that he can take afternoons off when I need help with childcare. It can't be easy – he's an accountant in a huge firm and I know he's hoping for a promotion soon, so taking so much time off in that way probably doesn't look good. But that's just the kind of thing he does for us. Sooner or later it's bound to take its toll, though.

Care of my daughter is not Will's responsibility; we're not married and we don't even live together – despite his numerous requests – so I owe him a huge debt of gratitude for doing so much for Freya. One day I will be able to do it. But he understands that I can't just replace Zach.

'Is there any way you can—'

'I can't stop seeing people if they need me, Will. But I won't take on anyone new for now.'

He nods. 'That's a good idea. And you're doing all right for money, aren't you? Because if you ever need anything, all you need to do is ask.'

Zach and I never took out life insurance but, financially speaking, I'm okay. I work hard to make sure Freya has everything she needs without being spoilt, and I will never let myself be dependent on anyone.

I grab Will's hand and pull him down next to me on the bench, while Freya screams in delight from up in the air and lets go of one side of the swing to wave to Will. I gesture for her to hold on with both hands. 'Thank you. That means a lot to me, but I'll be fine.'

Will waves back at Freya. 'I guess that means you won't think about me moving in yet? Or if that's too weird we could get a new place together? I know you love Ealing so I'm more than happy to live anywhere around here. I just had my flat valued and I can get quite a lot for it at the moment. Apparently, after all the turmoil with the housing market, it's a good time to sell.'

I picture Will's flat – a pristine new build in Chiswick – and have no doubt he'd do well if he sold it, but moving in together is not a decision I can make with my head. It's my heart that has to tell me the time is right.

Squeezing his hand, I hope that even some small part of him will understand how I feel. 'I'm just not ready yet, Will, I'm so sorry. I'm not saying never, but not just now. I need to get the business more established and, well, Freya's so happy right now. For the last five years it's just been the two of us in our house, so...' But Freya loves Will and he's been like a father to her for the last two years, so I shouldn't use that as an excuse. I correct myself. 'But I know she'd love it if you moved in...'

Will sighs and takes a moment to answer. 'It's okay, I know *you* have to be ready too.' He turns to watch Freya, unable to look me in the eye because yet again I have rejected him. The kindest man I could ever meet.

But didn't I think that about Zach? He had my complete trust and it was shattered into a thousand pieces. I won't let that affect my feelings for Will, though. I have to be fair to him: he is not Zach.

Oblivious to the thoughts swirling around my head, Will turns to me. 'Hey, isn't your client due in a minute? You'd better get going.'

I grab my phone to check the time. I've been so wrapped up in my claustrophobic bubble, while Freya played, that I didn't realise I needed to get back. A new client, a woman I haven't seen before, is coming at 2 p.m.

'Good job you only live across the road!' Will says. I know what he's doing: bringing humour to the moment so that I don't meet a new client while burdened with guilt.

'I'll take Freya to the cinema,' he suggests. '*Beauty and the Beast* is on, I think.' Knowing Will, he'll have already checked this and worked out the best showing to see, and calculated what time they will have to leave to get there so that they don't miss any of the film.

'Thank you so much,' I say, my words coming out as barely a whisper because I'm so choked up by his thoughtfulness.

I leave the park and glance towards my house. The house Zach and I saved all our money for all those years ago, with the hope of a future for our little family.

Before I cross the road, I turn back and see Freya wrapping her arms around Will. He lifts her up in the air and she squeals with delight. The elderly couple on the bench across the park nod and smile. They probably think Will is Freya's dad. Sometimes I really wish he was.

At home I head straight to my office to wait for my client. I'm lucky to be able to work from home and not have to rent office space, and my room is right next to the front door, a separate area from the rest of my home. It's important to me to have a clear division between work life and my life with Freya, and so far this has worked well. The downstairs toilet is also right by the office, so I can be sure no clients need to see the rest of the house. When Zach and I bought this place I never thought I'd be working here, or that he would be gone.

Now I'm in this space I immediately switch into work mode, pushing all other thoughts aside. I've become good at doing this. But Zach would probably say that I always was, even before. I need to give one hundred per cent to this woman, due at any moment. To remind myself of her name, I check my appointment book.

Alison Cummings. She only called a couple of days ago, informing me that she thought she needed counselling after being in an abusive relationship. That was all the information she offered. I have no clue how old she is or whether she has any children, but I'm sure I will find that out in good time.

She is late. Not a good start. Minutes tick by and I'm about to give up on her – it's to be expected that people have second thoughts when it comes to baring their souls – but then the doorbell chimes and I stand, straightening my jeans before I head to the front door. I don't dress formally for my sessions; I've found that wearing casual clothes helps put people at ease, enabling them to see me as someone just like them, someone they can open up to.

The first thing I notice about her is how young she is. She barely looks twenty, but when I study her further, I realise my assumption comes from her being so tiny in stature. I am only five foot four, but I seem to tower over her, even though we're on level ground. From head to foot she's dressed in black, despite the heat, and I can't tell whether she's wearing leggings or jeans, but they cling to her stick-like legs, further emphasising her petite frame.

'Mia Hamilton?' she asks, her voice quiet and unsure.

I hold out my hand. 'You must be Alison. Nice to meet you, come in.'

Her hand is fragile and thin like the rest of her, but also moist. She is nervous.

I stand back so she can enter the house, but she stands like a statue on the doorstep, making no move to go anywhere. 'Alison? Are you okay?'

She nods, but still doesn't move, and her eyes take in my home. 'So is this where you live?' she asks. 'I thought it would be… an office or something.'

'I work from home and my office is just there.' I point to the left to show her how close it is to the front door, to make her feel safer.

'Okay.' Finally she steps forward and I close the door behind us. 'Can I get you anything to drink?' I ask, as we head into my office. Now she is right by me I can smell her shampoo, or whatever hair product she's used today. It could even be perfume. For some reason it makes me think of Zach, although I have no idea why; it is definitely a female scent.

She eyes the cabinet in the corner where I keep a kettle, some mugs and a jug for water. 'No, I'm fine, thanks.'

'Not even a glass of water? It's very warm out there today. And in here, actually. I'm sorry I don't have air conditioning, but it is something I'm planning to sort out.' I am rambling as if I am nervous, but I don't know why. I always find first sessions tricky, before I've got to know a client, because it's hard not to feel judged. People have expectations; somehow they expect you to have all the answers, when the truth is it's a journey we have to go through together, and that means I need to get to know them. Know what puts them at ease and what makes them uncomfortable.

But there is more to it than that this afternoon, only I can't pinpoint what it is.

'Take a seat, Alison.' I open the window – the air in here feels thick and cloying – and the sounds from the park across the road immediately drift in. 'So, let me tell you a bit about myself first.'

She nods and her shoulders droop slightly; clearly she is relieved I'll be doing the talking first.

'I studied psychology at university, but then took a few years out to travel. I went all over the place, actually: Thailand, America, New Zealand, Europe…' As I recite some of the places I went to, I feel detached, as if I'm discussing someone else's life. Because it was all before, and I am a different person now. 'Then I met my husband and we had a little girl. She's seven now.' Of course I don't mention that Zach is dead, or that I never really knew the man I was married to.

Will would be devastated, would probably question our whole relationship, if he found out I never mention him in these introductions, but how can I? It would throw up questions I'm not able to answer, and I can't have my clients encroaching on my personal life: the boundaries have to be clear.

'Yes, I saw you in the park just now with your daughter. She's very sweet. I had no idea it was you, of course, until you opened the door just now.'

So I was right to believe someone was watching me in the park. Well, at least it was only this woman. 'Thank you. Anyway, a couple of years ago I trained as a counsellor and now here I am. Do you have any questions before we get started?'

Alison shakes her head and a curtain of dark red hair falls across her face.

'Okay. Well, you've made contact with me because you feel there are some things you could do with talking through. Do you want to tell me what it is that's causing you emotional pain?'

'It's hard to talk about,' she says, staring past me to the window. A stream of sunlight covers half her face, and I have to turn my chair to see her clearly. 'I… my partner… he… hits me.' She looks back at me to check my reaction, perhaps thinking I will judge her, but I remain impassive.

'I know I should leave him, but it's not that simple,' she continues. 'Oh, God, I know what I must sound like. But we have a history together, a complicated one. We've been through a lot together.'

On the phone, Alison had led me to believe she had come out of the relationship, and now she is telling me something different. But I cannot make a big deal of this; I'm just grateful she's being so open. Usually it takes longer than this to get to the root of things.

'Please don't tell me to go to the police,' she says, before I even open my mouth to speak. 'That's just not an option.'

'It's understandable that you're afraid, but there are safe places you can go, and they'd make sure he couldn't hurt you again. That's the number-one goal, isn't it?'

She doesn't answer, and a heavy silence fills the room, somehow stifling the roar of car engines and the shrieks from the park.

Alison sighs. 'Please, can we just talk about it without you trying to get me to report him? Aren't you supposed to help me find the strength to get away from him?'

Those expectations again. The belief that I can wave a magic wand and banish all problems. Life just isn't that straightforward – I know that well enough. We bear the scars of our past, permanent tattoos carved onto our skin, whoever we are.

'Okay,' I say. 'Then why don't you start by telling me more about what's going on? How does that sound? Don't worry about anything else for now.'

She clasps her hands together and sucks in a deep breath. 'I was young when we met. I mean, I'm only twenty-six now, but I was twenty-one at the time. He's a lot older than me. Forty-one when we met.' Her eyes scan my face, searching once again for signs of judgement, but that is the last thing she will find.

I do a quick calculation and work out he must be about forty-six now. With a nod, I wait for her to continue.

'I really didn't like him at first. That's the ironic thing. In fact, I would actually say I hated his guts. He was arrogant. So full of himself, as if the world owed him.' Her eyes drop to her lap. 'I suppose that makes it even worse, doesn't it? That I saw signs of the person he was before I even got involved with him.' She pauses for so long that I wonder if she will ever speak again.

'How did you meet?' I need to get the conversation moving, and this is a harmless enough question.

'At his work. Well, actually, it was university for me. He was a lecturer there. Not mine, but that doesn't matter, does it?'

My chest tightens and it feels as if it will collapse inwards. It's just a coincidence. I need to hold it together, but I can't seem to manage any words. It is all coming back to haunt me.

Alison leans forward, frowning. 'Mia? Are you okay?' Our roles have reversed and now Alison seems like the counsellor while I am the one needing help.

I manage a nod. 'Sorry, please continue.' For show I grab a tissue from the box on my desk. 'I get really bad hay fever and, well, the pollen levels are extra high today.'

She frowns, but carries on speaking, and I try to focus on each word she says, though they are now blurring into each other.

'We got together by accident. I was drunk and I shouldn't have gone anywhere near him, but I was feeling so bad about myself, so… I don't know… rejected, by everyone and everything, and I think I just needed to know someone wanted me. Does that make me a weak person?'

'No, definitely not. It makes you human.' It's a struggle to remain present, but I must force myself to focus if I'm to have any chance of helping this woman. 'It's understandable to feel like that, Alison. We all lapse in judgement sometimes, don't feel guilty about that.'

She shakes her head. 'It's not guilt I feel. I have more than enough to feel guilty about, but that's not it in this case.' She pauses. 'Stupid, that's how I feel.'

'Well, you'd been drinking.'

'A lot. And I never normally touch alcohol. If only I hadn't. Everything would be different and I'd be… free.'

'So you feel like a prisoner?'

'Yes, that's it. A prisoner in my own life.'

'Again, that's normal,' I say. 'But what we've got to do is work out how to get you out of this prison, and there's always a way.' Wasn't I evidence of exactly that?

'I've got to get the key from Dominic and set myself free,' she says, staring me straight in the eye.

And now there is no way to ignore the huge coincidence. I'm burning up, suffocating, and I can't escape. 'Dominic?'

'Yes, my partner.' And this time her voice is firmer, more controlled; she is almost a different person. 'And I think you know who he is.'

Her words are a punch to my gut. Who is this woman and what is she doing here?

'Dominic Bradford,' she says, when I cannot bring myself to speak. 'I believe he was a colleague of your husband, Zach.'

His name echoes into the room and bile rises in my throat. 'Who… who are you?'

'Exactly who I said I was. I just didn't mention that I know who you are, or that I'm here to tell you your husband didn't kill himself.'

TWO

Five years earlier

Josie

Do you ever get the feeling you don't fit in? Like you're the wrong piece of a jigsaw puzzle, trying to wedge yourself into a space you just can't squeeze into? Well, that's how I feel every day of my life. They all think I'm just a party girl, that I spend more time downing shots than studying, and do you know what? They're right.

It's a miracle I've even made it through the first three months of university, but I got this far to spite her, because she doesn't believe for one second that I'll make it. But here I am, Liv.

Although there are days, like today, when I want to just jack it all in.

The coffee shop is empty this evening so I've pretty much been left alone to deal with the customers, although Pierre is in the back office if I need help. It's suffocating me, being in this place, but I need to pay my rent so I just have to suck it up. I'm not one of those girls who's lucky enough to have parents supporting her. No, I'm the other kind. The kind nobody can believe has made it this far, one of those girls who ends up in trouble before they're out of their twenties. But I revel in their shock. It drives me, spurs me on to do even better with my life. I will not be like *her*.

I'm so wrapped up in these thoughts that I haven't noticed the middle-aged woman who has approached the counter and is now staring at me, hands on her hips and an impatient frown on her face. A designer handbag hangs from the crook of her arm and she teeters on heels that are too high for her. She shakes her head and huffs at me.

Screw her, I'm only human, and if she knew me she'd understand why I have trouble concentrating sometimes.

'A skinny cappuccino,' she says, with no greeting or smile. Maybe her tight, thin lips aren't capable of one. Perhaps it would just crack her face. She pulls out a matching designer purse and squints at me. 'Are you allowed to wear that thing in your nose when you're serving people?'

She's talking about the small diamond stud in my nose. But I'm used to it. Used to people silently, or not so silently sometimes, thinking, *She would be pretty if she lost that disgusting thing.*

Even though I want to scream at her to go and get her bloody coffee somewhere else and take her judgement with her, I plaster on my sweetest smile and say, in an exaggeratedly posh voice, 'Of course. Is there anything else I can get you?' The smile is painful, straining my face.

'No, that's all.' She pushes back her coat sleeve – on her thick wrist is a shiny gold watch, which probably cost more than my car – and shakes her head when she notices the time. It's all for show, to force me to hurry up, and because of this I take my time, pretending I'm having trouble with the coffee machine. I give her a shrug, as if to say I'm sorry, but inside I'm smirking.

Don't get me wrong – I have nothing against wealthy people. Good for them. What I can't take is people looking down on others, thinking they're better than you.

When she finally leaves, I silently pray she disliked me enough to never come back in here, no matter how desperate she gets for caffeine, and then I clean the coffee machine again, just for something to do. This shift is the worst; it's late and people are travelling home from work and probably not expecting us to be open, but Pierre insists on staying open until eight. He must know these last two hours are dead ones, but if he does, it doesn't faze him. Perhaps he makes extra money doing something else. It wouldn't surprise me. He's always getting calls on his phone and never lets anyone hear what he's saying. A bit dodgy, if you ask me. And believe me, I know how to spot it.

So I've got two more excruciating hours here, then an assignment waiting for me at home that I will probably fail, and each minute ticking by feels like a year. But then I turn around and a familiar face is smiling at me.

Zach Hamilton, one of my lecturers.

It takes me a moment to place him because he is so out of context here; I've never seen him outside of the university buildings.

'Hi,' he says. 'Josie, isn't it?'

How does he know my name? He must have a thousand students to teach and the academic year only started a couple of months ago. 'Yeah, hi. Um, what can I get you?'

He orders an espresso to have sitting in and hands me a crisp new five-pound note. And as I turn away to prepare it, I feel his eyes on me.

'Actually, I wanted to have a quick word with you after the lecture today, but you disappeared before I could catch you.'

This doesn't sound good. I search my brain for something I could have done to warrant him needing to speak to me. 'Yeah, I had to go home before I came to work.' I hand him his drink. 'What was it about?' But I already know. He's going to tell me my first assignment was rubbish, that I've got no chance of passing this module so I may as well give up now.

'Nothing bad at all. Um, maybe we could have a chat now? Do you get a break?'

I'm not really given a break at this time, but I'm allowed to have a cigarette out the front if I get desperate. Thankfully, Pierre smokes so he's happy to indulge me. I tell this to Zach.

He turns and glances through the window. 'Okay, I can have this sitting out there. It might be minus five degrees but what the hell?'

The first thing I do when I get outside is light up because I'm nervous. There is so much riding on my degree and I can't afford to fail a module. 'So are you going to put me out of my misery?' I ask, taking a deep pull on my cigarette and sitting opposite him. I don't mean for the smoke to head straight in Zach's direction, but it does and he tries to discreetly wave it away. 'Sorry. You're not a smoker, are you?'

'No, not now, but I used to be in my youth.'

I laugh because he must only be in his thirties. 'Yeah, I can see you're heading for retirement.' As soon as I say this I wonder where it's come from. This man is one of my lecturers, not someone to have friendly banter with, but it's too late to take it back now.

Thankfully he chuckles. 'Not just yet. Anyway, I want to talk to you about your short story assignment. I've just finished marking them and, well, quite frankly, I was blown away by yours.'

I stare at him, wondering if somehow I've misheard. Or misunderstood. Does he mean he liked it? He can't mean that. He must have got me mixed up with another student.

When I don't answer, he carries on speaking. 'Where did that come from? I mean, you're so young to have such insight. I don't mean to be patronising, but if I hadn't known who'd written it I would swear they were much older.'

So he liked it. Relief pumps through my body, but I am still in shock. Nobody has ever praised me before. Not for something I've done, or created. The only compliments I've ever had have been from lecherous men, right before they've tried to sleep with me. 'Um, thank you. I… I just wrote from the heart.'

He has no idea just how true this is. That I was able to bring my story to life because it was partly about *her*. I laid bare my soul with those words, but I guess it was worth it.

'And I'm older than you think,' I tell him. 'It took me a while to get my A-levels, so I'm already twenty-one.' The age of most third-year students.

Zach smiles. 'Well, you've got a real talent, Josie. I really felt the character's despair. What are you planning to do after university? I know you've only just started, but these years will fly by, you know. You really should think about what you want to do.'

But time isn't passing quickly for me, it is stagnant, and the end of these student days can't come soon enough. I need an accomplishment behind me, something to prove I really am nothing like *her*, that I'm not the selfish, heartless woman she is, because there are brief moments, tiny fragments of time, when I actually begin to wonder.

I don't want to tell Zach I'm not sure, that it's hard enough getting through each semester without the added pressure of deciding what to do with my qualification. But I'm not a fool – I know I need to decide quickly. The job market is tough and there is too much competition, too many people will be graduating with me. People who are much better than I am.

The answer comes to me without any thought. 'Teacher training, I think. English, of course. Secondary school. The truth is, English is the only subject I've ever been interested in. The only one I was good at.'

A smile spreads across his face. 'I'm sure that's not true. But that's great that you want to teach. It's difficult, but definitely rewarding, I'd say. It means another year of studying, though, after your degree.'

But hopefully by then I should be better able to deal with it. Once I know I can achieve something. Yes, I have my A-levels, but I barely scraped by with the bare minimum I needed, and had to wait for clearing to get my place at the University of West London. I had my heart set on London, but I would have gone anywhere I could to get away from Brighton.

I take another pull on my cigarette, careful this time to turn right round when I exhale, and then look at Zach's kind face. 'Can I ask you something?'

'Of course.' He lifts his espresso and takes a sip.

'Do you have any advice for… prioritising, I guess. I mean, things just keep getting in the way and I feel like I'm getting behind with it all. It's weird – I want this so badly yet… I just keep procrastinating. Going out when I should be studying, then everything gets done at the last minute.' I don't tell him that it's much deeper than this. That I need to be out of the flat and out of my mind – vodka or gin will usually do the trick – so I don't have to think about anything. Then the next day I hate myself, and cram in as much studying as I can to make up for it. I will burn out soon enough – it has to all catch up with me eventually.

'Hmm,' Zach says. 'That's a tricky one. I probably shouldn't say this but when I was in my first year at uni I didn't take it too seriously. I think I was out most nights, just getting used to, and making the most of, student life. But I knuckled down eventually. And do you know what? You will be fine. If you can produce work like you've just done for me then you've got nothing to worry about.'

His words flow over me, wrapping me in a warm blanket. This man really believes in me. Trouble is how do I believe in myself?

I don't know what makes me confide in him even more. Perhaps it's the kindness he's showing, or the belief he seems to have in me. 'Sometimes I just feel like walking away, to be honest.' But the second the words leave my mouth, I regret revealing so much. He will think I am a waste of time now, not worth his attention or advice.

He shakes his head. 'Don't ever do that, Josie. Don't be a quitter. At anything.'

'You're right. And I probably should stop going out so much. I need to be more focused.' But I already know the challenge this will bring: it's not easy to go against the grain of who you are.

'Well, remember to cut yourself some slack, too,' Zach says. 'You need a balance. But you know what? I really believe you can have anything you want if you put your mind to it.' He stares up at the dark sky. 'What I'm trying to say is, just never give up.'

Crushing out my cigarette in an ashtray that needs cleaning, I stand up. 'I've taken up too much of your time already,' I say. 'Enjoy your coffee.'

He reaches out his hand to shake mine and it's surprisingly warm. 'Nice chatting to you, Josie Carpenter.'

As I walk back inside, an unfamiliar feeling overcomes me. I can do this. Zach believes in me. He liked my story. I'm going to make a go of this.

When I step inside the café, I turn around and he's still watching me.

The flat stinks, as usual, of Alison's cheap perfume and the cloying vanilla scent of the candles she insists on placing in every room. She never says anything but I'm sure it's to hide the smell of my cigarettes. Even though I only ever smoke hanging out of my bedroom window, the smell somehow seeps into all the rooms.

Alison and I couldn't be more different from each other, yet here we are, sharing this poky flat, in each other's pockets, when both of us know we can't stand the sight of each other. We can't even make small talk about our studies as I know nothing about environmental science and she shows no interest in literature or creative writing.

The dopey woman who arranged our flat-share said she was sure we'd have a lot in common. That even though Alison was a third-year student and I was just beginning my first, we were the same age so should get along fabulously. Like that's all it takes. I hit it off better with my lecturer within minutes – as opposed to the months I've lived with Alison – and he said goodbye to his twenties some time ago.

I think Alison and I each expect the other to request an accommodation transfer from the university, but for some reason neither one of us has bothered so far. I would do it, but I don't need the hassle of uprooting myself again. I can stick it out until summer and then I will definitely not share with her again in my second year.

It's dark in here, other than the faint orange glow from the street light right outside, so I know she's not home, but we never tell each other where we're going.

As I always do when I find myself at home alone, I head to Alison's room and try the door handle. Just to see. But of course it's locked, as it always is. I don't know how she got a lock on her door when I don't have one, but I think her dad must have done it for her.

Either she doesn't trust me or she's got something to hide, but it's hard to imagine Miss Studious Bookworm has a dead body hidden under her bed. I laugh at the thought. She's so frail and skinny I doubt she'd have the strength to do anyone any harm. But then again, it's the quiet ones you have to watch out for. She's always staring at me, and I have no idea why.

My stomach rumbles so I head to the kitchen to get something to eat. There is nothing in my cupboard but a half-empty bottle of ketchup, not even bread, and the nearest shop is a half-hour walk away, so I ransack Alison's supplies. Another difference between us: her cupboard is full of food, all of it neatly arranged with all the labels facing forwards.

I grab a can of tomato soup and a couple of slices of bread; I've done it before on the odd occasion and she never says anything, so I don't think she notices. Or she's too afraid to confront me. Yes, I feel bad, but not too bad – her parents pay her rent every month and send extra money for food so she doesn't have to pull shifts in a coffee shop to get through her degree.

While I eat my soup I think of my conversation with Zach Hamilton and how he raved about my short story. I replay his words in my head and they fill me up, making me float.

My phone beeps with a text and I scoop it up, smearing the screen with a residue of butter. I wipe it off with a sheet of kitchen roll that's been left lying on the table, probably by me, earlier. I'm not messy, but Alison's ridiculous cleanliness drives me crazy, shouts out for me to defy it.

The text is from Anthony, a psychology student I met in a bar last week. Did something happen between us? I remember black hair, golden skin, stubble on his face, as if he was trying to prove he was a grown man, him leaning in to me, whispering something about me being hot, but I'm sure I pushed him away, as I always do.

I read his short message: *Wanna meet up tonight?*

No *How are you?* or *Hope you're okay.* He may as well just ask me if I'll screw him.

Sorry, busy. I press send and smile as I imagine the look on his face as he reads my rejection.

Another text comes through, this time from someone I'm actually happy to hear from: Vanessa, another student I met somewhere along the way, asking if I'm up for a night of tequila shots at her place. The thrill of the offer is hard to resist. Vanessa is a good laugh, and she doesn't judge me or anyone else. I wouldn't call her a friend, but it's nice to have superficial acquaintances in the absence of anything else.

I'm still eating when a key turns in the front door and Alison appears in the kitchen doorway, a ridiculously large bag slung over her arm, textbooks poking out. I'm surprised her body can bear the weight of it.

'Hi,' she says, her eyes flicking to my bowl of unfinished soup. Her reddish hair, set in pristine waves, glints in the light. She places her bag on the floor.

'Hi.' We may dislike each other but there's no harm in being polite if we're going to be stuck with each other until summer.

'I'm surprised you're home,' she says, in her passive aggressive way. Why doesn't she just come right out and say, *It's almost 9 p.m., shouldn't you be off your skull by now?*

I push my bowl aside. 'Felt like a night in.'

She doesn't reply, but opens her food cupboard and rummages around, turning back to glance at my bowl. I pray for her to say something this time, to confront me so we can have a huge row that will force one of us to call accommodation services to request an immediate transfer.

But all she does is rearrange her food to cover the gap her can of soup has left.

I almost feel guilty again now. Perhaps I will replace it tomorrow. After all, we can't help the families we're born into. Some of us are just dealt a shitty blow, while others, like Alison, have perfect, doting parents. Anyway, she may be weird but she's never actually done anything to me, apart from her freaky staring. I can live with that; I've lived with far worse.

I head to my room and lie on the bed, surprised to find I'm thinking about Zach Hamilton again. Minutes later, I jump up to sit at my desk. Before turning on my laptop, I text Vanessa to let her know I won't be going out tonight.

I've got studying to do.

THREE

Mia

It's no exaggeration to say that the walls are closing in on me, sucking out my breath. I stare at the frail young woman sitting opposite me, and in an instant her eyes change from defiant to frightened, as if someone has flicked a switch.

'What? What did you say?'

Her face crinkles. 'What do you mean? I was just telling you I need to get the key from my partner to set myself free. We were talking about me being a prisoner in my own life.' She leans forward. 'Are you okay, Mia?'

Panic floods through me. Perhaps I'm losing my mind. Post-traumatic stress disorder or something. It's only to be expected after what happened. It's a miracle I've held it together this long. But I heard her. I couldn't have imagined it. 'You just mentioned my husband, Alison.'

She frowns and shakes her head. 'No, I didn't. You must be mistaken. I was talking about my partner. I don't know your husband.'

I stare at her, shock rendering me speechless. But I know what I heard. 'What's your partner's name?'

'Aaron. I told you that. Didn't you write it down?'

But I don't take notes during my sessions, in case it intimidates people that I'm writing things they cannot see. I note down all the important details afterwards, once I'm alone. 'No, I didn't. But I know you said his name was Dominic. That's not a name I'd forget.'

She shakes her head again, wrapping her arms around herself. 'Oh, that's weird. But I didn't say that. You're freaking me out now. What sort of counsellor are you? You haven't even been listening to me and now you're making things up.'

I'm about to try and reason with her but before I can work out how to do that, Alison is standing up and storming out of my office, slamming the front door behind her, a trail of her flowery scent following her out.

From the window I watch her cross the road and head past the park, her black figure a sharp contrast to the blinding sunshine. I'm tempted to run after her, but what would I say? What if she's right and I didn't hear what I thought I had? But how is that possible? It's been five years since Zach died, why would my mind start reliving it so intensely now?

The shortness of breath comes quickly, along with the feeling that I'm about to suffocate. I rush to my chair to sit down, but it does little to stop me shaking.

I glance at the clock on the wall and it's only two twenty, which means she was only in here for twenty minutes. Opening my desk drawer, I pull out her folder and scan the contact sheet. I always get a phone number and address for my clients, but even as I key in the digits of her mobile number I know there will be no ringtone.

I'm right, and I disconnect the call, more confused than ever.

Desperate for fresh air, I run through the house to the back garden, falling to a heap on the decking.

'Mummy? Mummy, are you okay?' Freya's small hand is shaking me, and slowly I open my eyes. Her large brown eyes stare down at me and beside her Will kneels and helps pull me up.

'What happened? Are you okay?' His voice is steady; he is holding it together, despite how shocking it must be to come back and find me sprawled out here like this.

'I'm… I think so. I must have collapsed or fainted. I don't remember.'

But I do. I remember everything. Alison Cummings. The statement she made about Zach not committing suicide and then, two seconds later, her claim to have said no such thing. I feel dizzy, sick to my stomach.

'Can you get Mummy some water please, Freya?' Will helps me to one of the garden chairs and I sink into the cushion.

'What time is it?' I ask, patting my pockets for my mobile. But I feel nothing in there other than some tissues, so I must have left it in my office.

'Almost four. We didn't go to the cinema in the end. Freya changed her mind about the film so we went to Creams instead. I hope that's okay? I know you try not to give her too much sugar.'

I nod and thank him. Right now it doesn't matter if Freya had some ice cream; that's the least of my worries.

Will scans the garden. 'What were you doing out here?' he asks. 'Did you see your client at two?'

'Yes, I saw her,' I say, and he frowns, as if he doesn't believe my story, as if something doesn't quite make sense. But how can I tell him the rest without sounding delusional? Without sounding like I'm the one in need of help?

'And did it go okay?' Will asks. 'What happened after that? Can you really not remember?' He sighs. 'I'm worried about you, Mia, and I think we need to get you to a doctor. Or at least call 111 and see what they think?'

He asks so many questions that I don't know which one he expects me to answer first. Will means well, but there is no way I'm going to the hospital. 'No,' I say, 'I'm not sitting around in A&E

for hours just to be told I had heatstroke or something. Maybe I didn't drink enough today. That must be it. Honestly, I'm fine now.'

Physically, maybe, but what about my mind? I keep this thought to myself.

But Will won't let this go easily; he's not the type to accept something without questioning everything he's told, instead preferring to investigate and analyse for himself. 'Do you think that's what it is then? You were out in the sun too long? Got dehydrated?'

I grab his hand, in part to prove to him how hot and sticky my own is. 'Yes, I'm sure it's that. It's sweltering today.'

Will's mouth twists – he's not convinced – but he finally gives me the benefit of the doubt. At least for now. 'Okay, Mia, but if you won't get checked out then I'm not leaving you alone tonight. I should be here in case it happens again.' He puts his hands up. 'Don't worry, I'll sleep in the spare room again. I know you don't want Freya to see us sharing the same bed.'

What he's saying makes sense; I have my daughter to think about and I can't risk fainting again. I'm sure it's just the shock of what I heard – or thought I heard – Alison Cummings say, but I won't take any chances.

'Thanks,' I tell Will. 'That would be good.'

His face doesn't light up as I've expected, and the shadow of his frown remains there. 'I'll have to pop home quickly and get some things. I've got a presentation tomorrow and need my laptop.'

Freya appears, carefully holding a glass in both hands. She's overfilled it and water spills over the edges, sloshing onto her sandals and the decking. I rush to take it from her before it ends up all over her. 'Thank you, sweetheart.'

'Are you okay now, Mummy? I was really scared.'

Putting my glass on the garden table, I grab her and hold her tightly. 'I'm fine, nothing to worry about. I think the sun just made me a bit dizzy, that's all.'

She squints, and I know she's deciding whether or not to believe me. Even though she doesn't remember Zach, she knows he was taken from us and it gives her a lot of anxiety. It breaks my heart and I often have to reassure her that I'm not going anywhere.

But how can I be so sure? I didn't think Zach would be dead so young. None of us know what's around the corner.

Alison Cummings. Who the hell is she?

'Okay, Mummy.' Freya's little arms tighten around me and I wipe a smudge of vanilla ice cream from her hair.

'Hey, guess what? Will's going to stay the night, won't that be exciting?'

She jumps out of my arms and screams, 'Yay! Can we watch a film because we never got to see one today?'

I glance at Will but he's already nodding. He tells her of course they can and she skips off to the bottom of the garden, clambering onto her trampoline.

'Thanks,' I say. 'For everything.'

Will kisses my forehead. 'No problem. I'll make a move now so I can get back in time to watch a film.'

Once he's gone, I quickly make Freya fish fingers and sweet potato wedges. It's one of her favourite meals – the least I can do after giving her such a scare. Will and I can eat something later, once she's in bed.

I try to focus, to listen to every word Freya is saying in between mouthfuls of food, but I can't stop thinking about Alison Cummings. About Zach. I need to know who she is, and what possible reason she could have had to tell me something like that and then retract it so quickly. And the more I think about it, the more convinced I am that she *did* say those things. I am not falling apart, having some sort of crisis, that's just not me. Somehow I held it together when Zach died – yes, for Freya's sake, but having her gave me strength I never knew I had. So I'm not going to doubt myself now.

She said those words.

Your husband didn't kill himself.

And I need to know why. What does she think she knows? And why did she take it back?

While Freya's having a bath, I load up my laptop and wait for Google to appear. I don't know how much time I have before Will gets back, so I need to be quick. I can do more once we're all in bed, but even that amount of time feels too long to wait.

I type Alison's name into the search box and hits immediately appear. Most of them are Facebook profiles, though there are a few websites with her name highlighted. If it's even her real name, that is. But when I check them, one by one, none of them are the same woman I met today.

I don't have Facebook any more. After Zach died I deleted it, sick of the abuse I was getting for what he supposedly did, despairing of the vitriolic messages from strangers who had nothing to do with our lives. I will never put myself on social media again, never put myself in the firing line.

Maybe it's easier to look for people if you have an account? I know Will is on there, so I will have to think of a reason to get him logged in so I can check the profiles, but it won't be easy unless I tell him the truth.

For now, though, I check the profiles I can see, but after ten minutes I still haven't found the woman I'm looking for.

'Mummy, can you help me wash my hair?' Freya shouts from the bathroom.

I close the laptop, but keep it nearby for later – there won't be much sleep for me tonight.

'Is Will here yet?' Freya asks, when I join her in the bathroom. I stare at her countless bath toys and wonder when she'll no longer ask for them. Time passes too quickly in some ways, and much too slowly in others.

'Any minute now,' I say. 'When we're finished in here you can get your pyjamas on then we'll go down and pick a film out.'

She beams from beneath a crown of shampoo. 'Can I have a hot chocolate? Please, Mummy.'

'Okay, but I'm sure you had one yesterday too. And you've already had ice cream today. Probably a huge one, I'm guessing?' She smiles her cheeky grin, the one that's identical to her father's, and I begin to melt. 'Okay, but let's not make a habit of it.'

'I promise I won't keep asking.'

That's just one of the wonderful things about my daughter – I know she'll keep to her word.

Less than half an hour later we all sit huddled together on the sofa, Freya cushioned between Will and me, her head resting on my arm. This would be bliss, a perfect moment where I might actually believe things are going to be all right, but the heavy weight of Alison Cummings bears down on me.

Although I'm facing the television – Freya has chosen *Frozen* for about the twentieth time – I cannot take in anything the characters are saying or doing. It's lucky I've seen it all those times before, because I know she'll want to discuss it afterwards, as always. I just sit here, numb, counting the minutes until it's over and I can get back on the laptop.

After the film, once Freya is in bed, Will suggests we have a glass of wine. Although the idea of it is appealing – something to take the edge off this day – I am desperate to get back to my laptop.

'I really don't think I should after what happened earlier. I don't want to risk having alcohol,' I say.

Will agrees. 'I didn't think about that,' he says. 'You don't mind if I have one, though, do you? I could get you something else?'

I tell him how tired I am, that it's been a long day and I need to get some sleep. I still want to ask him about his Facebook page, but can't think of a legitimate reason for needing to see it. He will think I don't trust him, and I've spent our whole two-year relationship trying to prove that I'm not paranoid about what he does when I'm not with him, despite Zach.

'How about I join you for a bit?' His smile spreads across his face, making it even harder for me to disappoint him. Usually, once Freya is in bed, this is our time together, and even though he sleeps in the spare room when he stays over, for the first part of the night he is always in my bed.

'Will, I'm so sorry, but I think I just need to sleep tonight. Is that okay? I promise I'll make it up to you.'

'Okay,' he says. He tries to stay upbeat but I know he must be disappointed. 'I'll just pop to the shop and get some wine in. I noticed you didn't have any. Do you need anything?'

I tell him I don't and he stands up and plants a kiss on my forehead. He does this often and I like this way he has of reassuring me that everything's okay.

'My keys are on the phone table,' I say, and as he heads out of the door I add, again, that I'm sorry.

Once Will's gone, I stand up to get a glass of water from the kitchen and notice his iPhone tucked between the cushions of the sofa. I shouldn't do it. It's a complete abuse of his privacy and he is the last person who deserves that, but I lean forward, compelled to pick it up. I already know his passcode – he's told me before it's the day and month we met, that's how much he trusts me – and before I know it, it's in my hands. I type in 0-8-1-0 – his home screen greets me.

I'm doing this for you, Zach, because I need answers. I thought I had come to terms with it, that I'd accepted what you did and made my peace with it, but now this woman comes along and detonates a bomb right beside me. It's ticking – and I don't have much time.

I make a silent promise to Will that I will not snoop, I will only search for Alison Cummings and Dominic Bradford and nothing more.

The shop is only a five-minute walk away so Will won't be long; I need to be quick. But once again my search is futile. Although there are plenty of people named Alison Cummings and Dominic Bradford, nobody matches the people I'm looking for. There are some profiles without pictures, but nobody living in London who could match either of them.

But I won't give up. And I have an address – most likely fake – I can use as a starting point: Hawthorn Gardens. Although it's here in Ealing, I don't know the road, but my navigation app on my phone will help me with that. Keeping my silent promise to Will, I delete my search and put his phone back where I found it, but guilt wraps around me, squeezing me tighter.

Seconds later, Will is standing in the doorway, clutching a bottle of wine, his head turned slightly to the side.

'Oh, I didn't hear you come in.' How long has he been standing there? Long enough to see me on his phone? I panic and prepare to explain what I was doing. To tell him about Alison Cummings and risk his uncertainty about my sanity, because that's better than letting him think I don't trust him.

'I was extra quiet,' he says. 'Didn't want to wake Freya.' No mention of his phone or what I've been doing with it.

'You left your phone here,' I say, reaching across the sofa for it.

He takes it from me and slips it into his pocket. 'Thanks. Didn't even realise.'

I search his face for any clue that he might have seen me, any sign that this is some sort of test and he's waiting for me to admit what I've done, but his face is unreadable.

In the kitchen Will pours himself a glass of wine and kisses me goodnight. It's not the usual long kiss he gives me whenever we say goodbye, but I hope that's just disappointment that we won't be together tonight.

Once I'm ready for bed, I close the bedroom door, even though I usually leave it wide open in case Freya needs me, and get back to my search. This time I hunt for Dominic Bradford, and even though I start with the University of West London website, where he worked with Zach, there is no mention of him in the faculty list. It's no surprise he no longer works there – things change and people move on. I put his name into Google but no search results reveal the person I'm looking for.

I have a vague recollection of what he looks like – dark hair too slick and groomed – but I never knew this man. He wasn't a friend of Zach's, not really. They were colleagues, but didn't even work in the same department. The first time I met him was at the funeral, and I remember him taking my hand, telling me how sorry he was, that Zach was a great man, in spite of what people were saying. I remember being grateful he had turned up, when so many other colleagues – and even friends – had deliberately stayed away. He was clean-shaven, and had that look about him that advertised he thought too much of himself. Exactly how Alison Cummings described him.

I click to the next page of results and the top link is for a university website, and underneath the address is his name: Dominic Bradford. With a lump in my throat I click again and it takes me to the University of Westminster site. Moments later, I find out he is the head of the law department, and works at the Westminster Law School Site, near Euston station.

Finally, I am getting somewhere. This is the man who will lead me to Alison Cummings.

And then I will find out what she knows about my husband's death.

FOUR

Josie

Over the last few weeks I've really pulled myself together. I'm at home, cocooned in my bedroom with my books, more often than I can be found in a bar, and to my surprise I'm happier than I've ever been.

Don't get me wrong, I'm no saint – not like Little Miss Prim, Alison – and I did find myself in the back seat of Anthony's car last night, but I got out of there before things went too far. The thought of undressing him actually repulsed me, so he didn't get more than some drunken kisses I put no effort into. I deleted his phone number the second I got home.

It's the Christmas holidays now, but this morning I decided to come to university and study in peace. Alison's parents are visiting and the thought of them playing happy families only metres away from me was too much to bear. Actually, there's no playing involved. They are what anyone would consider a functional, happy family. They visit at least once every two weeks and whisk her off for lunch or dinner. I can't imagine going for lunch with a parent, as they smile proudly at you. She doesn't know how lucky she is, she really doesn't.

So here I am, and the place is like a ghost town, most people only too pleased to be having a break, back in the welcoming embraces of their families, so I have my pick of the computers for a change.

A couple of hours later I'm in the middle of making notes for my Shakespeare assignment when someone taps me on the shoulder. Assuming it must be one of the librarians telling me they're about to close up, I turn round, ready to beg for a bit more time, but it's Zach Hamilton standing behind me.

He smiles at me and when he squeezes my shoulder, it's like a bolt of electricity surging through me. I guess having a chat over an espresso and cigarette has made things more casual between us. 'Hey, Josie, I'm pleased to see you here.' There's a huge grin on his face to back up what he's saying.

'Is that because this is the last place you thought you'd ever see me?'

He chuckles. 'Let's just say it seems you've made good progress since our last chat. You know, the one where you tried to choke me with your cigarette smoke.'

'Very funny.' I flick my hair back and then wonder what the hell I'm doing. Am I flirting with him? My eyes dart to his left hand, to the band of silver – or perhaps it's platinum – circling his finger.

Of course he's married.

He takes a seat in the computer chair next to me. 'You know I'm just messing around. Seriously though, I'm proud of you. From what you were saying before, it's been a bit of a battle for you to stay here.'

And to get here, I think, but I won't tell him that. He doesn't need to know where I've come from. After all, isn't it where you're going that's more important?

'Why are you here, though?' I ask. 'Don't you have a family at home you should be with? Lecturers need a break too, don't they?'

For a second his eyes flick to his hand, but then he looks up again. 'I left my USB stick here in one of the computers,' he says. 'It's got all my lectures for next semester on it so I had to come in and get it.' He studies my face. 'The computer in my office broke and they're taking their time fixing it so I've been coming here to work. I'm not usually so disorganised, but never mind. Thankfully, Maggie over there' – he gestures to the librarian – 'checked the contents, realised it was mine and kept it for me.'

So he'll be leaving any second. An emptiness fills my body, a feeling I can't understand, and actually don't even want to try. 'Well, have a great Christmas,' I say, closing my textbook. It's nearly 3 p.m. and my stomach's just begun to remind me I haven't eaten a thing today.

'You off then?' he says. Is there disappointment in his tone, or do I just want there to be? People see and hear what they want to, don't they?

I nod. 'I need food. Need a break. I've been here over two hours.'

'In that case I'll walk out with you. Is your car in the car park?'

How does he know I drive? 'Um, yep.'

'Silver Polo, isn't it?'

Now my heart is starting to leap around my body. 'That's right. The cheap one that's about to fall apart any second. Are you my stalker or something?' I grin to let him know I'm just messing around, but I can't help wishing that he was.

He laughs. 'No. Sorry to disappoint, but you drove right past me the other day. You don't like speed limits, do you?'

This definitely sounds like me. Reckless. That's what Liv called me once, and the funny thing is it was the first time she'd actually got me a bit right. 'Well, I'm always in a rush,' I tell Zach. 'Life's too short, isn't it?'

He shakes his head at this. 'Not at your age it shouldn't be, Josie.'

Why does he keep saying my name? He needs to stop, because whenever he does, I melt like a silly schoolgirl.

'Do you live far from here, then?'

'Nope. I live by South Ealing station.' I hold up my hand. 'I know, I know, it's barely a few minutes' walk, and I usually do, but

I was running late the other day. Didn't want to miss my lecture.' I could have lied, told him I had somewhere I had to go afterwards, but somehow I knew he wouldn't judge me.

He grins. 'And today?'

'Um, today I have no excuse, actually.'

'Well, we all have days like that. I certainly do. And can I confide in you?'

My heart almost stops. 'Yeah. Course.'

'I live in Ealing too, so I could quite easily walk here. Only I'm never up early enough to leave the house in time. But to be fair it would be a pretty long walk.'

'Sod that!' I say, and then I clamp my hand to my mouth as if I've sworn in front of a priest.

He laughs again, and it's satisfying to know I can put a smile on his face.

'Anyway, Josie, are you ready to go?'

Outside, the bitter air hits me like a punch, so I pull my coat tighter around me. The car park is at the other side of the building and as we walk, Zach asks me about my plans for Christmas.

It's a question I dread having to answer, and I frantically search for a response, one that he will believe. 'Not sure yet,' I say. But I should have lied, because now he will ask me about my parents and that's a conversation I don't want to have with anyone, let alone this man who is doing something to my insides with every word he speaks.

'Oh,' he says. 'You must have a lot of options.'

I need to change the subject, and push from my mind the thought of another Christmas Day alone. 'What about you?'

'Oh, I'll be visiting my parents,' he says.

This perks me up. *Maybe he's divorced. Please let him be divorced.*

'They don't get to see us that much and our little one's almost two now.'

I feel like I've just been smacked across the face. But this is ridiculous. He's my lecturer and of course he's married, so why do I feel so disappointed?

Because you like him, Josie, you fool. He's seen what's inside you, not your looks or your body, and he genuinely seems to like you as a person.

'That's nice,' I say, quickly recovering. I can never let him get an inkling of how I've only just realised I feel.

'Yes, it will be,' he says.

We continue walking in silence until we round the corner and I see my car. 'I'm over there,' I say. 'Where are you parked?'

I feel half relieved and half disappointed when he tells me he's parked along the back too. It means more time with him, but that's more time with a man it's pointless even thinking about.

We reach the last row and he stops, turning to face me. 'Actually, Josie, I'm glad I've bumped into you today. There's something I wanted to say to you, that I meant to say the other day, but didn't get a chance.'

Stay calm. Be cool. 'Go on.' I distract myself by pulling my car keys from my pocket.

'Okay. Um, this is a bit weird, but I just had to tell you.' He avoids my eyes and stares past me, shuffling his feet like a nervous teenager. 'Your story really inspired me. I don't tell anyone this, except family, of course, but I'm actually writing a novel. Kind of a long story, but I started it years ago and, well, I'd hit a block and hadn't written anything for a long time, but when I read your story… it kick-started my motivation, I guess.'

It takes me a moment to register everything he's said, and then, when it dawns on me exactly what he's saying, I feel as if I'm floating, riding high on his huge compliment. 'I… er… thank you. That's unexpected but… wow.'

'It's me who wants to thank you. You're so talented, Josie, and I really don't want you to give up, no matter how tough things get.

Just keep remembering what we talked about in the coffee shop. Whenever you hit a low point, just think of that.'

I barely know what to say to this so I just thank him and watch him walk off, shocked that it meant so much to him that he had to tell me all this.

What does it mean?

I didn't go home after getting into my car. Instead, I waited until Zach had driven off – fiddling around in my glove compartment to make out I was searching for something – and then I got out of the car and walked to Walpole Park. I couldn't bear the thought of being alone now, and even if Alison was home, we were no company for each other.

Sitting on a bench, I'd got lost in the book I had to read for next semester: *The Handmaid's Tale*. It engrossed me so much, I lost track of time, and suddenly it was getting dark.

Now, as I drive home, Zach fills my thoughts, even though I know he shouldn't. He's my university lecturer, and married with a baby, so what am I doing even thinking about him?

I've done some pretty questionable things in my life so far, but never something like that. I have to pull it together. Besides, even if I was tempted, there's no evidence he feels the same.

The minute I step into the flat I hear voices in the living room. Alison's parents must still be here, trying to spend as much time as they can with their daughter.

A cloud of loneliness settles over me. Perhaps I'm envious of her, of what she has, because I just can't imagine anyone giving up their time to visit me, to check how my studies are going. Maybe this is what drives me to go in there. The feeling that, just for once, I want to be part of something normal, even if I'm only looking in from the outside.

I flounce through the door, plastering a smile on my face I know will annoy Alison. I'm the last person she'll want socialising with her family.

'Hi! Nice to…' But it's not Alison's parents sitting on the sofa. It's a young guy I've never seen before, with floppy hair, jeans and Converse trainers.

Alison's face drops, as though I've caught them naked in bed together instead of sitting metres apart on our tatty sofa. 'I thought you were working today,' she says, glancing at the guy then back to me.

'Nope, not today.'

The guy stands up and holds out his hand. 'I'm Aaron, nice to meet you. Josie, isn't it? I've heard a lot about you.' His smile is hard to read. No doubt everything he's heard has cast me in a dismal light.

'And I've heard nothing about you, Aaron,' I say. He takes too long to let go of my hand. 'Are you and Alison on the same course?'

'No. But we're just—'

'Let's go to my room, Aaron.' Alison jumps up, placing herself between us like a wall. That's when it dawns on me that she likes this guy. This is interesting. She's made no mention of having a boyfriend, or even just being interested in anyone – but then again, I'm the last person she would talk to about anything like that.

'Why don't we stay here?' Aaron suggests. 'Join us if you like, Josie? We're about to get a takeaway and have a few drinks.' He smiles at me, and that's when I know he has no interest in Alison. 'Well, *I'm* about to have a few drinks. Alison says she's got a headache.'

I glance at Alison and see the pained expression on her face as she silently begs me to leave. 'Nah. Think I'll leave you to it.' But then I think of my empty room, of spending the next few weeks alone while everyone else is celebrating Christmas. Sod it, I've got to eat, and spending a couple of hours with Alison isn't the worst thing in the world. Better than being in a bar, breaking the promise I made to myself, meeting another Anthony. Besides, it'll be fun finding out what's going on between them. 'Actually, I will join you. What are we having? Indian?'

'Sounds good to me,' Aaron says. 'What do you think, Ali?'

It's funny to hear her being addressed so informally. I've never even considered shortening her name. Somehow it doesn't fit with the uptight clean freak that she is.

'It's not my favourite, but that's fine,' she says quietly. She stands and walks over to the bookshelf, pulling out a folder and flicking through it. It takes me a moment to realise the folder is a menu organiser, and I can't help but chuckle. Only Alison would have one of these. 'Here,' she says, pulling out a sheet and handing it to Aaron. 'This is the best one around here.'

The food arrives and it isn't great, so when Aaron offers me a Beck's I'm grateful to have something strong to wash it down with. One won't do any harm, will it? I'm not going to do any more studying tonight anyway, and at least I'm at home.

Alison says very little while we eat, but Aaron doesn't seem to notice – he's too busy talking about himself. I consider making an excuse to go to my room, because it's cruel of me to stay here when she clearly wants to be alone with this guy, but when her phone rings and she excuses herself to talk to her parents, I decide I may as well stay where I am for the moment.

'Have another drink, Josie,' Aaron says.

'Go on, then,' I say, because I still don't want to be alone. All I'll do is mope about Zach and how the one man I've ever had any real interest in is married with a kid. And is my university lecturer.

He hands me another bottle, and I take it greedily, relishing the coldness of the glass on my fingers. 'So what's the deal with you and Alison?'

He flicks his head up and guzzles some beer before answering. 'Nothing. No deal, we're just friends.'

I narrow my eyes. 'Really? Because it doesn't look that way to me.'

He shrugs. 'So she likes me. That doesn't mean I have to like her, does it? I've never led her on or made her think I do.' No, of course he hasn't. Because drinking and eating a takeaway on a Friday night together could never be misconstrued.

I tell him this and he laughs. 'You're funny, you know, Josie. I like that.'

Here we go… Another loser who's out for what he can get. Now, despite my feelings towards Alison, I feel sorry for her. She clearly really likes this guy, and it will all come to nothing. A bit like with me and Zach, but at least I have other people interested – if I can be bothered with them. It's not that Alison is unattractive, but she's too strange. Too quiet and creepy. Thinking of this makes me feel even more sorry for her.

Perhaps she and I aren't so different after all. Both of us are screwed in different ways.

'I love this,' Aaron says, reaching across to touch my nose ring.

I shove his hand away. 'Yeah, well, I'm not a tat kind of girl, so this is as far as I go with decorating myself.

He rolls up his sleeve and half of his skinny arm is covered in ink.

'They don't interest me,' I say, and his face falls. Perhaps he's used to girls fawning over him – I suppose he's not bad-looking – but I'm surprised Alison finds him attractive. I'd have thought a stuffy older guy in a suit would be more her type. Or someone like Zach.

Aaron pulls down his sleeve and leans in towards me. 'Really? So what does interest you, then?'

This is an interesting question, and I wouldn't have known the answer until today. But I ignore Aaron, because I don't want to have this conversation with him – his pathetic attempt at flirting is an insult to Alison.

'Does she know you're not into her?' I ask. I'm still clutching my beer bottle but I don't want any now.

Aaron shrugs. 'I don't know, it's never come up.'

Sometimes I'm a decent person, and right now I feel an urgent need to defend Alison. She won't stick up for herself so I've got to do it, and I won't let this loser walk all over her. 'What exactly are you doing here? Trying to get a quick shag from her? People like you make me sick. You know she's not that type so what are you playing at? Bit low on offers this week, are you?'

His mouth hangs open. Perhaps he's not used to being confronted like this. Is that why he's picked someone like Alison?

I don't wait for him to answer. 'Think she's desperate, do you? That she'll be so grateful you're showing her any interest she'll jump into bed with you just like that?'

The fury is escalating within me and I'm losing control. But I can't stop. Perhaps it's years of my own abuse – although of a different kind – that has me championing Alison.

Proving he has no decent response, Aaron stands, letting his half-full bottle crash to the floor, a river of beer spilling all over the carpet. 'I don't have to listen to this bullshit. Screw both of you!'

And then he's gone, slamming the front door behind him.

I feel her behind me before I turn around. Alison is staring at me, her mobile clutched to her chest. Her eyes are wide with horror as she takes in the scene. And when she speaks, her voice is quiet, but her words speak volumes.

'What the hell have you just done?'

FIVE

Mia

Sleep was fitful for me last night, fear and anxiety keeping me awake, so I am up before 6 a.m. Still in my dressing gown, I head downstairs to the kitchen, surprised to open the door and find Will standing by the oven, already up and dressed, the smell of bacon and eggs wafting from the hob.

'Hey, how are you feeling? I thought you'd wake up around now after going to bed so early.' He points to the frying pan. 'Hope you don't mind, but I thought we could all do with a nice cooked breakfast.'

Food is the last thing I feel like but I appreciate his offer. 'Thank you. Is it nearly ready? I should go and wake Freya.'

'Just started. Actually, could we have a word before Freya gets up?'

This will be serious; normally Will doesn't preface things by asking if we can talk. He must know I used his phone without asking. Or somehow he's found out about Alison Cummings and wants to know why I've kept this from him.

'Is everything okay?' I ask. But of course it isn't. And I've got the feeling it won't be again, unless I can track down that woman and find out what she's playing at.

Will stirs the scrambled eggs and turns to me. 'Mia, I'm really worried about you. First, you collapse yesterday and then you were so quiet all evening. I know you were tired, but is there something else going on? I'm just not buying the dehydration thing, you're too good at looking after yourself.'

I try to reassure him I'm fine, that it was a one-off and won't happen again, but he's still not convinced.

'You can't know it won't happen again, can you? And if there's something physically wrong then you need to get checked.'

'Will, I love you for caring, and noticing so much, but honestly, I'm fine. Yesterday just wasn't a good day. Today will be better, I promise.' My words are hollow and riddled with deceit. Is this how Zach felt?

He leans forward and kisses my cheek. 'Okay, but if you start to feel ill again—'

'I won't,' I say. 'Now, I'd better get Freya up, breakfast looks like it's nearly ready.'

I turn away before I break down and tell him everything. I can't put that burden on Will. Not now. Not ever.

'Remember, I've taken the whole day off today,' Will says, as I clear away the breakfast things. Freya plays outside in the garden, alternating between her trampoline and her paddling pool, and I watch her from the window. She's the only thing that keeps me calm when everything else is threatening to crash down around me.

'Are we still doing something this afternoon?' Will continues. 'I thought we could take Freya to London Zoo?'

My heart sinks – I'd forgotten we'd made this arrangement last week, but I need to track down Alison today. I can't let any more time go by without finding out what she knows.

Freya has a playdate with her friend Megan this morning, while I see clients, and I can't cancel my appointments, so that only leaves me this afternoon to check the address Alison gave me when she called to make an appointment. My plan is to take Freya with me and combine it with a trip to Oxford Street, which is not too far from the Westminster Law School campus.

'Oh, Will, I'm so sorry. I have to go out this afternoon, and I was planning to take Freya with me. I know it won't be exciting for her, but… Anyway, how about we do something this evening?'

The smile drains from his face, and I know he wants to ask me where we're going, but he would never pry, just like I don't with him. 'That's fine.'

'You're welcome to come here this afternoon, though. You've got your key.'

'No, that's fine. I've got work to do at home.' He turns away from me and watches Freya through the kitchen door. 'Actually, why don't I have Freya this afternoon for you, if that will help you out?'

Even when he's dealing with disappointment, Will still finds it in his heart to show kindness by helping me out.

'Are you sure? I don't want to put you out,' I say, though I know this will be better for Freya. Better for all of us. If I do find Alison then I don't want my daughter anywhere near her.

'Of course. You know I see her as my own daughter.'

I pull him into me, squeezing him tightly because he is such a good man, and right now, I really don't deserve him.

Hawthorn Gardens is a tree-lined street full of Victorian houses. Most of them are well maintained, despite their age, and if Alison is telling the truth about living here then she and Dominic must be doing well for themselves. I remind myself he is a head of department at a prestigious university now, something Zach never got the chance to be.

As I head towards number 26, it strikes me that Alison could have been lying about Dominic Bradford being her partner – but

for what purpose? None of it makes sense, and the little that does
– Zach's death – I don't want to think about.

The house looms over me as I stand outside. What am I thinking, coming here? If, by some slim chance, Alison did give me
her genuine address, what can I possibly say to make her admit
what she told me yesterday? She fled my office without hesitation;
clearly, she's made up her mind.

But I've got to try. I can't walk away from this now.

I press the doorbell but can't hear anything on the other side
so have no idea if it even works.

Silence surrounds me, even on a busy London day. But it's past
2 p.m. now so most people will be at work. I'm turning away, sure
nobody is home, when the door creaks open.

'Can I help you?'

It's not Alison, of course it isn't. The woman addressing me is at
least eighty and she hunches over, leaning against the door frame.

'Hi, I'm looking for Alison Cummings?'

The woman frowns, appraising me from head to foot. 'No,
wrong house. It's just me here.'

'Okay, sorry. She must have moved.'

'Not likely. I've lived here my whole life and it was my parents'
house before that.'

Thanking her, I turn and leave. It was only as I expected, but
anxiety still floods through me. What if I never find her? What
is she up to?

It's been a long time since I set foot in a university, but walking
into one now brings back a flood of memories: starting adulthood;
meeting Zach; losing him years later. I didn't think coming here
would hit me this hard – this exact place had nothing to do with
Zach or anything else – but it's a struggle to keep going.

I should have called. It's the summer break and though I know university lecturers work most of the holidays, there's only a small chance he'll be here. I could have saved myself this pain. But I couldn't just sit at home. At least I'm doing something. Whether it's futile or not, I'm heading in the right direction. I just don't know what to expect when I get there.

The reception desk is manned by a young woman with glasses and shiny black hair. She smiles as I approach, putting me at ease. 'Hi, how can I help?'

'I was just wondering if Dominic Bradford is in today? Head of the law department? He's an old friend of mine and I wanted to catch up with him.'

She looks towards the main doors. 'Oh, you just missed him. But he only left a moment ago so if you hurry, you might catch up with him. He's probably heading to the tube station.'

I quickly step out into the street, but there are too many people around. Too many men who could be Dominic. From behind, I have no way to identify him, especially when I've only seen him once, five years ago. I spin around, both wanting and not wanting to find him, and then there he is, across the road, bending down to tie his shoelace.

Dominic is larger than I remember him, and at least a stone heavier, but his hair is the same and his face is unmistakable. At the funeral I'd considered it an arrogant face, but it's hard to believe he is an abusive man, although they don't come with warning signs or labels. It is always the people you least expect. *Like Zach*, I think.

Dominic straightens up and continues on his way, so I cross the road towards him. But what am I going to say? I can't just run up to him and demand to know if he's seeing someone called Alison Cummings. There's no way to tell him. Plus, if she *was* telling the truth about him being abusive, then what will Dominic do when he finds out she has come to see me? It would only fuel his rage.

Slowing down, I keep my distance but follow behind him. I've had a better idea.

I didn't have to follow him for too far, just one short tube trip from Euston to East Finchley, and after a short walk through some quiet streets, we turn into Abbots Gardens. He walks up to number 95, a large, white, semi-detached house with a front garden filled with huge trees, giving the house privacy from passers-by.

But I can see him clearly as he stands by the front door, fishing in his pocket for what I can only assume are his keys. And just as he pulls them out, the door opens and Alison is standing there, stepping aside to let him in, neither of them smiling or greeting each other.

I shrink back against a tree, hoping she doesn't spot me. At least I have made progress today, and I will come back here to get some answers.

'Mummy! Where have you been? We've been waiting ages for you!'

Freya rushes to the door as soon as she hears me turn the key in the lock, and she barges into me, folding her little arms around me as if she hasn't seen me for weeks.

I look past her to Will, who is shaking his head in the kitchen doorway. Shrugging an apology to him, I kiss my daughter on the head. 'Sorry, sweetheart, I just got held up. I'm here now, though.'

Freya pulls back. 'Will said it's probably too late to go anywhere now. And it's nearly my bedtime, isn't it?'

I hadn't meant to be back so late, but travelling halfway across London during rush hour eats away at time. 'How about pizza for dinner?' I suggest. It's another of Freya's favourite foods so that should at least cheer her up a bit. 'And we can play that game you love – Sequence.'

This brings a smile to her face. 'You won't just let me win this time, will you? I'm seven now, Mummy, I can win for myself.'

I ruffle her hair. 'No, I play to win.' And this is true today after finding Alison Cummings so easily, although that is no game.

Freya asks Will if he's staying, but he shakes his head. 'Sorry, I can't today. I've got some work to do later. But I'll have some pizza with you first, if that's okay?'

He addresses his question to me, and I nod. 'Of course. You know you don't have to ask.'

But does he know this? I've been so off with him since yesterday that it would be no surprise to me if he didn't quite feel comfortable.

I'm not being fair to Will. I owe it to him – to everyone – to get some closure. I thought I had it, but then Alison appeared and stirred everything up. I have to find out what's going on, and then maybe I can start living.

Will is quiet over dinner, but Freya's excited chatter fills the silence as she tells him about her trip to stay with her grandparents tomorrow. Zach's parents live in Reading, and I try to take Freya there as much as possible. They have always adored her, but now she is their only link to their son, so every moment with her is even more precious to them. She loves going there too; they can bring Zach to life for her, fill in the colours even more than I can.

When Will leaves, he kisses me quickly by the front door and tells me he'll call tomorrow. 'I know Freya's away for a few days, but I really need to catch up with some work this weekend. How about we get together on Monday?'

It's not unusual for us to go a few days without seeing each other – we both have busy lives – but it hasn't happened for a while. Lately there's usually been some point in the day when we've seen each other. But I could do with this time now, so I readily agree that Monday is fine.

*

Something startles me from sleep: a sharp piercing sound I can't place at first. It's my mobile phone, ringing from the bedside table.

With blurred vision, I check the screen, but there is no caller ID. Normally I would ignore it – these anonymous calls are usually nuisance ones – but it's 2 a.m. so it must be important.

I greet the caller and wait for what can only be bad news.

'Mia? Why did you come to my house today?' Alison's voice sounds different over the phone.

Ignoring her question, I demand to know why she told me my husband didn't kill himself.

'Leave this alone, Mia. And don't come to my house again. You have no idea what you're doing.'

And then there is silence as she cuts the connection.

SIX

Josie

Alison hasn't spoken to me since the incident with Aaron, and she won't give me even a second to explain what happened. Every time I try to talk to her she leaves the room without a word, and somehow this is worse than if she'd just have a go at me.

I have the truth on my side but she just doesn't want to hear it, which makes her even stranger than I'd thought. I don't know if she's tried to contact Aaron, but if the two of them have spoken then I'm sure he's fed her a stream of lies.

Today is the last day of the Christmas holidays, and somehow I've made it through these weeks by taking on extra shifts at the coffee shop and throwing myself into my coursework, in a strange mixture of determination to succeed and desperation to drown out my loneliness, to not give in to the call to go and have a drink somewhere.

But I'm not due at work today and I can't stand the thought of being stuck here, with Alison mooching around the place, punishing me with her silence, just as lost as I am, but in a different way. She's been staying with her parents for most of the holiday but now she's back and I don't know what's worse.

So I make a decision: today will be the day I go home. Not to see *her* of course, but I miss Kieren, and I know he must miss me too. He won't understand why I moved so far away, why I had to get away from her. She might try to poison him against me, but she shouldn't estimate how strong-willed Kieren is, even for a five-year-old. He's just like me – she'll love that.

The train journey to Brighton passes too quickly and I'm stepping onto the platform sooner than I'm prepared for, into the city I will never be able to think of as home. Yet, until a few months ago, it was the only place I'd ever lived, the only place I'd ever been.

Somehow she has friends here: too many of them, scattered all over the estate, watching out for her. I shudder to think just how many people she's turned against me, so I need to be on guard, ready to defend myself and my actions. But I can hold my head up high because I did the only thing I could do: I did the right thing.

There is only one person who hasn't turned their back on me since it happened: Sinead next door. Despite being around Liv's age and a mother of two herself, she's never found anything in common with Liv, has never liked her, so I wasn't surprised when she approached me in a shop one day and told me she believed my side of events. 'I know you wouldn't lie, Josie. That Liv, though… Sorry, I know she's your mum, but my God, what a nasty piece of work.'

Since that day, Sinead has texted and called with regular updates on Kieren – it's the only way I can know how he's doing. I think about knocking on her door before I go to Liv's, but I quickly decide against it. I don't want anyone to see me there; that will only cause problems for Sinead and her family.

Liv's house – not mine, it never was – is only a short bus ride from the beach, so I head to the pier first, just to buy myself some time. It's deserted at this time of year, the atmosphere nothing like the bustle of the summer months, but that suits me fine – I can be invisible.

This is the time when I could really do with a drink, just something to take the edge off, because I'm actually afraid of what she's capable of. But I've stayed away too long already. Four months is a hell of a long time for a kid, and I want Kieren to know I haven't forgotten him; that I never will.

If there was a way I could get him away from her now then I'd do it, whatever it took, but there isn't; I've already looked into it. I don't know what Kieren's life is like now, but I pray it's not as bad as it was for me. He's a boy, so she won't be jealous of him, but she still doesn't know how to be a mother – it's not in her nature. To her, kids are just mistakes, things that get in the way and stop her living her life. Things that drive all the men she's interested in away.

After staring at the waves for too long, I can't put it off any longer. I came here to see Kieren and to do that I'll need to deal with her. *Right, I'm ready. Bring on whatever you've got for me. I can handle anything.*

The house is just as shabby as it's always been, forcing home the fact that nothing has changed. I press my finger on the bell and hear it ring out inside, taking a deep breath, bracing myself as it slowly opens.

'JoJo!' Kieren shrieks my name and runs into me, gripping me in a tight hug.

I lean down to his level. 'Where's Mum? She is in, isn't she?' Because it would be just like her to think he can be left on his own at five years old.

He nods, and his smile vanishes. 'She's in the bath.' He turns and looks up the stairs. 'She said we're never to let you in,' he says. 'Why is she so horrible to you?'

One day I'll tell you, when you're old enough to understand what she did to me.

I look past him into the hallway, take in the rubbish bags – dumped there with their contents overflowing because she can't be bothered to walk the extra few metres to put them in the bins outside – and the shoes and coats piled everywhere. 'Kieren?' I lean down to his level. 'When did she get in the bath?'

My brother shrugs. 'Just now. She told me to watch TV, I'm not supposed to answer the door.'

That will be in case it's me. She knows I won't be able to stay away from Kieren for too long. She always takes her time in the bath, so I relax a little and tell him to grab his coat and join me on the doorstep. I'm not setting foot in that place, not unless I have to.

We sit down and snuggle close, keeping each other warm. 'I thought you'd gone away,' he says, pulling back so he can see my face. 'Mum said you were never coming back.'

'Well, here I am,' I say. It would be too easy to explain what an evil, lying bitch that woman is, but I could never do that to Kieren. As long as she is feeding him, not abusing him, and keeping him in clean clothes then I don't need to speak badly of her to him. He's at that age when parents mean everything, and he doesn't need his world shattered. And looking at him now, the apparently new and spotless Mickey Mouse sweatshirt and jeans he has on, everything appears to be okay.

The abuse and neglect were just for you, then, Josie. Does that make you feel better or worse?

'Have you had lunch?' I ask Kieren. I'm already reaching into my bag for the uneaten tuna and sweetcorn sandwich I bought at the station.

'No.' He eyes my sandwich.

'Here, take this.' I hand it to him but he doesn't reach for it.

He glances back at the stairs and shakes his head. 'No, I'll get in trouble. Richard is taking us to McDonald's later.'

I've never heard this name before but I don't need to ask who he is. Mum's new boyfriend, no doubt. Well, it didn't take her long to get over Johnny. Just thinking his name makes my stomach heave.

'Is Richard nice to you?' I ask. Because if he isn't, I'll take Kieren with me right now, and sod the consequences.

Kieren shrugs. 'He's okay, I don't know.' He buries his head in the crook of my arm. 'I miss you, JoJo.'

I ruffle his hair. 'Me too.'

'I can ask if you can come back… then we can be together again.'

It breaks my heart to tell him that can't happen. I try to explain I'm at university now, and I have to live away from home, but I'll come and visit him as much as I can.

'It's not fair!' he protests. 'Why does Mum hate you?'

'Because your sister is a nasty, filthy liar and she doesn't deserve to be alive.'

My heart almost stops when I hear Liv's gravelly voice. I barely take in what she's said because I'm too stunned that she's standing there and neither Kieren nor I heard her come downstairs. She's wearing a long, fluffy green dressing gown, stained with make-up, and her hair is wrapped in a pink towel. What did she just say? All I know is it was something along the lines of wishing me dead.

Kieren releases his hold on me but is frozen to the spot, just as I am. It would have been different if she'd answered the door and I'd been ready for her – I'm not good at being taken by surprise.

'Get out of my house,' she says, spitting her words at me.

'Actually, I'm not in your house.' It's a feeble attempt to stand my ground, but I won't be intimidated by this monster. How is it we share the same genes?

She lurches forward and grabs Kieren. 'Get upstairs, now.'

He doesn't protest but runs off, thudding up the stairs without even a glance in my direction. Fear, that's what that is. But when he reaches the top he stands and blows me a kiss that only I can see.

'You've got some balls coming here,' says Liv. 'D'you know how many people wanna see you hung, drawn and quartered for what you did?'

'And what exactly did I do, *Mother*?' The irony I lace this word with will be lost on her. To me she is, and always has been, Liv Carpenter.

'Really? You wanna play that game, do you? You put an innocent man in prison and walked away as if nothing happened!' She edges towards me, her eyes stone cold. 'He's suicidal, y'know. And if he tops himself then God help you, because there'll be a lynch mob after you. He's got loads of family, loads of friends. And every one of us wants justice.'

It is all I can do to stop myself vomiting across her cracked doorstep.

I lift up my arms. 'There's nobody around, Liv. No one listening. Why don't you just tell the truth? Because you know what he did. You *saw* him, I know you did, so cut this phoney act. You're as guilty as he is and what goes around comes around, Liv.'

I turn quickly and walk away – I can't listen to any more of this.

Her shouts follow me down the street. 'Don't show your face again, you dirty whore. D'you hear me? Just shrivel up and die in a corner somewhere, that's what you deserve.'

As I walk away, I think how strange it is that those words can hurt just as much as, or more than, what she's already done to me.

The flat is silent when I get home, but that doesn't mean I'm alone. Alison is always too quiet, creeping around the place undetected until she's standing right there, staring at me. Creepy as hell.

After the day I've had, I could do with her being here; I want to have it out with her and force her to listen. She needs to know the truth. *But that didn't work with Liv today, did it? When will you learn that people like her and Alison only hear what they want to hear, and you're wasting your breath trying to convince them otherwise?*

There is only one thing I can do, other than drink myself into oblivion, and that's prepare for my lectures tomorrow. I've got Zach's first thing in the morning, and our next assignment's due in, so I need to go through it one more time.

As I step into my room, I catch a waft of Alison's sickly-sweet floral perfume. It's bloody everywhere in this flat: the bathroom, the kitchen, and now it's seeped into my bedroom, the only place I can get away from her. And since the incident with Aaron, she's been wearing even more of it, probably just to annoy me.

Settling at my desk, I load up my laptop and hunt around for my USB. I usually leave it in my desk drawer, safely tucked out of the way, but it's not here. It's got all my uni work on it and I can't afford to lose it. I only feel a mild flutter of panic – I've been known to find it in pockets or my bag – but after an increasingly frantic search, there's no sign of it.

Swearing to myself, I scan my computer files, relieved that I back up my important work. But my assignment for Zach isn't there, and a search of the hard drive finds nothing with the name of my assignment.

How could I have been so dumb? But as I search my memory, I remember saving it on here. I swear I did. I even remember wondering if Zach would be as complimentary about this one as I copied it to my USB, convincing myself he wouldn't and that he'd realise he was wrong to think so highly of me.

I spend another half hour turning my room upside down, until it looks like I've been burgled, but the search is futile.

Alison – it has to be. She's trying to screw with me in her passive-aggressive way, and she's done the only thing she knows will get to me. I rush to her room and pound on the door, shouting her name just in case she's hiding in there. But there is only silence.

Not even bothering to get my coat, I grab my keys and leave the flat, slamming the door behind me, ignoring the bitter wind as my feet pound the pavement. I have no idea where I'm going, but I need to get the hell out of that flat.

After a few minutes, my head feeling like it's about to explode, I realise I'm running in the direction of the coffee shop. I'm drenched in sweat, despite the cold, and must look a mess, but it's as good a place as any to go. I can dose up on caffeine, let my heart rate slow down and get my mind around the momentous task of rewriting this damn assignment before tomorrow.

I've still got the handwritten notes for it, but I know without trying that I'll never be able to recreate the original story, that there's no chance I can match it. Damn that bitch, she's lost her head over a man – if Aaron can even be called that – and that's why she's done this. I've seen Liv behave like this too. I would never let a man drive me to that kind of psychotic behaviour.

There's only one customer in the coffee shop when I walk in: an elderly man whose hand trembles as he lifts his cup to his mouth. Lucia is serving today and she asks if I want my usual.

'No,' I tell her. 'A double espresso.' I'll be up late tonight and I need all the caffeine I can get.

She frowns and then laughs, almost simultaneously, and says something in Slovakian. 'Sorry. Sit. I bring.'

The elderly man has gone now so I take his seat in the corner by the window, pulling out my notebook while I wait for my drink. I stare at my notes and beg inspiration to hit me. Something. Anything. But the words just blur into a black scribble. This is useless; I can't do it.

'Hey, this is a sight for sore eyes.'

I look up and Zach Hamilton is standing by my table, smiling down at me.

'Hi, what are you doing here?' I try not to show how pleased I am to see him.

He sits at my table. 'I had to do some last-minute prep and thought I'd stop here before I head home. I did wonder if you were working.' He eyes the notes scattered across my table. 'But actually it doesn't look like you are.'

'Not today, but I needed to get out of the flat. I've got a lot of uni work to do.' He doesn't even know the half of it.

He frowns. 'Josie, is everything okay? You seem a bit... out of sorts? Oh, God, that's a stupid expression, isn't it? I must sound like I'm ninety.'

But I can't laugh. There's been no time in my life when anyone has ever asked if I'm okay, other than the police, so I forcefully blink back tears. 'No, not really. Not at all. Nothing's okay.'

Even as these words escape me, I know it will be a huge mistake to pull Zach Hamilton into my life.

SEVEN

Mia

Time stood still that night, when the police stood in my living room, telling me Zach was dead. Their mouths were moving but I only heard certain phrases: *body… flat… dead… suicide*. And then I was in a heap on the floor and sturdy arms were lifting me up, guiding me to the sofa, handing me a glass of water I didn't want. Some time later, someone accidentally kicked it over and I watched water fan out, soaking a dark patch into the beige carpet. It's funny how I remember this. I can barely recall the small details of Zach's face unless I look at photos, or remember exactly how he sounded, yet I remember that pool of water.

The other thing I will never forget is Pam's high-pitched wail, like a helpless animal being slaughtered, when, still numb and dazed, I made the call to his parents. The police offered to do it, but I couldn't let Pam and Graham hear it from anyone else. I had to be the one to tell them. The sounds of Pam's scream and Graham's gasping were the sounds of their hearts breaking, just as mine had already done.

This is what I think of as I drive along the M4 to Reading, Freya singing along to the radio in her car seat.

Traffic is always lighter in the summer holidays so we make it in just under an hour, which means I won't have to rush back. I don't usually see clients at weekends, but I've made an exception for Carlo, who has recently lost his wife, and I need to make sure I'm back before 1 p.m.

But first, I need to speak to Pam, preferably alone – and getting her to open up won't be easy or quick.

Pam and Graham are standing together at the front door as we pull up, and in the rear-view mirror I see Freya's face light up, her little hand reaching up to wave to them.

Despite being in their seventies, they're both fairly sprightly and Pam rushes to the car. I've barely switched off the engine before she pulls open Freya's door and begins helping her out of her car seat.

'Grandma!' Freya says, wrapping her arms around her.

'Oh darling, it's so good to see you! We've missed you so much.'

Graham blows her a kiss then opens my door for me. 'Hello, Mia. It's good to see you too, of course.'

I step out and hug him, but as usual it's a short, uncomfortable hug. Although he is a loving man in his own way, Graham has never felt at ease with physical affection, even with his own son. It never bothered Zach, though, and he never doubted how much his father loved him.

Graham makes more effort with Freya, scooping up her bag and grabbing her hand. 'Come on, Socks is waiting for you.' As they head into the house, I can't help thinking that, as old and frail as their cat is, he has somehow outlived Zach.

'Are you okay, love?' Pam asks, linking her arm in mine. 'You look a bit pale.'

I assure her I'm fine, but her eyes narrow. 'It's hard for you coming here, isn't it? All the memories.'

Although Pam and Graham only bought this bungalow when they retired, after I met Zach, we both lived here while we saved to get the deposit for our house, even though the daily commute into London was tough. So Pam is right; it's difficult not to feel as though Zach will walk through the door at any moment, as if he somehow lingers on in this place. I can't explain why it's not like this at my house, given that it was our home together for years. Maybe it's because Freya, older now, has brought something new to it, and I never got to see Zach interact with her as a little girl.

I smile at Pam. 'Yes. But it's nice to remember.'

Inside, Freya is already unpacking her colouring books, pencils and the Num Noms she insists on collecting, spreading everything out on the living-room floor. 'I need to show you my new ones,' she tells Pam, who of course humours her and kneels down to have a look.

I have given up apologising to Pam and Graham for the mess Freya always makes. They have assured me they love it, that it makes their house feel lived in, like a proper home.

After a few minutes Graham turns to Freya. 'Let's go outside, I'm sure Socks is under a tree somewhere. Grandma can get everyone drinks, if she doesn't mind.'

This is my opportunity. Following Pam into the kitchen, I watch Freya and Graham outside while she boils the kettle. I tell her I'll just have water, it's far too hot for anything else, but she still busies herself making tea. They will never go without it, whatever the weather.

'Can I talk to you, Pam? It's about Zach.' Normally I wouldn't jump straight in like this, for fear of her closing down, but I have to take this opportunity while Freya's busy outside.

Her body tenses but she continues making tea, avoiding looking at me. 'I'm sorry to bring this up, I really am, but I just wondered if you knew anything about one of Zach's colleagues, Dominic Bradford? I didn't know him but he was at the funeral and I remembered you talking to him for quite a while, and, well, I thought it would be nice if I could get in touch with him. To just remember Zach together, maybe.'

She stops what she's doing and turns to me. 'Dominic Bradford? But why now? It's been five years, Mia. Why do you want to do this now?'

'I know this must seem a bit out of the blue, but I just haven't felt ready to speak to anyone before now. You saw how I was after the funeral – I could barely speak to you. If I hadn't had a two-year-old to look after I don't know what I would have done. Shut myself off from the world even more, I suppose. But now I feel like I need to talk to people about him. People who knew him and cared for him. You must understand that?'

'Yes, I do. But what good will it do? You know what people think of Zach now. Nobody has a good word to say about him other than us.'

'But not Dominic,' I say. 'He never believed Zach was capable of what they said he did. He told me that at the funeral.'

Something crosses Pam's face and I know immediately what it is: she cannot bear to think of her son with one of his students. She shakes her head, but I've got to keep her talking before she completely shuts down. 'Please, Pam. This is just something I have to do.'

'Why now, Mia? You've moved on. You've got a beautiful little girl, so why dredge up so much unhappiness? If you talk to Zach's colleague you'll just end up going over the same old stuff again. And then you'll start doubting yourself. Thinking that he's guilty. Forgetting the man he really was.'

For five years I've not been able to tell Pam and Graham that I don't believe Zach was innocent, that the evidence stacked against him was too compelling to ignore. And, yes, I've hated myself every day for this, but rationality had to win out in the end. I couldn't let love blind me.

'He was depressed,' Pam continues, when I don't answer. 'That's why he took his life like that. I mean, he took enough of that horrible drug to make sure there was no chance anyone could save him, didn't he? It was nothing to do with that girl, nothing to do with guilt.' She dabs at her eyes. 'It was just desperation. Sadness. I don't know. It's hard to accept that none of us could see how desperate he was. And it's hard to understand why he'd leave Freya fatherless when he loved her so much, but that's what depression does.'

I hear Alison Cummings's words in my head: *Your husband didn't kill himself.*

There is no reply I can give Pam, so all I do is offer her a small nod. But I would have known if Zach had been depressed, wouldn't I? There would have been some sign of it, something I couldn't miss. And he had no history of depression.

I can't tell her my true thoughts, or about my counselling session with Alison Cummings, her huge revelation. Not until I know what's going on. I can't let Pam's world be torn apart all over again if nothing comes of this.

'Anyway, there's nothing that will bring him back, Mia,' she adds. 'And what's the good in talking to Dominic Bradford? They weren't that close and he's moved on with his life, I'm sure.'

I take a deep breath, wondering how much further I can push her. I don't need her to tell me where he lives, of course, but if there's a chance she knows anything more about him then I need to know it. 'You're probably right, Pam. I'm sure he doesn't want me turning up after all this time, reminding him of what happened.' I pause. 'He had a nice wife, didn't he? She was with him at the funeral, I think.' I hate having to play this game with Pam, of all people, but I need ammunition against what is to come.

She shakes her head, just as I knew she would. 'No, he was there alone. He got divorced not long after Zach died, so maybe there was trouble between them at that time... Anyway, I don't really know what happened. He kept in touch for a while, afterwards, but we haven't heard from him for years. I don't even know where he lives now.'

'Can you remember her name?' I'm pushing my luck now, but I need to try.

Pam frowns. 'I think it was Elaine. Why? Why are you asking me this, Mia? What's going on? Why do you want to know about Dominic's wife now?'

I turn back to the garden. Freya has finally located Socks and is walking round the garden, holding him in her arms. 'It's nothing. I just… I miss Zach, and I suppose I want to feel close to him, and be around people who knew him.' I can tell Pam's not convinced by my words, and I wouldn't be either; they make little sense even to me. I need to distract her. 'One of my clients has just lost his wife and it's bringing it all back to me.'

This seems to work and she walks over to me and gives me a hug. 'It will always be hard, dear. We just keep living with it, that's all we can do.' We stay holding each other for a moment until she pulls back and straightens herself up. 'How are things with Will? Are you going to let him move in yet?'

This is the amazing thing about Pam – she is able to put her pain aside and still want the best for me, even though she probably feels her only son is being replaced.

'I can't, Pam. Not yet. I'm not ready.'

She nods but I know she's preparing to question me about this. 'It's been five years, Mia. How long is long enough? From everything you've told us he sounds like a lovely man, and Freya loves him, doesn't she?'

There is no arguing with Pam's logic, but I cannot easily explain what's in my heart. 'Yes, Freya adores him. We both do.'

Her forehead creases. 'You do trust him, don't you? Because if this is about not wanting to get hurt, I'll say it again: I don't believe for one second Zach did anything wrong. Anything at all. You were a good wife to him, Mia, he would never have done anything to hurt you.' She pauses. 'Oh, I know that sounds wrong when he took his life, and he must have known how that would hurt you both – hurt us all – but you know what I mean.'

A familiar numbness takes hold of my body and I can't feel a thing. I clench my fist to shake some feeling into me but it's like watching someone else from afar. This can only be a protective mechanism I've developed over these years. To stop myself from falling.

'I try my best to believe that every day,' I say. *No, I don't. No, I don't. Zach ripped out my heart with his betrayal. But I know he loved Freya, and me too, in his own way, so I will focus on that, for Pam's sake.* 'Some days it's easier to be positive than others,' I say. 'Anyway, yes, Will is a good man.' The words stick in my throat; this is what people always said about Zach.

Pam nods. 'Graham and I were talking about it the other day and, well, we both think it's time we met Will. It's been long enough, hasn't it?'

This is the last thing I've been expecting and I'm momentarily stunned. 'I… um… yeah, that sounds good.' I know how hard meeting them will be for Will. He will do it for us, I have no doubt, but I don't want to put him through that. Still, I promise Pam I'll talk to him about it.

She smiles. It brings her pleasure to still be involved in my life. 'It doesn't have to be anything formal,' she says. 'There's no pressure. It's not like meeting the parents, is it?' She stops herself. 'Actually, it is, because that's what we feel we are, Mia. You're our daughter, as far as we're concerned.'

There are tears ready to burst from my eyes and all I can manage is to whisper a thank you.

'It's funny,' Pam says, 'when Zach first met you in… Tenerife, was it?'

'Fuerteventura.'

'Oh, yes, that's it. Well, I didn't think it would last five minutes – these holiday romances rarely do, and you were both so young. Zach was only twenty-five, wasn't he? And you must have been, what? Twenty-two?'

I nod. Pam has always been good at remembering dates and ages.

'But then he brought you home to us and I knew you were perfect for him. I just knew you were a good woman.'

I'm so choked up by her words I can't manage to speak. But it's funny to recall how Zach and I met. A lifetime ago now. I had assumed it was just a few nights of mostly drunken fun, and I certainly wasn't expecting him to call me once we both got home. But he did. And even when we got married three years later, and nobody thought it would last, we did. *How did we only have ten years together, Zach? Ten short years. Until death do us part.*

I'm glad I didn't eat breakfast this morning, because I would have definitely lost the contents of my stomach right about now. Luckily, Freya chooses this moment to bustle into the kitchen, still cradling a purring Socks in her arms. She is a welcome distraction. 'Can you stay for lunch, Mummy?' she asks.

As much as she loves her grandparents, she always hates it when I leave – at least until they distract her with some game or other.

'I can't, sweetheart, I have a client this afternoon. But I'll see you on Monday, okay?' I bend down to give her a kiss on the cheek. 'Be good.'

'I always am,' she protests, but I ruffle her hair to let her know that I know this.

And when I leave the house and step outside it's like breathing again after being close to suffocation.

EIGHT

Josie

I've always tried to be strong, to keep my emotions in check and never reveal any vulnerability, despite the circumstances I find myself in. Even after what Johnny did to me, I refused to shed a tear in front of him. I focused on my anger instead, and it protected me like a wall so he couldn't get in.

Now though, sitting in front of my lecturer, I feel like I am breaking down, crumbling from the inside. This is not me, but I can't seem to shake it.

'Come on,' Zach says, 'we need to get out of here.' He doesn't wait for a response but gently grabs my arm and takes me outside. Like a damsel in distress. I'll hate myself tomorrow. And I will never be able to face him again; I already know that.

'Is this about university?' he asks. 'Is there anything I can do? You know, if you're struggling with your work then there isn't a single tutor who wouldn't help you if you needed it. You just have to ask.'

I shrug. 'It's not that, really. Well, partly, but it's not the whole of it.' I reach into my pocket for a tissue but the only one I find is old and I know it has chewing gum stuck in it somewhere. I use it anyway, to get rid of these annoying tears. 'I'm not making sense, am I?' I say to Zach. 'Look, I'll just go.' I start to walk off but he reaches for my arm.

'I can't let you go like this, Josie. You're clearly upset about something.'

This is weird. He shouldn't be so concerned. He should be more than happy to say, *okay, great, see you around.* 'Don't worry about it, I'll be fine.'

But he's not buying it. 'No, you won't. Your hands are shaking.'

Are they? I can't tell. I can't feel anything. It's his kindness that's doing this to me. The other stuff too, but mostly the fact that he's bothering with me.

'Look,' he says. 'Is there anyone you can be with? Anyone you can talk to? It seems like you could use a chat. I just don't think you should be alone. Who do you live with?'

Ha, Alison! Yeah, she'd be a great person to talk to right now. 'My flatmate,' I say. 'But she's out.' I don't tell him that she's the cause of this; that she would probably love to see me this way.

I feel a surge of defiance, and have no idea where it's come from so suddenly. I don't want special treatment from Zach or anyone else. I'm going to get my assignment done if it kills me. I won't let anyone – especially Alison – get the better of me.

Zach checks his watch and looks around. 'I'll walk you to your car. Where did you park?'

'Actually, I didn't drive here.'

'Come on then, I'll drop you home.'

I can't let him do this. It's not fair. He's got a nice life and a nice wife and kid; he doesn't need to be around damaged goods. 'No, it's fine. I can walk.'

'Josie, it's getting dark now, and I just want to make sure you get back safely. Come on.'

So I give in, just because it's easier, and I get the feeling he's as stubborn as I am and we'll be out here debating it all evening if one of us doesn't admit defeat.

Zach's car has that brand-new smell, like he's just driven it out of a showroom, but inside it looks well used. There are CDs scattered all over the place, and books piled on the back seat. A pair of little pink shoes.

I turn to him. 'CDs? You actually buy CDs?'

'Yeah, why? Is that not cool?' His smile tells me he doesn't take my surprise personally.

'I just haven't seen one for a long time.' Since I left *her* house. But this comes as no surprise. Liv had me at sixteen and is probably around the same age as Zach.

We drive in silence for a few minutes and I get lost in the radio station Zach's put on. It's rock music – not really my thing – but somehow it suits him. I lean my head back and close my eyes, trying to make the moment last, when in reality we are only minutes from my flat.

'Are you okay, Josie?' Zach says.

My eyes snap open. Am I? It's hard to tell, but right now, being with Zach, I feel better. His car is a cocoon, keeping the outside world at bay. Here, everything that's wrong in my life is too far away to touch me. I can write another story. Maybe it won't be as good as the original, but I'll do it anyway. Alison, despite everything, is harmless, and that woman is miles away in Brighton. She can threaten me all she wants, I'm not going to let her – or anyone else – scare me.

'I'm getting there,' I tell Zach. 'Sorry about just now, I don't usually lose control like that.'

He shakes his head. 'Josie, it's okay to have those moments. You're only human. We all are. You can't be superwoman all the time.'

I throw my head back. 'Ha, is that what you think I am? You couldn't be further from the truth.'

'Well, that's good to hear. Perfection is exhausting. It makes other people feel as though they're not good enough, that they'll never live up to your expectations. You don't want to be perfect.'

I wonder if he is speaking from personal experience here, if it's his wife he's referring to.

'So what was it about?' he continues. 'It must have taken something important to upset you so much – in front of me, of all people.'

I don't know what he means by that, but it doesn't matter. What counts is that he's asking me, wanting to know.

'I can't... I'm sorry.'

'No, no! I'm the one who should be sorry. I shouldn't be asking you, it's inappropriate. It's probably personal, and I'm your lecturer, so you really don't have to tell me anything. But, well, I'm here if you want to talk. About anything. I'm quite open-minded, you know.'

This is easy to believe. I could jump to the worst conclusion and assume that Zach has an agenda, but I don't sense that from him at all. I barely know him, but I feel that he's genuine. And believe me, I've had enough experience to know when a guy is sleazy and after something.

Maybe I'm dumb to trust him so easily, and maybe part of that's because I find him attractive, but I like to think I can trust my instincts.

'Thanks, Zach. Maybe some other time. Turn right here. I live on this road, about halfway down.'

He pulls up just outside my flat but keeps the engine running. 'You'll get through it, Josie, whatever it is.'

Yes, I will. I've come this far, I'm not about to let myself down now.

'Thanks for the lift, Zach,' I say, reaching for the door handle.

'See you tomorrow, Josie.'

I stop and turn to face him. I've never been one to hold back, and I have to ask this. 'Why are you doing this? Being so kind to me, I mean. I'm not your only student. There can't be enough time in your day to help us all.'

He doesn't seem fazed by my question. 'No, you're right,' he says, looking me in the eye. 'But I'd be there for any of my students if they needed help with anything. I don't think my job stops the second you all leave the lecture hall.' He turns away and stares through the window. 'Plus, I'd like to think we've kind of become, well, friends, in a funny way. Connected through our writing or something.'

'Friends.' I try the word out and find that I like it. I don't tell him that I long ago gave up on the idea of having friends. That when you're at rock bottom you turn around and find they've all disappeared, that there's nobody there to hold out their hand and lift you up.

I open the car door and jump out.

'Can I be honest with you, Josie?' Zach calls.

I walk around to the driver's side. 'Course. About anything.'

He smiles. 'I feel like I can, at least, but I just need to say this. I'm married, with a young toddler, and I love my home life, so please don't think I have any kind of weird thoughts or anything. I just have to get that out of the way. I shouldn't have to. I mean, if you were male, we probably wouldn't even need to address it, but I just want you to know that when I say friendship, that's exactly what I mean.'

'That's great to know!' I say, keeping my voice upbeat even though something inside me feels like it's just torn. 'But just for the record, I never thought you had any… dishonourable intentions.' I laugh to reinforce what I'm saying.

'People are too uptight these days,' he says, almost to himself. 'I like to just go with the flow, be friends with who you want to, without having to feel judged by society. We can feel a connection to all kinds of people, and just because I'm your lecturer – for three hours a week, I have to add – why shouldn't we chat and talk about our writing together? We're both adults. And you've really helped me with my writing, Josie, without even doing anything but hand in your assignments.' He laughs. 'God, what do I sound like?'

'Like you're being honest,' I say. 'And I agree with it all. Plus, it's nice to know I'm helping you get your novel finished.'

He smiles and I sense he is relieved that I understand what he's saying. I do understand it, but I don't have to like it.

I lean closer into his window. 'Can I ask you something? Seeing as we're such good friends now?'

He laughs. 'Of course.'

'Sorry to ask such a personal question, but, before you got married, how did you know she was the one? I'm not prying, I just wonder how you can ever know that when none of us know what the future holds.'

'That's a bit cynical, isn't it?'

You would understand why I'm like this if you knew where I came from.

'I know, but just humour me.'

He lets out a deep breath and drums his fingers on the steering wheel. 'Okay, well, the minute I saw Mia I knew there was something different about her. She was so... in control of everything. Of herself. I just found her a refreshing change from the women I'd met before. She wasn't needy at all, and I could just... be myself, I suppose.' He looks at me and shrugs. 'We weren't much older than you are now, so I can't say I knew I wanted to marry her immediately, but in time it felt like the natural thing to do. The only thing to do.'

'I can't imagine that happening to me,' I say, almost forgetting who I'm talking to, because this is the thing about Zach: he makes me feel as if I've known him forever. I know, such a cliché, right? But it's true.

'And surely people change?' I continue. 'You can't be the same person you were in your twenties.' I sound jealous and bitter, but that's not how I feel really. It's more an intense sadness, and loneliness. But, hey, at least I can admit this.

'No, but you just have to hope you grow together. And I couldn't imagine it happening to me either, until it did. That's the beauty of life. The unexpected. Embrace it, Josie. I think it's exciting that you never know what might happen tomorrow.' He stops and waits for a man walking his dog to pass the car. 'What I'm trying to say is, be positive – like you're being with your studies now. Let that spill over into all aspects of your life.'

'That's exactly what I'm doing.'

'Good. Anyway, you shouldn't be worrying about relationships or marriage or anything like that. You've got plenty of time for all that.' He stares ahead, out of the windscreen, and I wonder what he's thinking.

'Anyway,' he says, turning back to me. 'I'd better get back. Mia will be wondering where I am.'

'Thanks again. For everything.'

I stand back and fumble in my pocket for my keys, watching Zach's car pull away and disappear round the corner.

Mia. It's such a pretty name and I bet his wife is beautiful to match it. She sounds perfect. But surely perfection can't exist? And Zach was only just saying that we're only human and should be allowed to make mistakes. That perfection is exhausting. Something like that anyway.

So just how happy *is* his marriage?

I close the front door behind me and lean against it, not bothering to turn on the hall light, my heart pounding in my chest. Was Zach trying to tell me something other than what he appeared to be saying when he described his wife? Or am I just blinded by his kindness, desperate for someone important to be in my life? Because other than Kieren, there really is no one. Yeah, I have plenty of people I could go drinking with, but what does that really mean? None of them would give me the time of day if I needed help with anything, other than offering to buy the next round of drinks.

Suck it up, Josie, there are people far worse off than you. And nobody ever died of loneliness, did they?

I look up and Alison is standing in the darkness by her bedroom door, watching me. I gasp. 'What the hell?'

'Who was that in that car? New boyfriend? Glad things are working out for you. Hope it lasts longer than it did for me and Aaron.' Her smile is a snide grin.

I'm shocked she's actually speaking to me, and having a dig at me, but I quickly recover; ready as always to defend myself. 'You have no clue what you're talking about, Alison. If you stopped to let me explain, then you'd know Aaron was a sleaze and you're well rid of him. Even you can do better than that.' I hadn't meant it to come out that way but it's too late to take it back now.

'But that wasn't for you to decide, Josie, was it? It's my choice to decide who I will and won't be with.' Her voice is so soft now I can barely hear her. I take a step closer.

'He just wasn't interested in you, Alison. I'm sorry, that sucks, I know, but you can't blame *me* for it. Maybe you'll choose better next time.'

Her mouth turns into an ugly grimace. I wait for a further onslaught but all she does is glare at me with her wide green eyes.

I look towards my door, which is slightly ajar. 'Have you been in my room, Alison?' I don't know why I'm bothering to give her a chance to deny it.

Her nose crinkles, but the mad stare stays on her face. 'Why would I go in your room?'

What do I do now? I can't just accuse her of deleting my assignment; she'll only deny it and I'll sound like a nutjob. 'No, I guess you wouldn't, would you? You wouldn't go in there when I'm out. Because that would just be, I don't know, *crazy.* And you're not some sort of crazy stalker or freak, are you?'

Without another word she turns and disappears inside her room, closing the door silently behind her.

And I am left with a bitter taste in my mouth.

NINE

Mia

Carlo, like me, is too young to have lost a spouse. It's hard enough when you've shared your whole life with someone, but when those years are cut short, stolen from you, the impact is devastating.

This young man is the only client I've spoken with about what I've been through, and I think it's partly why he keeps coming to me, though he initially admitted he would have preferred a male counsellor. 'Please don't take it personally,' he'd said during our first session. 'But I don't find it easy talking to women, apart from Jenny. I tried to find a man but there weren't any suitable round here.'

But it's been five months now, and he continues to make appointments, and open up to me, so I like to think I'm helping in some way. I told him about losing my husband after a few sessions, when he seemed to be putting up resistance, not believing in me or himself. It is the only time I've ever done it, and actually I don't regret it. It's what he needed to hear.

'I constantly feel like I take one step forward and then two back,' he says, sitting across from me. As always he is leaning forward in his chair, his elbows resting on his knees.

Even though it's the weekend, I'm glad I let Carlo book this appointment; it's what I need to take my mind off the mess of my own life at the moment. Alison made it clear she won't talk to me, so I just need to work out what to do, and in the meantime, helping this poor man is what I will throw myself into.

'That's normal, Carlo, I promise you. And it can be like that even after five years.'

'Five years.' He lets out a sigh that turns into a whistle. He knows this is how long it's been for me. 'Do you know what scares me the most? That I'll forget Jenny. That in a year, maybe two, I'll wake up and she won't be the first person I think of. That freaks me out, Mia. I don't want to forget the things she said to me, or her funny little ways.' He smiles. 'She had this funny laugh that would always turn into a snort, like a pig. But it was so cute. Just so… *Jenny.*'

I don't tell him that eventually he might forget exactly how it sounded. 'But do you know what that will be, Carlo? Progress. It won't mean you're forgetting her, just that you've come to terms with it.'

He takes a moment to consider this and then nods, confident that I know what I'm talking about, that my guidance doesn't just come from studying textbooks. But there is a huge difference between his situation and mine. The death of his wife isn't tainted by horrific acts of betrayal – and worse. Carlo can grieve normally, remember the moments they shared without the memories being overshadowed. But for me, Zach's death is synonymous with Josie Carpenter. The two of them are forever entwined.

'There's something you could try,' I say, pushing my thoughts aside. 'I think it might help you.'

One evening, after Zach died, I put Freya to bed and went out in the back garden. Just as the sun set and it grew dark, I lit a Chinese lantern and watched it float away, saying goodbye to Zach as it ascended. It took ages for the light to get so small I could no longer see it, and in the time it was drifting upwards, away from me and off to some new place, I remembered Zach, told him all the things I would miss about him, and ignored anything else that had happened surrounding his death.

I suggest to Carlo that he tries this and his face actually brightens. 'You're saying it actually works? I guess it sounds like a good idea. I'll do it.'

I nod. 'It's a nice way to say goodbye when someone dies, or even when you lose something, or life changes in some way. It might help you in your grieving process.'

Still leaning forward, he clamps his hands together. 'Thank you, I would never have thought of that. D'you know what I think of sometimes? And it makes me even sadder. Jenny would have loved you. I know she would. She was strong and kind like you, with a huge heart. But then if she hadn't died, I wouldn't be here to have met you, so… well, life's just a bit weird, isn't it?'

'Yes, it is, Carlo. And Jenny sounds like an amazing woman. To be diagnosed with terminal cancer and still keep positive for the people around you takes tremendous courage.'

He nods, a proud smile on his face. 'So does what you've been through,' he says, but then looks away.

I knew when I told him I'd lost my husband that there was a chance he'd Google it and find out about Zach's suicide. And about Josie Carpenter. And now I'm convinced he has. Carlo is too polite to say anything, but he knows, I'm sure of it. I wonder when he found out. Maybe it was even before his first session. It's only natural that he would check out the counsellor he's planning to open his heart to. Although I had the option of reverting to my maiden name, and there were times I was desperate to escape the stigma of Zach's name, I couldn't bring myself to do it. I didn't want to have to change Freya's, or to have a different surname from her.

For a second I feel the flood of shame I used to get whenever I encountered anyone who knew. But there is no judgement emanating from Carlo, and clearly nothing he's found out has stopped him from coming to me.

I need to change the direction of this conversation, turn it away from me and back to him. 'How are you finding your local support group, Carlo?'

He shrugs. 'Yeah, it's good. But, the thing is… most of the people there are much older than me, so I kind of find it hard to relate to them. I'm the only one in my thirties. That's why I prefer coming here. I feel like you really get me.'

'That's nice of you to say, and I'm glad you feel supported, but surrounding yourself with people who understand at all is the most important thing. You don't have to be the same age or share the same interests. There's something much more important that will bond you together. Maybe you don't want to see them all the time but I wouldn't recommend leaving the group. Not at this early stage. In time you might find you don't need the meetings as much, but it's all still so fresh for you, Carlo, and I don't want you to be so alone in this.' Alone like I was, because who could I talk to when everyone hated Zach?

I remember what Carlo has told me about his family. 'Your parents and siblings are in Italy, aren't they?'

He nods. 'And America. But at least when I'm feeling up to it, I'll get to travel. Can't imagine doing it now but eventually I will.'

'That's true. Just don't cut yourself off from people. Being isolated makes everything so much harder.' I know this only too well. My mum passed away soon after Zach and I were married and Dad moved to Canada to live near his sister, so he wasn't around much after Zach died. I understood this; he just couldn't deal with any more death. I was lucky enough to have friends who stood by me, even after what Zach was accused of, but I didn't, and still don't, like to burden people with my problems.

'I hear you,' Carlo says.

By the end of the session, he seems in better spirits, but I know this hour will only be a temporary fix. As soon as he walks out of the door it will hit him all over again, and my words and support will fade into the background until I see him next week.

The house is too quiet without Freya around, and although I wanted time and space to think, now I've got it I desperately want the hustle and bustle of normal life.

I sit at my desk, long after Carlo has gone, and stare at my notes. I'm pleased with his progress but my mind is clouded and I can't focus on writing up the details of our session. What am I supposed to do with the information Alison gave me? What kind of sick game is she playing? I could try to talk to Dominic, but if Alison was telling the truth about him being abusive then I can't risk him doing anything to her. Regardless of whether she ever comes back, she's my client and I owe her confidentiality, but, more than that, I would never risk causing her harm. Despite what she's said and why she may have said it.

But there is one person I can speak to and that's Dominic's ex-wife, Elaine. I expect she won't be forthcoming if it's got anything to do with her ex-husband, but it's the only thing I have left to try.

I Google Elaine Bradford; even though they're divorced there's a slim chance she's kept her married name. Just like when I was searching for Alison, several hits come up, but it only makes me realise how futile this is. I don't know what this woman looks like, or her age, or anything that could help me identify her. All I know is she got divorced around five years ago.

Frustrated, I scroll through the list of links, hoping something will jump out at me, but nothing does.

My mobile phone rings and I snatch it up when I see it's Will.

'Hey,' he says. 'How's everything? Did you drop Freya off okay?' His voice is filled with warmth, as it always is, and just for a second I can almost pretend everything is normal. That it's just the three of us.

I should let this Alison thing go; I have a life now and nothing can bring Zach back. He's gone, and so is the person I was, so I need to put it behind me. Alison doesn't seem to want to pursue it either so there can't be anything in what she said. *But still. There was a reason for her visit. A reason for what she said.*

'Yeah, all fine. They want to meet you soon. For dinner.' I hesitate. 'How do you feel about that?'

A few seconds of silence follow before Will answers. 'Actually, that would be nice. It's a big step for them so I appreciate the offer. I know how important they are to you, they're practically your family.'

'It's a big step for you too, though, Will. Are you ready?'

'The main thing is are *you* ready, Mia?'

The truth is I don't know. But I need to prove to Will that he's important to me and that I believe we have a future together. 'Let's do it,' I say. 'I'll let them know.'

'If you change your mind, though—'

'I won't.' And now I've made that promise, I need to make sure I can keep it.

Feeling more optimistic, and certain I can get past this, I spend the rest of the day catching up on paperwork. I even write up Alison's notes, though it's unlikely she will return.

As I'm putting away my folders, I spot the corner of my wedding photograph. It shouldn't be in this drawer after so long, but I can't bring myself to put it away with all the others. It makes me feel as though Zach is with me, somehow, when I'm helping other people.

I can rarely bring myself to look at it, but I slip it out from beneath the papers it's hiding under, and stare at my husband's face. He smiles back at me, his hazel eyes shining with all the promise that lay ahead of us. The promise that came to nothing.

What did you do to that girl, Zach?

I don't notice the tears falling from my eyes until they splatter onto the photo, blurring my face. The face I perfected with make-up because it was the most important day of my life, at least until Freya was born.

Zach always told me things didn't need to be perfect, they just needed to be what they are, but he understood that day that I wanted everything to be right. And it was. A fairy-tale wedding. There was no glimpse of the nightmare that was to follow.

The doorbell rings, snapping me out of thoughts I'm only too glad to be distracted from.

I'm not expecting anyone, but it crosses my mind that it might be Will, wanting to surprise me. He said he had a lot of work on, but it would be just like him to turn up when I need him the most.

The last person I'm expecting to see when I open the door is Dominic Bradford.

TEN

Josie

I haven't had a chance to speak to Zach for a couple of weeks. I've seen him, though, in my lectures, and hung around afterwards to try and grab a word with him, but there's always a queue of students waiting for him. I don't even know what I want to say to him, I only know I have to say something.

He saw me waiting for him today, and I thought he might make some sort of gesture that I should wait around, but his eyes only met mine briefly, giving nothing away, and then he turned back to the person he was speaking to. That loudmouth bleached-blonde woman who looks old enough to have kids at uni herself.

I need to get real. Zach's trying to distance himself from me after giving me a lift home that night. He regrets it now. But what was all that talk about friendship? He said we had a connection.

Sod him. I don't need this shit in my life. I've managed without any so-called friends since I came to London so I don't need his *friendship*. It's so much easier not to bother with people.

So now I'm in a bar getting wrecked; Vanessa and a group of her friends surround me and I have no interest in what any of them are saying. One of them – Harry, is it? Something with an H – sits nudged up against me. He's pretending he's got no choice because six of us are crammed into a small booth, but even in my state I can see there is room on his other side.

I push him away and dig my nails into his thigh just to ram home my message, but he's too far gone to feel any pain. It's not even 9 p.m. But then, who am I to judge?

I almost will this guy to try something because the mood I'm in means I'll enjoy ripping into him, shrinking him to the size of a woodlouse.

Opposite me, Vanessa is shouting about something but laughing at the same time. I have no idea what she's saying because all I can hear is noise – loud thudding music and everyone's voices mixing together so that nobody makes any sense.

Harry leans in to me. 'So how d'you know Nessie?' His voice pierces my ear.

'Who?'

'Nessie.' He points to Vanessa, who's gesticulating wildly about something to some girl I've never seen before.

'No idea,' I say. 'We just know each other.' I can't be bothered to explain how I met Vanessa on my second day in London. I was drinking alone in a student bar and she started talking to me while we waited to be served. I didn't want her to think I'd come out to drink on my own so I told her I'd been stood up by some guy.

'Yeah, me too,' he says, downing another tequila shot. At least I think that's what he said, even though it makes no sense.

He leans in towards me again and I edge away. 'Look, Harry, I—'

'It's Hugh,'

'Okay, Hugh. Look, I'm not feeling very sociable tonight so how about you back off? I just want to sit here and finish my drink and then get the hell out of here. Okay?'

He hesitates for a moment, probably shocked I've been so outspoken. 'Whatever,' he says eventually, turning away from me. And under his breath I hear him say, 'Nessie needs to be more picky about the friends she chooses.' Somehow I hear every word in perfect clarity. But it's okay – I don't give a damn what Harry, or Hugh, or whatever the hell his name is, thinks of me.

Someone ends up buying another round before I've finished my last drink so I end up staying for just one more. Thankfully, Hugh has moved on and is now harassing Vanessa's pretty Chinese friend, who, unlike me, is polite enough, or drunk enough, to bother talking to him.

What am I doing here? This isn't me. Or at least if it is, it shouldn't be. This isn't the life I want, and I'm not like these people. Not only are they younger than me they've got nothing to worry about. All they want to do is have fun, while I'm just here to escape.

I need to get out of here.

Nobody notices when I slip away. At least it feels like I'm slipping away, when in reality I'm staggering, stumbling all over the place.

Outside the icy air sobers me up enough for me to get my bearings. I'm in Chiswick and I need to get a bus back to Ealing. But what bus do I need? The stop across the road looks vaguely familiar so I try my luck and head towards it.

Somehow I end up on the right bus, sitting close to the driver because he took pity on me and told me he'd let me know when I get to my stop. 'Just in case you fall asleep,' he'd said.

But there's no chance of that. Every second closer to home sobers me up another notch as I wonder if I'll have to see Alison, if she'll confront me again. Knowing all I'll do when I get into bed is think about Zach, even though I've vowed not to. Worrying about that damn assignment I had to rewrite that I still haven't had back.

When my phone pings with an email alert I almost can't be bothered to check it, but habit compels me to have a look. And when I see it's from Zach, with the subject heading *Assignment*, my heart feels like it's in my throat. He's never emailed me before so this is bad. Very bad. I did the best I could with that assignment, in the few hours I had to rewrite it after Alison deleted it, but now I have to face not only a terrible mark, but Zach's disappointment too.

I take a deep breath then open the message. It's three words long. *95%. You star!*

That's it. Three short but powerful words that send me soaring. I jump up and grab hold of the pole by the bus driver and press the stop button. I'm smiling so hard I must look like a lunatic, but then I'm already drunk so nobody will be surprised.

'This isn't your stop,' the bus driver says.

But I ignore him. I know where I am now and it's only two more stops. The walk will do me good. He pulls the bus to a halt and I jump off, walking on air.

Now the effects of the alcohol are wearing off, I begin to feel the cold as I head home. It's quiet out here and my footsteps echo into the night. I'm almost at the flat when an arm grabs me from behind and a rough, large hand covers my mouth. I'm dragged backwards, and shoved into the back seat of a car before I even have a chance to panic.

Within seconds, fear sets in. But I won't scream. I need to stay calm.

I turn around to face my attacker, who has me pinned down now so I can't move. He's a large man and even though I don't recognise his face – narrow eyes set too close together, receding hair that looks brown, though it's hard to tell in the dark – I know this is not random.

This man has been waiting for me.

'Josie,' he says, his voice deep and familiar. He sounds a bit like Johnny. Memories flood back to me. 'Finally we meet. I think we need to have a bit of a chat, don't you?'

I struggle beneath his heavy arms. 'No. Let me out of this fucking car.'

'Or what? You'll scream? There's no one around, Josie. Besides, we're going for a little drive in a sec. Once I've made sure you're not going anywhere.' He reaches to the floor and grabs a roll of duct tape, wrapping it around my wrists and ankles so tightly it burns into my skin. Then he reaches into my pocket and grabs my mobile. He's right about one thing: I'm not going anywhere.

Despite my vulnerable situation, I still refuse to show any fear, even though my insides have turned to liquid. 'What do you want? Friend of Johnny's, are you? Or Liv's? Just get this over with and tell me what the hell you want.'

He laughs. 'Johnny was right about you – he said you had balls. But I don't care about that.' He slams the back door shut and jumps in the driver's seat. I lurch backwards as he drives off.

'You're one of his cousins, aren't you?' I think I knew this the second I saw him. He has that same twisted look about him. Similar arrogance in his voice, as if they've grown up together and learned from each other.

'It doesn't matter who I am. Listen to me. You're gonna shut the fuck up while I get to where we're going. And then you're gonna listen to me and do exactly what I say. Got it?'

I fake a loud, exaggerated laugh. It's all I can do to stop myself throwing up. 'Someone's been watching too many gangster movies, haven't they?'

But rather than show his anger and hit back with some remark designed to scare me, he says nothing, keeping his eyes fixed on the road. And somehow his lack of words is more sinister than anything he could have said.

During the silence I try to keep calm. This man won't hurt me, I'm certain of that, or he would have already done it. With a cousin already in prison he's unlikely to come after the girl who had to put him there.

But the longer he drives, the less convinced I become that he won't do anything to me. I stare through the window and eventually realise from the signs that we're heading towards north London. Why is he driving me so far away?

To stop myself thinking about this, I focus on the positive things in my life. There's Kieren, of course. And my degree. I've got to get a good career so that I can look after Kieren and get him away from her. From people like this man. There shouldn't be a court in the world that will allow him to stay with her if I'm in a strong enough position to oppose it.

And there's Zach. I replay the conversation we had in his car until I believe his words again. He hasn't been avoiding me, he's just busy, a professional man doing his best for his students. I'm not the kind of girl who imagines these kinds of things and I'm not some silly young fool with a crush on her lecturer. This isn't like that at all. But whatever it is can't be easily explained.

Human imperfection. That's all I can describe it as.

Although I'm not familiar with any of the buildings or roads we're passing through, a sign lets me know we're in Enfield. I haven't lived in London long enough to venture much further than the West End, and not knowing where I am makes me feel even more uneasy.

Finally he pulls into a narrow road, just past a large block of flats. Perhaps he lives here. When Liv was with Johnny I spent so little time in his presence that I know barely anything about his family. I only know he has three sisters and loads of cousins, but none of them ever visited the house when I lived there. I try to memorise my surroundings, just in case I make it out of here alive.

He cuts off the engine and turns to face me. 'Right. This is simple, Josie. I just need you to do one thing. That's it. One simple little thing, and then you can get on with the cosy little life you've made for yourself here in London.'

And now I know what he wants before he even says it. 'I'm not withdrawing my statement. Never. So you can just kill me right now, if that's what you want, but it won't make any difference. That bastard can rot in prison.'

A fist flies into my face, knocking me back against the seat. I want to press my hands to the source of the pain, but they are tied tightly together.

'Don't even think about reporting this,' he says, smirking. 'I've got an airtight alibi and was nowhere near London tonight.'

'Shame Johnny didn't have one the night he attacked me, isn't it?'

'Attacked' isn't even the right word. That suggests it was something quick, spur of the moment, a done in anger kind of thing. But, no, what he did to me was far worse than that.

'That's the problem, isn't it, Josie? It wasn't Johnny. Never. He wouldn't do something like that, especially to his girlfriend's daughter, so why don't you just be a good little girl for once in your sorry life and admit to the police that you lied?'

'Why would I lie? What possible reason would I have?'

'Because you hated Johnny, didn't you? Jealous, weren't you? You probably wanted him for yourself and couldn't stand the thought of your mum having him. Little slut! What were you – seventeen, eighteen? A bloody kid.'

And that's what makes it so much worse that Liv defended him, refused to believe he'd done that to me. I wasn't even an adult, not really.

I almost laugh; is this man really saying these words to me? 'I only ever told the truth, and I won't lie now to save that monster. 'You can threaten me all you want, nothing's worse than what he's already done.' I try to keep my voice firm, even though I'm shaking.

He slams his fists on the steering wheel then turns back, grabbing me by the neck. 'Listen, you little bitch. If you think what he did was bad you'd better think again, because that will seem like a trip to Disneyland compared to what'll happen if you don't put this right. Understand?' He doesn't wait for an answer. 'It's simple. All you have to do is tell the police you lied. Maybe you'll get in a bit of trouble for that, but believe me, that's the easier option.'

'They'll never believe it. There are photos, evidence of what Johnny did.'

'Tell them it happened on your way home and it was a stranger. Simple.' Without any warning he draws a knife from the glove compartment, and just as I'm praying for this to be as painless as possible, he cuts through the duct tape I'm bound with. 'Now get the hell out of my car. The clock's ticking, Josie. Tick tock, tick tock.'

I don't respond well to threats. There's too much of a fighter in me, too much stubbornness, which can be an asset but often gets me into trouble. Yes, I'm shaken up as I walk away from that man's car – I still don't know his name – but I'm also more determined than I've ever been. I won't be a victim. I had no choice but to become one when Johnny came at me that night, but never again will I let that happen.

Liv, my so-called mother. Johnny. His cousin. Even Alison. 'Bring it on,' I scream into the night. 'I'm ready for you all.'

ELEVEN

Mia

'Hi. Mia, isn't it?' Dominic offers his hand while I can only stare, open-mouthed, unable to form any words or take his hand. 'I'm so sorry to just turn up like this, but I thought it would be better if we spoke in person. Is that okay?' When I still can't speak, he puts his hand down and continues speaking. 'You probably don't remember me, but I was a colleague of Zach's. We spoke at the funeral.'

Finally, I find my voice, but the frown remains on my face. I know why he's here – Alison must have told him I followed him home the other day, and he's about to tell me to back off. 'Yes, I remember. Um…'

'I can see you're confused, and rightly so, but could we just have a quick chat? I won't take up too much of your time, I know how busy you must be. How is your little one? I remember her being about two, so she must be seven now?'

This is strange. It doesn't add up; his voice is apologetic – kind, even – when he should be angry.

I tell him he's right, that Freya's seven now, but make no move to let him in. 'What's this about, Dominic?'

He lets out a heavy sigh. 'I know Alison came to see you on Wednesday, and I just thought I'd better explain a few things.'

So he's here to tell me what Alison meant about Zach. Nausea bubbles in my stomach. This is worse than I thought. 'Okay, but let's go across to the park.' There is no way I will let him in the house.

Although Dominic seems surprised I've suggested this, he quickly agrees and less than a minute later we're sitting on the bench I usually share with Freya, while kids flurry past us, their shouts and screams mingling in the air. At least we're in public.

'Before you say anything,' I say, 'I can't discuss anything Alison said during our session, even if she doesn't intend to come and see me again. You have to understand that.'

He nods. 'Yes, I thought that would be the case. But I can talk to you about her, can't I? You don't need to tell me anything she's said. Actually, I'm not even sure I *want* to know what she's said, although I can hazard a guess.'

I'm not sure about talking to this man; it's dodgy ground, a grey area I've never had to think about before, but if I tread carefully I shouldn't get in any trouble. 'What's this about, Dominic?' I know the answer but I can't be the one to bring it up.

A dog runs past us, barking excitedly as it chases a tennis ball. 'I think I might know what Alison said to you, and I'm so sorry, but, well, she's a bit disturbed. And if I'm right, she should never have mentioned Zach like that.' He looks at me and I give a small nod, even though I probably shouldn't. Dominic takes it as his sign to continue. 'Telling you he didn't kill himself, it's just awful. I don't know why she said it, and I know you probably need some kind of explanation, but the best I can offer is that she doesn't even know what she's saying herself.'

My whole body tenses when I hear Dominic's words. It's bad enough that Alison said them to me but now I'm hearing it all over again. From another person I don't know or trust. And if this man *is* abusing Alison, then it makes no sense that she'd talk to him about Zach. 'How do you know what she did or didn't say to me? Have you talked to her about what she's claiming?'

He shakes his head. 'No, but sometimes she mumbles to herself and I don't think she even realises what she's saying. She just blurted it out the other day. I don't think she even knew I heard her.'

The more this man says, the more I struggle to believe him. 'But why would she say what you're suggesting?' I ask. 'She didn't even know Zach. It doesn't make sense.'

'You're right. She didn't know Zach. Look, this is really hard to talk about, especially considering how you lost your husband, but, well, Alison has issues. She's on heavy medication for depression and anxiety, has been for years and... God, I feel awful talking about her like this, but she's been prone to concocting stories.'

It takes me a moment to fully understand what he's saying, and even when I've got to grips with it, there is still so much not adding up. 'But that still doesn't explain why she would track me down.'

He raises his eyes. 'Damn it, I probably shouldn't be saying any of this, but I don't know what else to do. Here's the thing: when she was in her third year at university, Alison shared a flat with Josie Carpenter. The flat Zach was found in.'

The ground begins to sink beneath my feet. Hearing that name still cuts like a blade, even now. And this is just one more thing that doesn't make sense. 'No, you're wrong. She couldn't have. The police said Josie lived alone. She didn't have a flatmate.'

He nods. 'She *was* living alone at the time. Alison had moved out a couple of months before. I guess the police didn't think that was important.'

Every word he says pierces my gut, but I need to know everything. 'So they never interviewed her?'

'No. But why would they? She wasn't friends with Josie, she hadn't seen her since she'd moved out. She couldn't tell them anything that would help.'

But this is not why I'm asking. It's not Josie Carpenter I need to know about, it's Zach. 'So you're saying I can't believe anything Alison said?'

He turns around on the bench so his whole body faces me, and for the first time I notice specks of grey in his black hair. 'Yes, that's exactly what I'm saying. I'm so sorry, Mia. After everything you've been through, that must have been the last thing you needed to hear, five years later. I can only apologise for what she did.'

I shake my head, the one thing I need to know still pounding against my skull. 'But why did she say it? It doesn't make sense.'

'That's the trouble. Alison rarely does. And I should know, I've been with her for years, and she's rarely been okay in that time. I mean there've been glimpses of hope when I thought she'd just... be all right, I suppose, but they're always short-lived.'

'How long have you been together?'

'Three years,' he says. 'But I knew of her before that. She was a student at the University of West London when Zach and I were both there. I didn't teach her, and neither did Zach, as she was studying environmental science. But I'd seen her around. She was hard to miss, with that red hair. It was wavy then, though she straightens it now, of course, and looks quite different, but I guess she was young. The same age as Josie Carpenter.' His hand flies to his mouth, but the gesture feels fake. 'Sorry, I shouldn't keep bringing her up.'

When I don't speak, Dominic fills in the gaps. 'Don't get me wrong – I wasn't involved with her when she was a student. I was married at that time, but years later, after my divorce, I met Alison in a hospital waiting room.' He pauses and his eyes flick upwards. 'Oh, man, that sounds so bad, doesn't it? But we'd both been in A&E for hours and once we'd realised she was a student when I was teaching there we just spent the whole time chatting.' He holds up his wrist. 'Turns out I'd broken this.'

'Why... why was Alison there?' It seems so much of a coincidence.

'She... Well, it turns out she was feeling a bit low and thought she'd get checked out. Apparently she'd had thoughts of... harming herself. Sorry, Mia, that must be hard to hear after Zach.'

He doesn't realise that in my job I hear this a lot, and I can't think about myself at these times. 'It's okay.'

'Anyway,' Dominic continues, 'at the time she told me she was there for stomach pain, which she thought might be appendicitis. I was even getting angry with the doctors, cursing them for leaving her waiting so long. So she was pretty much lying to me right from the start. But they say love is blind, don't they? And it's not her fault. She just needs help.'

Dominic's story is convincing. Almost *too* convincing. How do I know he's telling me the truth, and that it really is Alison who has been lying? How can I trust anything either of them says?

'Sorry for rambling,' he says. 'Here's the thing – I said this to you at the funeral, but I still don't believe Zach had anything to do with what happened to Josie. I really don't. I don't know if Alison said anything about that to you – or what she might have said if she did – but I hope you don't ever believe that Zach was guilty.'

I want to scream at him: *How can you know that when you barely knew him? You were just colleagues, passing in the hallway and maybe saying hello to each other. You weren't friends and he never once mentioned you.* But I bite my tongue. If I'm to get information out of Dominic then I need to stay calm. 'You weren't close friends, though, were you?'

He shakes his head. 'We spoke quite a bit. We were in different departments so it wasn't that easy to find time to get together, but we always meant to go for a drink or something.'

And yet at the funeral Dominic had insisted that Zach was a good man, as if he had evidence of this and knew it without a doubt. But this type of thing is typical of certain people when someone they know dies. They want to be part of it, act as though the loss is theirs.

'Why did you get divorced?' I feel as though I'm interrogating him, as if I'm somehow investigating Zach's death, but I just want answers.

He looks down and stares at his left hand, absent of any rings. 'Yeah. I messed that one up. We divorced shortly after… you know.'

'Elaine, wasn't it?'

His eyes widen. 'Yeah. Do you know her?'

An image of one of the website links I found flashes into my head. 'She's an estate agent, isn't she? With her own business?' I have no idea whether or not this is the right woman I'm talking about, but it's worth taking a chance.

To my relief he nods, seeming not to notice I've avoided answering his question. 'Yep. I helped her set it up and then a few years later she was forcing me to sign divorce papers. But, looking back, she did me a favour, because now I've got Alison. I know she's got her issues but I do love her.'

His face lights up when he says this, and it's impossible to picture him as the man Alison described, but I can't simply trust everything he's telling me. Though when I picture Alison in my office the other day, how bizarre her behaviour was, I can't help but lean towards him.

'So you have no idea why she'd say that about Zach?'

'I wish I could tell you, Mia, I really do. And again, I'm so sorry for her dragging all this up. Look, I'll talk to her and make her promise to leave you alone, but I just had to come and speak to you personally. I kind of feel responsible. I told her to come off her medication against the doctor's advice because she was just so sick on it. But maybe this is worse.'

I don't say anything; I'm still taking it all in and trying to make the pieces fit together so I won't just blindly believe every word he says.

Dominic shifts forward on the bench. 'Listen, I'd better get back. Alison was quite agitated this afternoon so I don't want to leave her on her own for too long.' He reaches into his pocket and pulls out a business card. 'Here's my number, though. My mobile. Call me any time if I can help with anything.'

As I reach for the card, I think how unusual it is that a university lecturer has a business card. Zach never did – at least not that I knew of. *But there were lots of things I didn't know about you, Zach, weren't there?*

Dominic reaches for my hand before standing up, and this time I shake it, his firm grasp catching me off guard. And as I watch him walk away I remind myself not to be fooled, no matter how genuine he seems. People are good at masking things when they have to.

As evening draws in I realise that I don't feel any better after Dominic's visit. Although a lot of what he said could explain Alison's behaviour, he still couldn't give me a reason for why she came to me, so now I have a whole new set of questions. But, without realising it, he has told me exactly where I can find his ex-wife, and she might shed some light on whether or not I can trust him. I won't be able to let this go until I know for sure that Alison is safe, and what she thinks she knows about Zach's death. The fact that she so quickly retracted her statement – pretended, in fact, that she hadn't said anything at all – only makes me believe that she's scared. But of whom? And why?

These are the questions I need answers to, and my starting point is finding out whether it's Alison or Dominic who has things to hide.

It's too late in the evening to track down Elaine Bradford today, and most estate agents' offices are closed on Sundays, but on Monday I will see if she can provide me with any answers. Until then I have to sit tight, knowing that, for now at least, there is nothing more I can do.

Although it's nearly 8 p.m. it's still warm outside, so I sit in the garden while I attempt to write up some notes for my client files. The neighbours to my right are having a barbeque and their guests are already raucous, so I eventually give up trying to get anything done.

Will calls as I'm about to go inside, and asks if I'm okay. 'No more fainting episodes, I hope?'

I assure him I'm fine and distract him from worrying by asking what his plans are for tonight.

He hesitates. 'I have to meet a client. She's having real problems with her tax return and her business is in a huge mess. It's the only time she could meet so I couldn't say no.'

A lump forms in my throat but I will not give in to fear. I won't ask him where they're meeting or what she's like because Will is not Zach and I refuse to mistrust him, unless I ever have evidence that he doesn't deserve my trust. But still, it's hard not to feel a pang of pain. That it could be happening all over again.

'You don't mind, do you?' he asks.

'No, of course not. It sounds like she needs help so that's what you've got to do. I think I'll just have an early night.'

'Get some rest,' he says. 'I'm still worried about you. I'll see you on Monday. And Mia? Don't forget I love you.'

I go to bed, comforted by Will's words and assurance, laying my head on my pillow and drifting off with thoughts of him, thoughts of our future together. But when I wake suddenly in the middle of the night, my body drenched in sweat and tears sliding down my cheeks, it is Zach I have been dreaming about.

TWELVE

Josie

The last thing I will ever do is go to the police and change my statement, so Johnny's cousin – or whoever he is – can go to hell. But for weeks now I've been constantly looking over my shoulder, my stomach lurching each time a new customer walks into the coffee shop, never heading out alone once it's dark.

University is the only place I feel remotely safe – it's always brimming with people so he'd be stupid to try anything here, at least during the day. But I know one thing for sure: I can't live like this, constantly on edge, waiting for something to happen – and it *will* happen. I have no doubt he intends to carry through on his threat.

This is why I'm standing outside Zach's office this lunchtime. There is nobody else I can go to. I don't knock at first, but watch him through the narrow window in the door. His head is bent forward as he pores over some papers, so he doesn't notice me. He looks so peaceful that it gives me second thoughts. How can I bring all my problems to him? The burden should be mine alone to share.

I'm about to walk away when his head jolts up and he sees me. A smile spreads across his face and he beckons me in.

'Actually, don't worry,' I say, popping my head through the door. 'It's nothing.'

'Come in, Josie. I've been meaning to catch up with you. Sorry we haven't chatted for a while. Do you mind closing the door?'

So now it's too late and I walk towards him and sit in front of his desk.

'My novel,' he says, shuffling together the papers he was reading and putting them in his drawer. 'I'm struggling a bit with chapter eleven so I printed it out to read it on paper to see if that makes a difference. Sometimes it helps, but not today. I just can't get my mind into it.'

'You need to distance yourself from it for a bit and then go back to it.' I say this as if I'm an expert when the truth is I have no idea what I'm talking about. I can't even imagine writing anything longer than a short story. Unless I wrote about *her* – then I'd have plenty to say.

'You're right,' he says. 'I know that, but… I don't know. I feel a huge sense of panic sometimes, like time's running out and I have to get everything done now, before it's too late. Sometimes it feels like there'll be no tomorrow. Like I'm in a race and I can't even see the finish line but I've just got to get there.'

This surprises me – Zach always seems so laid-back. 'What do you mean by "too late"?'

'Oh, I'm not being morbid. I just feel this huge sense of urgency about everything. Anyway, just ignore me. How's everything going with you?'

But now I don't want to talk about me. I want to hear all his thoughts, soak up every part of him I can. But there's no way I'll tell him this. Instead, I say, 'Actually, things aren't too good. That's why I'm here. I was wondering if your offer still stands of listening to me if I ever needed to talk?'

He smiles. 'Of course, I meant what I said. Tell you what, though, shall we get out of here? I could do with some air. Freezing-cold air, but at least it's fresher than in here.'

'Sounds good.'

'Great. Just give me a few minutes – I need to quickly speak to someone – but how about meeting me in the park in ten minutes? I'll find you there.'

*

Zach was right about it being freezing, and my short biker jacket is no barrier against the wind. I'm in desperate need of a new coat but I need all the money I can get right now. I can just about manage to pay my rent and keep my car running, but I've also got to be able to provide for Kieren if anything happens before I graduate. I can't believe for one second that Liv has changed and is actually looking after my brother properly, so I need to be prepared for anything. What happened the other night with that man threatening me has made me realise this more than ever.

I wait for Zach on a bench by the lake, watching people as they walk past. Most of them are mothers with kids – something I can't ever imagine being – and I wonder what's behind their smiles and aura of normality, because we're never just what we seem on the outside. Anyone passing me would think I'm a typical student. If only they knew.

A hand taps my shoulder and I flinch.

'Whoa, sorry!' Zach says, holding up his hands. 'Didn't mean to scare you.' His smile fades. 'Josie, what's wrong?'

I shake my head. 'I'm not okay, Zach. And I don't know what to do.'

And that's when I tell him, avoiding his eyes most of the time because I can't bear to see his reaction.

When I was eighteen my so-called mother's boyfriend attacked me and left me for dead. With his fists. With a knife. With anything he could get his hands on. He never liked me. Said I was too mouthy and didn't know my place. He also said I should never have been born, which was pretty much what my mum had been telling me my whole life.

Liv's probably right about that. She had no business having a child. She was sixteen, a kid herself, but that excuses nothing. My grandmother – an angel before she died – helped her out whenever she could and plenty of teenagers don't have that support and still make a good go of parenting. But not Liv Carpenter. No, she gave birth to me and then treated me as though I had ruined her life with my mere existence. I was stopping her doing anything, meeting anyone decent, having a job. Partying. So she decided I would suffer for it.

As a young child, half the time she starved me, refusing to give me any food but eating her own dinner right in front of me. If anyone ever asked why I was so skinny, she would tell them I refused to eat, that she was doing everything she could to help me but I just wouldn't open my mouth. And they believed her – because what kind of person would starve their child? That kind of thing only happened on TV, didn't it?

She wouldn't bath me for endless days and I'd smell so bad it used to make me feel sick. Once I snuck into the bathroom and tried to fill my own bath, but I didn't realise I had to put the plug in and the water just kept disappearing. She came in and found me. *Shame you didn't get it right and accidentally drown yourself.* Those were her exact words. I must have only been about three or four.

There are tears in my eyes as I recall this and I look at Zach and see his disbelief and shock. He is a parent himself so probably can't imagine the horrors I'm describing, can't believe that anyone could behave this way to their own child. To *any* child.

I can tell he has a thousand questions he wants to ask but doesn't quite know where to start. 'Where was your—'

'My dad? Ha, she didn't even know who my father was! Sixteen years old and sleeping with so many men she couldn't work out who it was. I tried asking her who she thought it could be when I was old enough to understand, but her reply was always the same. She'd just say "Who cares?" and laugh in my face.'

Zach shakes his head. 'My God, Josie. I don't know what to say.'

But at least he's not looking at me as though I'm a victim – I couldn't handle that. I'm here, despite my childhood, despite everything, so I don't need sympathy.

He urges me to carry on but I warn him it only gets worse.

I explain that Liv met Johnny when I was around sixteen and things got much worse for me then. She'd had boyfriends before, some of them even lived with us, but none of them had paid me any attention. I kept out of their way and they kept out of mine, so there weren't many problems. I'd long ago stopped needing a mother and had taught myself how to pretty much do everything I needed to do to survive. But Liv hated that. She didn't want me to be self-sufficient, because then she couldn't mentally torture me.

But Johnny was different. I don't know why, but he despised me from the second he saw me. It couldn't have been because he hated her having a child – Kieren was a baby, so if Johnny had just hated kids then he would have resented my brother too. More, probably, because Kieren still needed a lot of attention. At least I kept out of Johnny's way. Or I tried to, at least. So all I can think of is that Liv must have told him how I'd ruined her life, that she'd had big plans before she got pregnant with me and now she was stuck, jobless and sponging off the government.

Johnny took every opportunity to make my life miserable. I think he saw how she treated me and knew he could do the same, and the worst thing was that she stood by and enjoyed what he was doing. We fought a lot because I couldn't just sit back and take his verbal abuse. I had to fight back.

One day, in the summer when I'd just turned eighteen, Liv had some friends round and everyone was in the back garden. I don't know how I was allowed out there, or even why I wanted to be, but somehow I was. I can't even remember what it was about now, but Johnny and I ended up in a huge row that ended with me spitting in his face. Not just a tiny fleck of saliva, more like a spray that ended up in his eyes, his mouth, all over him. Everyone saw it and the whole garden was suddenly silent. The weird thing was, Johnny didn't say a thing. He just wiped it off and calmly carried on drinking his beer. I took that as my chance to run.

Blinking back tears, I have to pause for breath. Telling Zach what came next will be like reliving the nightmare. Since giving my statement to the police, I've not had to speak these words again. I buried them somewhere they couldn't find a way out.

As soon as I begin to speak, the memory hits me like a punch in the gut. I'd just finished my last A-level exam and I was on a high. I knew I probably hadn't done that well, but hoped it was enough to get me to university. I'd managed to convince a friend to let me stay with her for a few weeks while I found a job and looked for my own place, so I couldn't wait to get back to Liv's and pack up all my stuff.

The house was empty when I got there and I was relieved. Part of me was scared she'd try to stop me, even though she'd wanted me gone, or dead, since the minute I was born. But to Liv, me leaving home meant that I was going to have that life she never would, and I worried she would do anything to make sure that didn't happen.

I was so engrossed in shoving all my belongings – not much more than a few clothes, and definitely no childhood mementos – into a bag that I didn't hear him come in, but suddenly he was standing in my room, his mouth twisted into an evil grimace.

I've never been so scared in my life. And I never will be again. Because once you've known – and survived – fear like that, you can handle anything.

The certainty that Johnny was going to do his worst came even before he flew at me, his fist slamming into my face, knocking me back with such force I crashed against the wall, cracking my head. I was sure my whole skull had shattered. I saw the pool of blood, but was strangely detached. It didn't feel like it belonged to me.

I thought that would be it, Johnny had taught me a lesson and that would be the end of it, but I couldn't have been more wrong. He was only just getting started.

Zach grabs my hand. It's smooth and warm. 'Josie, you don't have to tell me any more – if it's too difficult.'

But now I've started I can't seem to stop. Perhaps this is like therapy, baring my soul, and afterwards the poison will be out of my body and I'll be free of it. I know what Zach's thinking: that Johnny raped me. And it might make him uncomfortable to hear those details, but that's not what happened. That was never what he wanted.

There were fleeting moments when I thought this might be what Johnny wanted to do, but it never happened. Instead, he battered me with his fists, until there was barely a patch of unblemished skin on my body, and then he used any piece of furniture he could smash into me. But that still wasn't it. He saved the knife for last, carving slits into my body until I was lying in a bath of blood, which this time I was in no doubt was my own because I could almost feel it draining from my body.

'I enjoyed that,' he said, as he left me there.

I turn to Zach, able to look him in the eye again now that I've described what Johnny did. 'But that's not quite the worst of it,' I say, and watch as his jaw drops. 'As he walked out of my room, I saw a shadow in the hall. Liv was there, Zach. The woman who was supposed to be my mother, who was supposed to always protect me. I might have even forgiven her for everything she'd done if at that moment she had tried to stop Johnny, or at least comforted me afterwards, but she just stood there, with a nasty smirk on her face. She must have seen the whole thing.'

Zach pulls me towards him and hugs me. I'm sure he doesn't mean to but his whole body presses into mine. 'I know this might be inappropriate but right now I don't give a shit,' he says. 'You need a bloody hug and that's what you're going to get.'

I don't argue but go with it, breathing in his calming scent. A natural smell, not aftershave or anything stifling. Just Zach.

We stay like that for too long, yet not long enough, until finally Zach pulls back. 'What happened to you after that? Did you go to the police?'

I nod. 'I woke up in hospital and didn't know how I'd got there until the police told me. Apparently my friend Alexa had come round to find me. She's the one I was supposed to be moving in with, and she got worried when I didn't turn up. Somehow, thankfully, even though Liv and Johnny had gone out to get pissed down the pub, they'd left the back door open and Alexa had found me. Otherwise...'

'Fuck! Sorry, I don't usually swear, but this calls for it, I reckon.'

I want to hug him again now – just for being able to make me smile at this painful moment.

'I told the police everything. He's in prison.'

'Good. That's good, Josie.' He shakes his head. 'I can't believe you've gone through all this and you're still, well, *you*. Strong.'

'I can't let them win, Zach. That's what stops me being a victim. They wanted to destroy my life but I won't let them. I can't pretend it's always easy, but I've got my little brother to think of.' I tell him about my visit to Brighton, and how although it doesn't seem that Kieren's being neglected, I can't take any chances. 'I want him to come and live with me, Zach. Once I've got my degree and hopefully a good job. I can't let him be around that woman.'

'Did social services not get involved? I don't know much about how the system works, but surely after your mum's boyfriend did that they would be worried about your brother?'

'Oh, Liv knows how to lie. She's fooled everyone. She told them she'd have nothing more to do with Johnny and made up some lies about me having a relationship with him. And because I was eighteen, and not a child, they didn't take Kieren from her. But everyone who knows her, and that's a lot of people in Brighton, knows that she can't be without that man.'

Now I've filled Zach in on my past, I bring him up to date by telling him about Johnny's cousin visiting me a few weeks ago.

He shakes his head and sighs heavily. 'You need to tell the police he's threatened you, Josie. Why haven't you done that?'

'Because I don't really know who he is. I'm just assuming he's Johnny's cousin, but I've never seen him before and I was too shocked to think about getting his registration number or anything like that. He told me he has an alibi sorted for that night anyway so there's no point. And most of all, I just want the past behind me.'

'But it's not behind you, Josie, if this man carries out his threat.'

'I know. That's why I wanted to talk to you – to get another opinion. I know it sounds stupid but I really don't have anyone I can talk to. After the attack, nobody on my estate bothered with me. I guess they thought I was tainted and didn't want anything to do with me. People are scared of Johnny – they knew what he was like and what he was capable of, even before he attacked me. And Liv. Nobody ever gets on her wrong side. So I really had no one. I couldn't wait to leave, to start a fresh life in London.'

'What about your friend, Alexa? What happened to her?'

'She was the one person who would have stood by me, but she went to study in Edinburgh not long after and we lost touch. I wouldn't even know how to find her now. I've checked and, like me, she's not on Facebook or Twitter or anything so that's that.'

Zach squeezes my hand but doesn't let go. 'Well, I'm glad our paths crossed.'

I grip his hand back, more tightly than I should, but in this moment I no longer care. Just for this brief flash of time, it feels as though it's just me and him. Nobody else exists.

THIRTEEN

Mia

The house has been so silent this weekend, the atmosphere so cold, without Freya. I've missed her constant chatter, the way she can distract me from everything, the way that when I'm with her nothing else seems important. Without her here I've had too much time to focus on Alison and Dominic. And what happened to Zach.

But now it's Monday morning, and before I pick up Freya I will visit Elaine Bradford, and hopefully get some answers. There must be something she can tell me to help me understand Dominic, and whether or not he can be trusted.

Her office is in Muswell Hill, a part of London I'm not familiar with, but my satnav gets me there in just under an hour. It's in the completely opposite direction from Reading, but I should still make it in plenty of time to pick Freya up after lunch.

Bradford Estate Agents is a large office in a row of upmarket high street shops. I should have called ahead to check Elaine was actually in this morning, but I couldn't think of any reason why I'd need to ask that. Still, I'm happy to take this chance. I have no clients scheduled in and at least it feels like I am doing something.

Before I step inside, I scan the faces sitting at desks, but see no sign of Elaine. I know from her website picture that she's got dark hair, almost the same colour as Dominic's, and it's cut in a neat bob. She is definitely not in there.

But I walk through the doors anyway; it's likely she's out on a showing or something else work-related.

A tall young man, smartly dressed in a suit, comes to greet me, jangling some keys in his hand. 'Hi, how can I help you?'

'Um, I'm looking for Elaine, if she's around.'

His smile fades a bit. He must have been hoping for my commission. 'She's in her office. I'm just on my way to a viewing, but it's right over there.' He points towards a glass door at the back, where I can just about make out a dark-haired woman sitting at her desk.

'Thanks,' I say, but he's already disappeared.

As I walk towards her, the first thing I notice is how different Elaine Bradford is from Alison. Not everyone has a type – Zach and Will couldn't be more different in looks – but the woman before me is so much more together, so much more confident than Alison. I can tell this within two seconds.

She smiles at me. 'Hi, how can I help you?' she says. Then she frowns. 'Don't I know you?'

It's impossible. I've never seen her before and she wasn't with Dominic at the funeral, so there's no way, unless of course…

'No, that's it – you're Zach Hamilton's wife. Sorry, I recognise you from the Internet.' She offers a half-smile. 'Oh, I know how awful that must sound, but, well, there's no point pretending it's anything other than it is.' Her smile widens and she holds out her hand to me. 'Nice to meet you anyway. It's a small world, isn't it?'

I take her hand, puzzled that she recognised me so quickly. I look different now, I've made sure of that. I needed to shed the past, so my hair is now shorter and a chestnut colour, no longer the almost black that it was, and I iron out my natural waves with straighteners. But it hasn't fooled Elaine – or others, probably.

'Don't worry about it,' I tell her, taking her hand. 'And yes, I'm Mia.'

She offers a warm smile. 'Well, for what it's worth, it's no reflection on you. I heard years ago that you had some trouble from people. I just wish everyone would mind their own business.'

As much as it's painful to hear this woman talk of the abuse I received, allowing her to discuss it could be my way to bring up Dominic. 'It was hard,' I say. 'I couldn't even leave my house without someone confronting me. Most of the time they'd just scream and shout in my face, but sometimes it got even nastier than that.' Memories flood my mind of smashed car windows, abusive words spray-painted onto my front door. It got so bad that I barely left the house for months.

Elaine shakes her head. 'I can't believe the nerve of people. It's outrageous that you had to go through that. They claimed to be friends of that student, didn't they? Although by all accounts she didn't really have any close friends. Not surprising, given the way she carried on.'

'No close friends apart from my husband,' I say.

Elaine's eyes widen and she stares at me for a moment, probably wondering just how far I will let this conversation go. 'Yes, well, we don't always choose right the first time round, do we?' She snatches a glance at my left hand. 'I certainly didn't. You probably know my ex-husband, Dominic? He worked with Zach.'

'Yes, we only met briefly at the funeral—'

'Oh, I'm so sorry I didn't go, but Dominic and I had been having so many problems and I'd actually left him by then. Thank God!'

'Don't worry about that. You didn't even know Zach so I wouldn't have expected you to be there.'

'Actually, I did meet him. Well, "meet" is probably the wrong word for it, but I saw him at the university once when I went to visit Dominic. He was... I'm sorry to say this now, but he was with that girl. They were just walking along the corridor and I remember he held the door open for me. Very polite man. I thought nothing of it at the time, but after what happened it stuck in my mind.' She finally pauses for breath.

Elaine is right about that. The whole time I was with Zach I never heard him say a bad word, or even an angry word, to or about anyone. He was always so calm, able to keep level-headed about everything. It's hard to understand how he could have snapped that night.

An awkward silence hangs between us for a moment until, to my relief, Elaine attempts to move the conversation on. 'How are you doing anyway?' she asks, as if we are suddenly close friends.

'Time heals all wounds, doesn't it?' I say this to avoid directly answering her question.

She studies my face for too long. 'Yes, but it must have changed you. Something as horrific as that is bound to have scarred you, you poor thing.'

There is no way I want to talk about all this to Elaine, even though I can tell she means well and her concern is genuine. But if I want her to open up then I've got to be prepared to do that myself. So I tell her that it *has* changed me, more than I can put into words. I used to be a sociable person, making time for my friends whenever I could, but afterwards I could barely bring myself to look anyone in the face, even those I knew wouldn't make any judgements. Eventually, I cut myself off from the world, and the loneliness and isolation might have finished me off if it wasn't for Freya. It was only three years later that Will's kindness and warmth brought me out of myself.

Elaine nods as if she knows exactly what I'm talking about, as if she's been through something similar herself, rather than being on the outside looking in at the spectacle that was my life five years ago. 'I'm so glad you met someone special. What do you do now? You weren't working at the time, were you?'

I start to feel on edge. This woman knows too much about me and I know nothing about her other than who she was married to. We are on unequal footing. This can never be a good thing. 'No, I took some time off work to look after my young daughter, then when she started school I trained as a counsellor and now I have my own business. Like you.'

'Well, that's fantastic! Good for you. I know it's not an easy thing to do. So what brings you to see me?' she asks, changing the subject. 'Did you say you were looking for a property?'

She must know full well I haven't even had a chance to explain my visit. 'I could be. My partner and I are considering moving in together and, to be honest, a move from Ealing might do me good.'

'You still live there? In the same house?'

I'm not ashamed to admit it. It was my house too, and I can't let what Zach did taint the memories it holds. I tell her this and she seems to understand.

'I suppose I get that. I'll tell you this much, though – after my divorce I couldn't wait to sell up and move away. Even this side of London didn't seem to put enough miles between me and that part of my life.'

This is perfect; she has referred to her divorce without me having to. 'I'm sorry to hear that.'

Her expression changes and her eyes seem to darken. 'It's a time of my life I'd rather forget. But then, a divorce is nothing compared to what you had to go through.'

'Well, that doesn't mean you haven't suffered. Was it really acrimonious? It's funny, Zach always spoke so well of Dominic.' She won't know that until the funeral I had no idea who her ex-husband was.

'Well, that's the trouble when people have two sides to them. Their colleagues only see the good – the kind, helpful man who will do anything to support them – while the wife gets the bitter, twisted and resentful part when he gets home. Perhaps all those hours of being nice get too much and they just have to let it out.' She laughs but I can tell it is forced, that this is hard for her to speak about.

I recall talking with Dominic in the park. It really is hard to picture him being the man she is describing – the man Alison described, too – but then maybe she's right about people having a side they keep from the world.

'It was a totally loveless marriage,' Elaine continues, seeming not to notice I haven't responded. 'Pretty much right from the start. Wasted years. I would have loved to have children but now it's too late because I spent so much time with him.' She looks around her. 'Mind you, I might not have done all this if I'd had kids, so maybe things work out for the best. Anyway, I haven't actually seen him for years and don't even know what he's doing or if he remarried or anything. It's easier this way. Pretending he doesn't exist.'

'Maybe he's changed?' I say. 'Become a better person?'

She shakes her head. 'I don't believe any of us are capable of changing. Not really. We're still always who we are inside, no matter what we try to show to the world. Don't you think?'

'Perhaps.' I think of Zach. Was he always capable of such betrayal? How did I not notice it? 'That's if we see it in the first place,' I tell Elaine.

She offers her sympathetic smile again. 'Don't blame yourself for anything. I spent a long time wondering if I'd pushed Dominic away, or turned him into the uncaring person he became, and it was ages before I woke up and realised none of it was my fault. I gave all I could to that marriage and I'm sure you did too.'

Although Elaine is being more forthcoming than I could have hoped for, I still don't know whether Dominic Bradford was physically abusive towards her. I make one last attempt to find out for sure. 'Still, divorce is one of the most stressful things you can go through. It's funny, people get divorced for so many reasons: infidelity, abuse—'

She starts to say something but we're interrupted by a knock at her door. Through the glass I see a young couple standing together, their arms wrapped around each other. Elaine smiles and holds up her hand to signal them to wait. 'Oh, that's my appointment. I have to go and show them a property now.' She lowers her voice. 'Between you and me, they're bloody time-wasters. I think this must be the thirtieth house they've viewed and none are anywhere near good enough.' She stands up and holds out her hand. 'Anyway, it was lovely to meet you, Mia. If you just leave your details with Tina, the lady sitting nearest the front door, I'll give you a call and we can get started with your search.'

I thank her and leave her office. As I head to the front door I see the woman who must be Tina. I consider stopping to leave my details, to keep up the charade in the hope that I can get more information about Dominic from Elaine, but I decide it's not fair to deceive her this way. Besides, she doesn't know anything about Dominic now – and she won't be able to tell me a thing about Alison – so I need to move on.

I glance back at Elaine's office and see she is busy talking the ears off the loved-up couple, so I smile at Tina and head through the doors, out into the oppressive heat.

Freya was quiet when I picked her up from Graham and Pam's, and although I asked her about her weekend, she only offered mumbled responses. I didn't push her, but now we're back at home and she still won't talk much. This isn't like her.

'Sweetheart, are you okay?'

She shrugs. 'Yeah, I'm okay.'

She's half-heartedly doing a jigsaw on the living room floor, and I sit down next to her. 'You don't seem okay. Can you tell me what's wrong?'

Again she gives a shrug, but then immediately starts talking. 'My daddy was a nasty man, wasn't he?'

Her question is such a shock that for a moment I think I must have misheard her. She has never said anything like this before. But then she repeats herself.

I reach across and hold her hand. 'No, sweetheart, of course he wasn't. Why do you say that?'

She pulls her hand away. 'Mummy, you're lying. I know he was. He was a bad man.' She tries to crush a jigsaw piece in her palm but it's too sturdy so she gives up and throws it down instead. My daughter never behaves like this, at least not since she was a toddler and could only express her frustration with tantrums.

'Freya, you need to tell me why you're saying this and then we can talk about it properly, okay?' I put the jigsaw piece back with the others.

Seconds pass until she finally nods. 'I read it. On Grandad's iPad.'

My chest tightens. 'Read what, Freya?'

There are tears in her eyes now so I pull her towards me and wrap my arms around her. 'It's okay, sweetheart, just tell me everything. What did you read?'

Through her sniffs and snorts, I have to strain to hear all her words. 'Megan told me how to Google stuff on her iPad so I used it to look up my dad.'

I knew this time would come eventually, I just didn't think it would be when Freya was only seven. There is no way I can expect her to understand what happened, so all I can do is try to control the damage. I urge her to carry on.

'It said he did a bad thing to a girl he was teaching. Mummy, what did he do? I didn't understand it all. But they said she must be dead and that's why he... made himself dead.'

Her tears come faster now so I hold her even tighter. I have always been honest with Freya and told her Zach took his own life. There was no way I was going to lie to her only for her to find out the truth years later and question everything she's ever known. But I have never mentioned the circumstances surrounding it, only telling her that he felt very sad.

'Listen to me, sweetheart. Daddy loved you very much – more than anything – and don't you ever forget that.'

She thinks about this for a moment, staring at me with glassy eyes and a trembling lip. 'Okay. But it's horrible, Mummy. Was he really nasty, like they're saying?'

'What you've got to remember, honey, is that he loved you.'

'And you, Mummy.'

My chest tightens. 'Yes, and me. He loved us both and that's all that matters. Don't listen to anything else. As you get older you might hear more things about him, but you've got to just ignore it. And just keep remembering what I've said. He loved us, and nothing else matters. Sometimes people make bad mistakes – it doesn't always mean they're bad people.'

The words stick in my throat, threatening to choke me.

Will is in good spirits this evening, bounding through the door with a box of chocolates for me and a pack of the *Frozen* stickers he knows Freya collects.

I half-heartedly cook us a meal while they watch television together and I can't bring myself to speak much as we eat. Thankfully, Freya has perked up after our chat and is keeping Will busy enough not to question me.

The talk I had today with Elaine plays on my mind. She didn't come out and say that Dominic was abusive, but I know she was about to tell me something when we were interrupted. But it's too dangerous to make assumptions. The only thing I know for sure is that either Alison or Dominic is lying to me. Was Alison scared of him? Is that why she quickly retracted her statement and practically ran from my office? Or is Dominic right and she's extremely troubled? I can't ignore the fact that she's chosen to focus on me: there's a reason for that and I need to find out what it is.

Drop it, Mia. You've fought hard to move on after what Zach did, and to build a life for yourself and Freya, so don't step backwards now. That would be a huge mistake. But how can I forget Alison's words, constantly whirring in my head?

Later, in bed, Will questions me about my reticence during dinner, just as I knew he would. 'Are you sure you're okay? Are you feeling ill again?'

Normally I don't like to burden him – I try to solve problems on my own, and so far I've kept him out of anything to do with Zach, but tonight I'm exhausted, and just in this moment it feels right to share some things with him.

'Oh, Will, something happened with Freya this afternoon and, well, it's kind of thrown me. More than thrown me, actually.'

He sits up straighter, a frown on his face. 'Tell me.'

I repeat what Freya said, trying to remember the words she used, but I know I won't have them exactly right. I was too shocked to notice exactly how she put everything.

'Oh shit,' says Will, when I've finished. 'That's not good.' He very rarely swears so I know this is a shock to him. 'What did you tell her?'

'The only thing I could. That Zach loved her and nothing else matters.'

He nods. 'Hmmm. I'm guessing that was hard for you to say.'

When I first met Will I couldn't bring myself to tell him exactly what had happened. I didn't lie to him, but told him it was too difficult to talk about, and that I'd appreciate it if he didn't push me. I didn't know if he'd heard anything, from other people or from social media.

Will's sister was a teacher at Freya's school so I had no doubt people were gossiping about it when Freya first started, even though it was three years later at that point. So the more time went on, the more I realised I didn't want his mind filled with anyone's version of events but mine.

Of course I thought about moving, before Freya started school – that would have been the easier option – but I refused to be chased out of my home.

We were on our first date when I broached the subject with Will. I'd reluctantly agreed to have a coffee with him after brushing him off a few times – he'd never given up and had taken to giving his sister lifts to school, which she didn't need or particularly want, just so he'd have an excuse to see me. He took my hand and told me he didn't listen to other people and had no opinion about it either way. 'I wasn't there,' he said, 'so I'm not going to judge.' But he added that when I was ready to talk about it, he would listen with an open mind.

And he was true to his word. 'Life deals us horrendous blows sometimes,' he'd said, 'but never let it define you, Mia. Whatever Zach did had nothing to do with you.'

So now, as painful memories once again stir within me, I realise how blessed I am to have Will, and the second chance at life he has given me.

'Do you know what makes all this harder?' I say. 'The fact they never found her body. It's like there's a permanent question mark hanging over me and Freya, and I just want it gone.'

'I know this is hard to hear, but sometimes people are never found, even though everything points to them no longer being alive. Even if they do find her, it could be years before that happens, it might not even be in our lifetime.'

I don't know if finding Josie Carpenter would be better or worse than how it already is, but at least the ghost of her would no longer haunt me – I could lay all this to rest.

Will grabs my hand. 'Listen, I know this probably isn't the best time… Actually, it's the worst possible time, but I need to ask you something – again – and I need you to at least consider it. I love you and Freya – you know that, don't you?'

I nod, already knowing where this conversation will go.

'You both make me so happy, and I can't… actually I don't want to be without you.' He must notice the panic on my face, and he smiles and squeezes my shoulder. 'Don't worry, Mia, I'm not proposing. But I am asking you again. Officially. Will you think about us living together?'

So many times he's asked me this, but never quite in this way. And he's right, his timing couldn't be worse, but as I look at his face, full of hope, I know there is only one answer I can give. Maybe, after all, fate has him asking me right now for a reason. To show me everything will be okay.

I lift his hand and kiss it. 'Yes, let's do it. But I don't think we should live here. It just wouldn't feel right. Let's buy somewhere new together, have a fresh start. It will be good for Freya too, especially after what she said today.'

Will grabs me and pulls me into him, letting out a huge cheer and punching the air. 'Do you know how happy you've just made me? In fact, don't answer that, let me just show you.'

And I let him, because I need to cleanse Zach away and focus on Will. On the future. And I won't let Alison or Dominic or anyone else ruin it for us.

Later, when Will has snuck to the spare room and I'm beginning to drift off, my phone pings with an email alert. Something in my gut warns me not to check, but my hand still reaches for it. I need to stop being paranoid; it's probably just junk mail, like it always seems to be at this time of night. I squint at the screen until the words come into focus.

I need to make another appointment to see you. It's urgent. Please. I can come any time tomorrow.

It's from Alison Cummings.

FOURTEEN

Josie

'I don't think I should come in with you when we get there,' Zach says. 'But I'll wait in the car park for you. And you've got my mobile number now, so you can just text if you need me.'

We're on our way to the police station and it's taken him days to convince me to go. Even though I would have come on my own, it's nice that he's here with me. But I've spent my whole life not depending on anyone so I won't allow myself to need him now.

'What if I'm in there for hours?' I say. This is more than likely; there's a lot of ground to cover. 'You should probably go, I'll be fine.' And I will – I always am. 'Anyway, don't you need to be at home? It's Saturday. Surely that's a family day?'

He lets out a heavy sigh. 'Unfortunately my work and the book mean there's not really such a thing as a family day. Anyway, Mia's taking Freya out this morning, so no, I don't need to be there. She's got it covered, she always has.' He sighs again. 'I actually don't know how she does it. Leave me alone with Freya for five minutes and I'm pulling my hair out, wondering what I'm supposed to do, why she won't stop moaning or crying.'

Although I hate to think of Zach in distress at all, I feel a tiny flutter at hearing that his family life might not be so perfect. Shit, I must be a horrible person. 'Well, obviously I don't have my own yet, but I pretty much did everything for Kieren when he was a baby so I know how hard it is. At least, it is when you're trying to be a good parent.' Of course, Liv didn't care. Kieren could be wailing his head off for hours and she wouldn't bat an eyelid, wouldn't even attempt to find out what he needed. It was always up to me to take care of him. But I never minded – I would die for that little boy.

'It's just effortless to Mia,' Zach continues. 'But for me… well, let's just say I'm struggling a bit.'

Even though I'm grateful he is opening up to me, I hate to think of him going through any kind of shit. 'I'm sure she appreciates that you're trying,' I say.

'Oh, she does. Mia's always telling me what a great job I'm doing, and that she couldn't manage without me, but it's not true because she totally would. Anyway, she never sees me struggling – I don't want her to worry.' He turns to me. 'Sorry, I shouldn't be going on about my crap when you're about to walk in there.' He gestures to the police station. 'Sorry, Josie.'

I brush off his apology. 'Remember what you said to me a while ago – you more or less said that we're human beings and not meant to be perfect, so stop being so hard on yourself. Whatever you're feeling now, it will pass. Trust me, I know.'

He stares at me for too long and my insides burn. It's a painful feeling, but nice too. 'You've got a wise head on your young shoulders,' he says eventually. 'You know, I actually kind of envy you in a way.'

'What? Are you kidding me?' I almost choke on my words. '*You* envy *me*?'

'Hey, I said "almost", remember? Anyway, maybe envy's the wrong word. I just mean that you have a freedom I can only dream of. I had it once, of course, when I was younger, but I didn't appreciate it then. Took it for granted, like most people do. Don't get me wrong, I know what you've been through, and it was horrendous, I'm just talking about the freedom to wake up in the morning and do what you like. To go where you like, whenever you want.' He pauses. 'Oh, Josie, I'm sorry. I shouldn't have said that – it was insensitive of me. I'm sorry.'

'Don't worry about it. Anyway, I might have that, but I'm not really free, am I? And actually, if you really think about it, none of us truly are. Doesn't true freedom mean having no desires? Not wanting anything other than what we need to live?'

He laughs. 'You're right, Josie. And that's exactly why you need to keep writing, keep creating. Don't bottle up what you've got in your head.'

My cheeks heat up and I know I must be turning red but luckily we are approaching the police station so I try to focus on the task ahead.

Zach pulls into the only free parking space and turns off the engine. 'Right, are you ready?'

'Look, you need to go, Zach. Home or wherever. I'll be fine.'

He turns around and points to the laptop sitting on the back seat. 'I'm sure you will be but I've got writing to do. And after philosophising with you all the way here, I'm getting in the zone now, so off you go. Don't put this off any longer, Josie. And one more thing – just ignore what I've said. I have no right to complain about my life, I truly am blessed.'

As I walk away from the car and light a cigarette, guilt consumes me. This kind man, who I'm growing more attached to every day, shouldn't be here with me. He should be at home with his wife and daughter, giving them every second of his time that he's not working or writing.

But as I turn around, ready to tap on his window and tell him to leave again, I see he is already focused on his laptop, and I can't bring myself to disturb him. Perhaps he needs this time alone. After all, he wouldn't be here if he didn't want to.

But why is he choosing to spend his time with you – his student, and a messed-up one at that – instead of his family? Ask yourself that question, Josie.

I ignore the voice in my head. I find it hard to even think of him as my lecturer now; it feels as though we've crossed a barrier somehow. Not physically, of course, but there is something emotional between us.

It's harder than I thought it would be, being inside this police station. Although my previous statements were taken in the hospital, the atmosphere here is a stark reminder of what happened. But I get through it, grateful that the woman interviewing me has a kind voice and soft eyes that seem to smile even when her mouth is a straight line.

'We'll be looking into this immediately,' she assures me. 'I can't make you any promises – with no evidence of anything, and no bruising on you this time, it will be very difficult to prove anything, even if you could identify the man. We'll check CCTV around that area, but it sounds like he planned this carefully so I'm expecting him to have avoided all cameras.'

'I'm sure he was Johnny's cousin,' I say. 'There was too much of a resemblance for them to not be related.'

'But you do understand that we can't just start accusing all his family members of threatening you, can we? We can see if any of them are known to us but then how many cousins does your attacker even have?'

I admit that I don't know, but it's likely there are several as he comes from a big family. Although I never met any of them, I know he has three sisters and Liv was always going on about how large his extended family is. *Nobody ever fucks with them, Josie, just you remember that.*

The police officer is right: this is hopeless. Coming here is beginning to feel like a mistake. 'It will be bad enough that I haven't withdrawn my statement about Johnny,' I tell her, 'but when this man finds out I came to the police about him too, surely that will make things worse? There's no way he was bluffing about carrying out his threat.'

'Believe me, you've done exactly the right thing. Now, just be careful. No going out alone at night, just be sensible. And call us if anything else happens. But don't leave it so long next time.'

'I don't have a choice but to just be careful, do I? It's not as if you can offer me protection.'

She shakes her head. 'Sadly, no. But here's my card. Call me any time.'

Taking the card, I thank her and leave, grateful to be heading back outside, even though it scares me that nothing has been resolved. There is nothing to protect me and, as usual, the only person I can rely on is myself.

It's cold out here, although the sun is so bright I have to squint to find Zach's car. But it's not in the same place I remember him parking, the only one that was free, by the entrance. Instead, there is a silver Golf parked there, the driver sitting inside, talking on his phone.

Puzzled, I shade my eyes and scan the car park, but there is no sign of Zach's car. Wondering if he had to move it or leave to get something, I text him.

Finished now. Just wondering where you are?

After another scan of the car park, I sit on the police station steps and wait for a reply. But almost half an hour later I still haven't heard from Zach.

'We need to talk.' Alison's voice is firmer than I've ever heard it, as if she's been practising, waiting for me to get home so she can try out what she's rehearsed.

'Can it wait? I've just done a shift at work and I'm knackered. I need to get something to eat and I'm really not in the mood for an argument.' But more than that, I'm confused that I still haven't heard back from Zach. Perhaps I typed in his number incorrectly when he gave it to me, but that doesn't explain why he disappeared.

Why would he leave without a word? Especially when he knew I didn't want to report that man in the first place. But I won't text him again. He will contact me if he really wants to. And it's been hours now, so if there had been an emergency I'm sure he could have found a way to let me know.

'No, it can't,' Alison says. 'Don't you think it's waited long enough?' Her words are tough but her voice is less confident now. Her arms are folded across her body and I notice she's already wearing her pyjamas, even though it's barely 8 p.m.

'I don't even know what you're talking about, but if this is about Aaron then I've said my piece. I told you what happened and if you don't believe me there's nothing I can do about that.' I walk towards the fridge but don't bother opening it. Not when Alison is right there, watching everything I do.

She takes a step back so she's almost leaning against the kitchen door. 'I know girls like you, Josie. I've met plenty of you. You think you've got it made, don't you? That the world owes you and you can have anything you want.' She snorts. 'You think that you can use men to get your own way, but that doesn't work with women, Josie. Unfortunately for you.'

Even more than her freaky words, it's creeping me out the way she keeps saying my name. Every sentence she speaks blurs into the next because she couldn't have got me more wrong. I am not the person she's describing. 'What are you talking about? I'm really not in the mood for this.'

'Sooner or later it will all catch up with you, Josie.'

'Oh, for Christ's sake, Alison, I don't have to listen to this! Look, if you hate me so much then why don't you just move out? That will be the best thing for both of us.'

'Don't you think I've tried? That I'd be out of here in a second if I could? But there's nowhere else at the moment and I'm not uprooting myself in the middle of term. Anyway, why should you get your own way? You'd love for me to move out so that I'm out of your hair – I'm just the annoying weird girl you can't relate to. Well, tough! I'm not going anywhere for now.'

I could mention my deleted assignment now, tell her I know it was her, but I won't give her the satisfaction. Much better to let her think she deleted something that wasn't important. That I still haven't even noticed.

'Good for you,' I say. 'Now can I have some dinner in peace?'

'You want peace, Josie? Good luck with that!' She storms out, slamming the kitchen door behind her.

Deciding I'm not going to let Alison make me feel even worse, I focus on the hunger pangs I need to stifle. But when I open the fridge to check what's in there, already knowing all the food will be Alison's, I'm shocked to find it completely bare. Nothing but a yellowing milk stain in the door compartment where the bottles are usually kept.

Even though I already know what I'll find, I check all the cupboards, just to be sure, and it's the same story. Completely empty other than a few mugs and plates, all of them chipped.

I let out a howl of laughter – because this is the best Alison can do. I've been beaten half to death, threatened with worse, and she thinks getting rid of all the food in the house can even bother me?

My hysterical shrieks echo around the flat, and I can only imagine what she is doing now, holed up in her bedroom, wondering why I'm not reacting the way she expected me to.

And when I finally calm down, the realisation dawns on me that this situation is actually not funny at all.

Alison Cummings clearly has issues, and I'm stuck here living in this place with her.

FIFTEEN

Mia

How different it is this time, to be sitting across from this woman. This time I am ready for whatever Alison will throw at me. I am armed with the ammunition Dominic provided me with – even though I still don't know who to believe, at least it's something to fall back on, if necessary.

I'm still Alison's counsellor so I need to tread carefully, and if she does need my help then I will be there for her.

'I can only imagine what you must think of me,' she says, staring at her hands. Her fingers are long and thin, spindly veins showing through the skin. But today she's not dressed as if she's in mourning, although I notice her dark purple shirt clashes with her hair.

'I'm not here to judge you, Alison. I just want to help you, that's all.' I can't tell her that Dominic came to see me – it would undoubtedly freak her out – so I have to let her do this at her own pace. Hopefully, she will admit to me that she's been lying about everything, and that this has got nothing to do with Zach after all.

Her eyes narrow. 'And this is all confidential? Even after… last time?'

I nod. 'Nobody outside these walls will ever know what we've spoken about. Unless, of course, I feel you may be a threat to yourself or others. Then I will have no choice but to inform the police.'

She stares at me, unblinking. 'I'm the last person who's a threat to anyone, believe me.'

It's hard to imagine, but just because she is small and frail-looking, it doesn't mean she isn't capable of harming anyone. People are never what they seem. I know that better than most. 'So you asked for this appointment, Alison. Can you tell me why you wanted to see me again?'

She picks up the cup of water I've poured for her but puts it down again untouched, clearing her throat as if she's about to deliver a carefully rehearsed speech. 'Last time I came here I was fully intending to tell you everything. It wasn't a game or some sick joke, I would never do that to anyone. But once I started talking, I got… scared. Actually, terrified. I thought it would be a relief to come to you with it but it made me feel worse. Talking to you about your husband, it was suddenly too hard. But I couldn't take the words back.'

So, as I feared, she is here to talk about Zach, not to seek my help for her issues, something I could do much more easily. She's not going to let this go, so maybe Dominic was right: she's clearly disturbed and needs help. But what if she's telling the truth? I need to know, even if it means letting her gouge out my wounds so I feel the pain all over again, ten times worse. She looks questioningly at me and I nod for her to continue.

'The thing is, I need your help, and I think I can help you too. I know that sounds strange but you'll understand when you know everything.'

'What is it I need to know, Alison? Can you tell me now?' *Or will you just run away again? Jump up and sprint to the door before I can even blink.*

She takes a deep breath and her bony shoulders rise and fall. 'Can you promise me you'll just let me talk without interrupting? That you'll hear everything I've got to say before you make up your mind?'

'That's what I'm here for, Alison.'

'Okay. What I said to you last time is true: I don't think your husband killed himself.' She stares at me now, waiting for a reaction, even though seconds ago she asked me to just let her speak. 'You need to see this and then you'll understand.' She reaches into her bag and I shift backwards, unsure what she's about to draw out of it.

But it's only her mobile phone. She taps away at it and turns it towards me as a video starts to play. To start with I'm not sure what I'm looking at but then I realise it's someone's computer screen, and the name on the log-in box is Dominic Bradford's. Then Alison's slender hand appears, tapping keyboard buttons and jiggling the mouse until she's brought up a photo library.

I stare at the photos – there are hundreds of them – sickened by the thought of what I might see. On the video she scrolls through them. Unknown faces smiling and posing. Places I've never been. And then a bright young face I know only too well appears, and Alison pauses the video.

Josie Carpenter.

The girl people think Zach murdered.

Her face is too close to the camera, a mocking smile spread across it. Alison pauses the video.

I don't understand. 'What... what is this, Alison?'

'This is Dominic's computer. It's usually password protected and he never leaves it on, but a few weeks ago I found he hadn't turned it off when he went out. So I looked through it. And when I found this photo I started filming the whole computer. Just so I could prove this photo was on it.'

'But—'

'You recognise her, don't you? Just like I did. But there's no reason why Dominic should have a picture of her on his computer. But there it is, and it must have been downloaded from his phone. He didn't even know her. At least, he's never admitted that he did. Clearly they knew each other, though.'

A cloud of fog swirls around my head as I try to make sense of what I'm seeing and hearing. But seconds tick by and nothing becomes clearer.

Impatient for my response, Alison continues, 'Mia, you have to help me. I think Dominic might have had something to do with Josie's murder.'

I'm stunned into silence by her words. The police could never determine what happened to Josie Carpenter. There was enough of her blood in her flat for them to suspect she'd been killed, but in the absence of a body, nothing could be proved. Their thinking was that whoever did it – Zach, in their eyes – probably killed her somewhere else, a place they could easily dump her body. And even now, five years later, they still haven't found it. They're probably no longer even looking, especially as their main suspect is dead.

I try to control my breathing. 'But… I don't understand what you're telling me, Alison. So he's got a photo of her – that doesn't necessarily mean anything.'

She holds the phone out again. 'But it might if it was taken on the same day it happened. Look, keep watching.'

And sure enough, the next part of the video shows the date that's etched in my memory. The day my husband was taken from me. From my daughter.

The familiar panic rises in my body but I need to control it, stifle it until I can be alone and let it temporarily take over. I've learned that's the only way to deal with these attacks.

'Do you see?' Alison says.

I nod but I can't speak.

'Mia, I'm so scared. After everything Dominic's done to me, and now I've found this.'

Dominic's words swim around my head. Is Alison so disturbed that she'd concoct this story, even the evidence? But the computer is clearly Dominic's, and the picture was added on the day Zach died. I don't think she could have planted it on there, but I'm no technical expert.

None of this makes sense. Dominic gave no impression that Alison was fabricating stories about him in any way, and surely he would have mentioned that when he was telling me the things she had done. It's one thing to accuse your partner of abuse, but quite another to claim they may have killed someone.

'So do you understand now?' Alison says, snapping me back to the present. 'Why I said I don't think Zach killed himself?' She's using his name as if she knows him and it turns me cold.

'No, actually, I don't. Yes, it seems there's a picture of Josie Carpenter on Dominic's computer, but what's that got to do with Zach's death?'

Alison moves her phone back. 'Okay, I know what you mean. This doesn't exactly prove anything, but don't you think it's strange that he has a photo of the girl your husband is thought to have killed? Taken on the day she disappeared?'

'Yes, I admit there's no easy explanation.'

'Think about it, Mia. Dominic has never told the police that he knew Josie, and they definitely questioned all the staff at the uni. Why would he keep that from them?'

She's right, there doesn't seem to be an obvious explanation. But I tell her I still don't see how this proves Zach didn't kill himself.

'That's why I need your help, Mia. I really think Dominic is responsible for whatever happened to Josie. And to Zach.'

Silence, heavy and claustrophobic, fills the room, swirling around me as I take in this huge bombshell Alison's just dropped. I need to clarify exactly what she is telling me. 'You think Dominic killed Josie? And then – what? Killed Zach too?'

There are tears in her eyes and she shakes her head. 'I don't know, Mia. I… I think he might have. I know how it sounds. Like some film or something, but… but I really think this is what happened, Mia.'

I stand up, unable to bear my body being still, and pace the room. 'But why? Why would Dominic do that? This is crazy.'

Alison remains in her chair but swivels round to face me. 'I only know a couple of things for sure, Mia. My partner is a violent man. And if he can hurt me like he does, then what else is he capable of?'

'*If* he's a violent man,' I say. I don't mean these words to come from my mouth but it's too late now.

She stares at me with huge wide eyes. 'What do you mean by that?'

I can't tell her Dominic came to see me or that I have doubts about her honesty, but this issue needs to be addressed.

'You don't believe me, do you? Anything I've said?' She grabs her phone from the desk and begins searching for something on it. How is this the same timid woman who walked into my office moments ago? 'Here, look at this.'

This time the pictures I'm looking at are all self-taken photos of Alison, battered and bruised, her skin a grotesque rainbow of black, purple and red. In one of them her eyes are so inflated they can barely open.

She decides I've seen enough and pulls her phone away. 'Now tell me this: do you still think I'm lying?'

I shake my head. 'Why haven't you gone to the police? You've got clear evidence here that he's abusing you.'

'I'm sure I told you this last time – there's no point reporting him. He'll come after me. He'll find me, and then what? I'll just end up like Josie.'

'Then why did you come here, Alison? What help can I possibly give you?'

'I'm here because I need to find proof that Dominic is responsible for killing at least two people: Josie Carpenter and probably your husband. So this involves you too, doesn't it? I thought you would want to know the truth.'

My legs buckle beneath me and it's a struggle to remain upright. Seconds tick by before I can compose my thoughts. She's right, of course: I need to know the truth. 'Okay,' I say, 'even if Dominic did harm that girl, that doesn't mean he had anything to do with Zach's death, does it?'

Alison stands now and walks across to me. 'Mia, do you really believe your husband would take his own life?'

'He was desperate,' I say. 'He... whatever happened with Josie, he couldn't deal with it. So he...' I struggle to say the words. 'Her blood was everywhere and he was dead in her flat.'

The silence again. Somehow it's worse than the horrific words I'm being forced to say.

Alison takes my arm. 'All I know is that Dominic is tied up in this somehow. I know it like I know the sun is shining outside right now. But the police won't take that picture as proof, and even if it did make them listen it would never be enough to convict him of anything. I need to find more to go to them with.'

I want to scream at her but I force myself to stay calm. 'But that's not your job, Alison. Or mine. And even if Dominic is guilty of anything, he won't exactly have a signed confession lying around for you to find, will he? This isn't TV, Alison, it's real life.' *Real life, which can be far worse than any film or TV programme.*

She nods. 'You're right. But sooner or later the guilty always slip up.'

I don't answer but start pacing again.

'Okay,' Alison cuts into the silence. 'I was hoping I wouldn't have to tell you this, but I can see you need more convincing.'

My head snaps up and I stare at this woman who may or may not be a delusional liar.

'I was there that night. I... saw your husband. And I spoke to him.'

SIXTEEN

Josie

Zach is avoiding me. It's been days since he dropped me off at the police station, and I haven't heard a thing from him. It's fine that he hasn't texted – perhaps he feels weird doing that, and he did tell me he was giving me his number for emergencies – but in his lectures he acts as if I'm invisible. As if no hint of anything has passed between us.

But I won't contact him again. I don't force myself on people; if they don't want to be around me then that's their call, but some kind of explanation would be nice. So that's why I'm standing outside his empty office, hoping to catch him, clutching my course module guide to my chest so it looks like I need to speak to him about an assignment.

Alison walks past, staring at the floor, pretending she hasn't noticed me, even though our shoulders touch as she brushes past me. I can count on one hand the amount of times I've seen her at university, so it's weird that she's here now.

I watch her head down the corridor and am surprised to feel a glimmer of sadness. Perhaps we could have been friends, if only she'd given me a chance. Or I'd given her one.

I haven't given any thought to how long I'll wait for Zach, but I've checked his timetable and he has no lectures until 3 p.m. so I have an hour left to hope he turns up.

I sense him before I see him, coming from behind me. I know it's him before he appears and reaches for his door handle, barely acknowledging that I'm standing right here. But there is a faint flicker of a smile – he's not that evil that he would completely ignore me.

'Zach, hey! Can we talk?'

He immediately looks uncomfortable, or more uncomfortable than he did already, and flicks his wrist to look at his watch. 'Hi, Josie. Um, I don't have long. Someone's coming for a tutorial in ten minutes.'

But I won't be fobbed off. 'That's okay, this won't take that long.'

He notices the course guide in my hand and his shoulders drop slightly. 'Sure, come in.' Maybe he's just remembered that he's still my lecturer.

For some reason, despite it being about two degrees outside, the window's open in his office and it feels like a fridge in here. I give an involuntary shiver and wrap my too-thin and too-short coat tighter around me. 'What happened?' I say, as soon as the door clicks shut.

'Have a seat, Josie.' He gestures to the chair I've sat in several times before, never once feeling the way I do now. Out of sync with everything, like nothing is right.

'Okay, I think I owe you an apology,' he says, once I've sat down. 'I know I promised I'd wait until you came out of the police station and I'm so sorry about leaving, but… Well, the truth is I have no excuse. I just had to go. Again, I'm sorry. I hope it went okay.'

I stare at him, unable to understand where this is coming from. 'You just had to go. Okay. Right.'

'I needed you to go to the police, Josie, that was the main thing. That's all that matters here. You did do it, didn't you? Please tell me you went through with it.'

I don't answer. It feels like this is no longer his business. He's clearly decided to wash his hands of it, and me, so I won't provide him with details now.

'Well, I hope you did,' he says when he realises he's getting nothing out of me. 'I really hope you'll be okay now. But...'

Ever since I was a child I've always believed there was one thing I could do quite well – and that's being able to know what people think of me. To see beyond their words, their actions, and know for sure whether they like me or not, and to what degree. It's not something I've ever questioned, and maybe everyone has this ability, but right now I know that Zach Hamilton has feelings for me that go beyond student and lecturer, beyond friendship. Despite the fact that he's trying his best to dismiss me.

I could stop him right now and save him the trouble of what he's about to say, but I need to hear it. He needs to be honest with me, just as I've been with him about my past.

He lets out a huge sigh. 'Oh, Josie, you're... I just think we need to take a step back a bit. I'm happy to help you with any university things, but I... I think we need to... I'm just... I feel like I'm in a bit of a sticky situation here. It's tricky with friendships, isn't it? People get invested in each other and then all kinds of things can happen. I just... I need—'

'I get it,' I say. He needs his life to go back to the way it was before he met me, before I crowded his mind too much with my baggage. With *me*. But I want him to say it. 'But just tell me one thing. I'm not imagining things, am I?'

He glances at the door then gives the tiniest shake of his head.

Without another word I stand up and leave. I completely understand it now.

A few hours later I have reached a new low. It's one thing to drown your sorrows with alcohol in a club or bar, but another to do it totally alone in your bedroom, the soundtrack to your despair your flatmate's hushed tones as she speaks to someone on the phone, trying her best to make sure you can't hear a word.

But here I am, sprawled on my bed and drinking straight from a bottle of vodka, my throat burning as it goes down. Usually the stuff makes me gag, but tonight it's an anaesthetic, taking me further away from Zach, and Alison, and Liv.

In the next room, Alison's voice starts to get louder, and there can only be one reason for this. 'I just can't stand her,' she says – and I don't have to be a genius to know she's talking about me. There's a long pause while the person on the other end of the line speaks. It must be one of her parents; nobody else calls her.

I tune out when she begins again, blasting music from my mobile to mask her nasty comments. I've already heard her opinion of me, straight to my face, and I don't need to hear any more. Nothing she can say about me makes me the person she thinks I am.

For the next couple of hours I stay like this, barely moving, letting music and vodka wash over me. I close my eyes and pretend I'm somewhere else – a scorching beach in a place I've never been. I'm twenty-one years old and I've never felt sand beneath my feet. And although I come from a coastal town, the beach is a pebble one and I've rarely dipped a toe in the sea.

There is so much I haven't done because of Liv, so much of my life wasted so far. I need to sober up, because I'm just wasting more time like this, but my body is too heavy, and moving seems way beyond my control.

Just give in to it, Josie. You are more like her than you want to believe. You are your mother's child.

This is the thought I close my eyes to, and when they snap open again it's because my phone is vibrating. It's a text message, and when I realise who it's from I stare at the words, wondering if the alcohol is playing tricks on my mind. But the message is still there when I look again. I sit up straight and force my eyes to focus.

We need to talk. Please. It's urgent.

*

I could be walking into a trap. I know this, but I still push through the doors of the pub, scanning the room quickly so that I'm not taken by surprise. And there she is, cradling a pint of beer, her hair tied up in a scruffy knot on top of her head. She suits this place, looks comfortable in it, and blends into the background even though she has never set foot in here.

But am I any better? I'm still in a half-drunken daze and don't quite know how I've managed to get here, but somehow I did. The tiny amount of sleep I had, and the cold, bitter air, has helped.

She looks up as I approach her table but doesn't smile. Of course she doesn't. Even though she is the one who asked me to come here. I should have ignored her message. This can only lead to trouble. But it's the first time she has shown willing to talk to me since my attack.

'Well, well, well… I didn't think you'd come,' she snorts. 'You're full of surprises, aren't you?'

I slide into a chair opposite her. 'I'm not scared of you, Liv. Or that man you sent after me. Or Johnny, or anyone else.'

She laughs and swigs her beer. But it's all an act. She wants something from me – no, *needs* something from me – otherwise we wouldn't be here. I have the upper hand. I have to keep that in mind, whatever she says.

'No, you're actually not scared, are you?' She scrunches her face. 'You've come here on your own, not knowing what to expect. That's either brave or stupid.'

'What do you want, Liv?' I sit back in my chair, trying to relax my body so my mind will follow suit.

'Don't you even want a drink? Although from the smell of you I'd say you've already had more than enough tonight, haven't you? Like mother, like daughter. You're so busy trying to prove you're nothing like me when we both know the truth, don't we?' Her laugh is coarse and throaty. Too many years of smoking… I really have to quit.

'No, Liv, that's where you're wrong. And I'd top myself if I thought for one second I was anything like you.'

She doesn't answer and the smirk remains on her face. Nothing I ever say bothers her. She doesn't care who or what she is. But we've all got a weakness, haven't we? And I know exactly what hers is.

'Why have you come all the way to London tonight? You've never stepped out of Brighton before, so what the hell do you want? And who's looking after Kieren?'

She takes another sip of beer and swills it around her mouth. 'Actually, I'm here to reason with you, Josie. We're family, after all, aren't we?' She can't even say the word properly, it sounds like it's sticking in her throat and she's choking on the lie.

'Just cut the shit and tell me what you want, Liv.'

Her eyes narrow and her mouth twists. 'You need to go to the police, Josie. Tell them it was a mistake and Johnny didn't do anything to you, like Richard said.'

And now it's my turn to laugh. 'Really? You came all this way to say that? Do you actually believe I'll do it? You're lucky you're not rotting in prison with him. That's what you deserve.'

She rolls her eyes. 'Oh, this bullshit again. I've told you a thousand times I wasn't at home, I didn't see anything that happened to you. Why are you always lying, Josie?' Her eyes burn into me, defying me to contradict her.

'There's no one listening, Liv. I'm not recording this.' I pull out my mobile to prove it. 'See. So why don't you just admit you were there? I *saw* you.'

She throws her head back. 'But how could you have seen anything after what that person did to you, whoever it was? You could barely open your eyes. Look, if you tell the police the truth then I suppose we can all make allowances for you, given the state you were in. I mean, you maybe just *thought* it was Johnny, right? Maybe it was someone who looked like him? But you've got to stop lying, Josie. About Johnny, and about me being there.'

I'm transported back. I see the outline of my mother, her thick frame familiar and unmistakable. I can even hear her laugh – the nasty chuckle she gave as she relished in my battering. She'd finally paid me back for being born.

I shake my head. '*I* know what the truth is and that's all that matters. Just because the police couldn't prove you were there it doesn't make you innocent.'

Her eyes narrow. I know she must be finding it hard not to explode in public. 'I thought you'd run off to start a new life, Josie?'

'Yes, I did, and I have. I'm at uni now, Liv, something you could never have even dreamed of. So—'

'Then what the hell is it to you if Johnny gets out of prison?' She shouts this at me; I knew it was only a matter of time. Thankfully, it's too noisy in here for anyone to notice, or care. 'He won't come after you, he wouldn't want to go anywhere near you after what you've done, so why can't you just leave us to it?'

Her question doesn't even deserve an answer. 'It's Kieren I feel sorry for, stuck there with you. He deserves better.'

She snorts again, an animal disguised as a human. 'Kieren is just fine. D'you know what? He's actually a decent kid, not like you were.'

I should walk away now; I don't have to sit here and let this woman, one who's supposed to be a mother, insult me, but I need some answers and I'm too stubborn to leave without them.

'What did I do that was so bad you had to neglect me, emotionally abuse me and then let that monster almost batter me to death? And don't give me that shit about me being mouthy. Yeah, I speak my mind, but I wasn't out of control. I generally kept to myself as a kid and hardly bothered you.' I take a breath. 'I know you think having me ruined your life, but surely you're not stupid enough to think that's my fault? I didn't bloody ask to be here. And you had a choice to make – you could have just got rid of me.' I stare at her cold, piercing eyes and wait for a response.

'It was too late to get rid of you by the time I realised I was pregnant. So actually, I didn't have a bloody choice. And you were a rope around my neck.'

I stand up and turn away. This is the only answer I'll ever get from her and I don't need, or want, to hear any more. I accepted long ago that she's a despicable creature and I'm not wasting any more time on her.

'You might want to hear what else I've got to say before you walk off.'

I turn back and there's a smug smile on her face. 'I've tried to warn you, Josie, but you're just not listening. I can't control what Richard does, but believe me he's not going to let this go. No chance. Sooner or later it will catch up with you.'

'I'm not interested,' I say. I've had these threats ever since I reported the attack and nothing's happened yet, so I'm not going to be bullied by her or anyone else.

She nods her head, as if she's known I would say this. 'Not even for your brother's sake?'

'What's that supposed to mean? This has got nothing to do with Kieren.'

'I can't be responsible for anything that happens. This is Richard's business as much as it is mine. So maybe you want to go away and have a think about it all.' She stands up and pulls on her coat. 'See you, Josie.'

And then she is gone, leaving me standing in the pub, hoping I'm wrong about what the woman is capable of.

SEVENTEEN

Mia

Of all the things Alison has come out with, this is the biggest shock. She's now claiming to have spoken to Zach on the night he died. It feels as though I'm going to vomit, but I have to keep in mind she could be lying, and the more she says, the more I have to believe that.

'How is that possible? There's no way. You couldn't have been there.'

'Mia, I'm telling you I was. Only for a few minutes, but I was. I know how this sounds, but you have to believe me. What reason would I have to lie?'

Because you're deluded, and for some reason you've picked me to play your sick games with.

I force myself to tell her I'm listening. And even though the windows are open as usual, and there must be noise drifting in from the busy road and park outside, I can only hear silence until she continues. Loud and threatening silence.

'I was at Josie's flat that night and I spoke to your husband. It must have been way before he… before he died, and as I said, it was only for a few minutes, but that was long enough for me to be convinced that he had no intention of harming himself.'

I take a deep breath. Whatever she has to say – lie or not – I need to hear it, every last detail. 'Start from the beginning, Alison, and don't leave anything out. If you're going to tell me this then I need to hear everything this time, not just snatches of information as and when you feel like giving them to me.'

'But anything I say is still confidential, isn't it?' Her forehead creases.

I nod. 'Unless I think you had anything to do with what happened.'

Her pause reveals that she's nervous. If she's lying, surely she has nothing to fear except being caught out in her deceit? 'Okay, well, that's not the case.' She tucks a loose strand of thick red hair behind her ear. 'I really didn't like Josie, that's no secret, and she felt the same about me. We'd been placed together in that flat so didn't really have much choice about living together. I tried several times to get a transfer but there was nothing close enough to the uni. Eventually I took out another student loan just so I could get my own place. It was a tiny one-bedroom flat, and far too expensive, but at least I was away from her. And after my experience living with her, I definitely wasn't going to share with anyone again. Even if it bankrupted me.'

Part of me wants her to hurry up and get to the Zach part, but I need this information too, so I have to be patient. I need to take note of every word she says, in order to be able to trip her up in any lies. The only things I'd ever learned about Josie were that she'd left home and didn't keep in touch with her family. At the time of Zach's death it was reported that she'd suffered a brutal attack a few years before but the police didn't think there was any connection; the man responsible was behind bars.

'Why did you hate her so much?' I ask. I have to know. What can make someone so loathsome to one person yet so appealing to another?

Alison looks me up and down. 'Haven't you ever met someone and they instantly repel you? Maybe there's no simple explanation for it, but no matter how hard you try, you just can't get along with them? Everything they do or say just puts you on edge.'

This hasn't happened to me but I understand what she means. The closest I've come to it is happening here, right now. 'Well, we're not meant to get along with everyone. We just need to try and be courteous, treat people with respect.'

She doesn't look convinced. 'Even if they don't deserve it?'

'Yes, Alison. It's not for us to judge other people. Anyway, please carry on. Where are you going with this?'

'I'm getting to it. But you need to know everything first, you need the whole picture. I don't want you to jump to conclusions about me.'

'I just said I don't judge, Alison. And it looks like you've got no choice but to trust that I mean that. So, please, go on.' I am trying my absolute best to remain calm and patient, because no matter what we're discussing here, Alison is still my client. She is clearly still in need of some sort of help.

'Well, I suppose it doesn't matter why we disliked each other, just that we did. So I'd moved out weeks before the night she… whatever happened to her, but I'd kept a front-door key. I'd had a spare one cut for my parents, for emergencies, and forgotten to give it back to the landlady.' She pauses, as if waiting for some admonishment, but keeping a door key is the least of my concerns.

When I don't respond she continues, 'It's just coincidence, but that night I let myself into the flat. I'd lost a bracelet my mum had got me and I wanted to check the flat to see if I could find it. I was sure it was in there somewhere. I was planning to knock on the door and ask Josie if she'd seen it, but when I got there I saw her running off in the other direction, so I knew it was safe for me to let myself into the flat.' She stops talking and looks at me. 'I'm not proud of myself for any of this. But I was young and a bit… naïve, probably.'

This is not the word I'd use, but again, none of that matters.

Alison tilts her head to the side. 'You don't believe me, do you, Mia? But I swear it's the truth.'

None of what she says sounds genuine, but I can't tell her that. I need her to keep talking. 'What did you do next?'

'I let myself in. And got a huge shock when I walked into the front room and saw Zach there.'

My stomach flips. 'What… what was he doing?'

'He was just sitting on the sofa, leaning forward with his head buried in his hands, as if he was in pain. I can still picture him. I didn't recognise him until he looked up, but then I realised he was a lecturer from uni. I didn't know him but I'd seen him around quite a bit.'

It's a struggle to force the words out. 'Why didn't you tell the police this, Alison?'

She lowers her head and stares at her feet. The boots she's wearing are more suited to winter than this summer we're having. 'I'm not proud of myself, Mia. I know now that I should have gone to them and told them everything, but don't you see the predicament I was in? I couldn't let anyone know I was there and get caught up in the investigation. The police would have found out I hated her and then what? I'd have been a suspect. And I couldn't prove where I'd been that evening, as I was just alone in my flat. They would have hounded me non-stop.'

Like they did to me, as the wife of a man who became involved with one of his students, a man who took someone's life and then ended his own when he couldn't face the consequences of what he'd done.

'But they already had their suspect,' I say. 'My husband.'

She shakes her head. 'But there was no real proof that he did it, was there? Other than him being in her flat. And he wasn't alive to tell them I was innocent, that I was long gone before anything happened. With Zach dead, the police were looking for another suspect, and they would have pounced on me, rightly or wrongly. At least then another crime wouldn't go unsolved.'

'Alison, that's a bit cynical, isn't it? The police only want to see the guilty punished. I think you're being paranoid.' Dominic's words flash into my head – how Alison has rarely made sense, rarely been okay since he's known her. Was he telling the truth after all? 'Anyway, without a body it would never have got as far as going to trial. Even for Zach, if he'd lived.'

'That didn't stop them accusing him, though. As far as the media and the public are concerned, he's guilty. I was too scared to let that happen to me. Even if I wasn't sent to prison for something I didn't do, how would I have got a good job?' She pauses. 'As it turns out, I ended up working in temporary admin jobs. What a waste of three years. But like I said, I was terrified. That's why I kept quiet. Until now.'

'At least you would have had a voice to defend yourself. Zach never got the chance, Alison. He's gone to his grave guilty, whether or not he actually is.' It's ironic that, despite everything, I still defend Zach in this way. I wish he'd had a chance to explain.

'So you don't believe he did it?' Alison says. 'That's good. So you must believe me that he also didn't kill himself.'

'The truth is, Alison, I stopped knowing what to believe long ago. At first I couldn't get my head around how Zach could have done that, but then I never would have believed him capable of getting involved with one of his students. I had to face the fact that I didn't know my husband at all. But you still haven't told me how you've drawn this conclusion about his suicide.' I don't know how I'm remaining so calm, despite it feeling as though the walls are crumbling down around me.

'I'm getting to that. So, like I said, he was there on the sofa. He looked pretty upset. I couldn't say anything at first as I was so shocked to find him there, but then he said hello and asked me if I was a friend of Josie's. He was so polite, even in that bizarre situation. And when I explained who I was, and what I was doing, he just told me sometimes we find ourselves in weird situations, but we have to take a step back and question what we're doing so we can get ourselves out. Something like that. I can't remember his exact words but it was along those lines. I don't even know why he said all that when I was just looking for my bracelet, but maybe Josie had already told him how much she hated me.'

I almost smile now because this sounds exactly like something Zach would say. He was always philosophising, always analysing everything. Alison must be telling the truth, at least about seeing Zach, otherwise how could she be able to give him words that are so accurate? I ask her what else he said.

'He said he knew he probably shouldn't be in the flat but he was only there to help Josie. She was having some troubles and he was worried about her. Really worried about her. I must have looked sceptical because he pulled out his phone and showed me a picture of you and your little baby girl. He said he would never do anything to hurt either of you.'

Tears are rolling down my cheeks now but I can't stop them.

Although Alison must notice, she carries on. 'Until that point I thought maybe he was protesting too much, and that maybe there was something weird going on between them, but do you know what? As soon as he mentioned you I believed him, even though I didn't trust Josie. There was no way he could fake the shine in his eyes as he looked at your photo.'

But that doesn't mean he was innocent. It just means that somehow, in the midst of it all, he still loved me.

Alison, unaware of the conflict within me, continues. 'I asked him where Josie was and he said she'd be back in a minute. I almost mentioned that I'd seen her staggering off, but for some reason I didn't. Now, obviously, I wish so badly I'd asked him, but, well, it's too late now.'

'So what happened next?' I say.

'I didn't want Josie to come back and find me so I told Zach I was leaving. He promised not to mention I'd been there if I'd do the same about him. Now why would he do that if he was planning to kill himself in that flat? It wouldn't have mattered who I told then, would it? That just doesn't add up, does it?'

Alison is right: if everything she's telling me is true then it does suggest Zach didn't take his own life. I feel another panic attack coming on, and this time I can't suppress it.

Immediately, Alison notices. 'Mia, can I get you something? I'm sorry, I'm so, so sorry.' She rushes to the corner where I keep the drinks and pours me a glass of water. 'Here, have this.'

I sip it gratefully and wait for the attack to pass. 'I'm okay,' I say eventually, once I'm in control of my breathing again. 'I just… have a condition. This happens quite a lot. I'm fine, though.'

She reaches out her arm and takes my hand. 'Has this been happening since Zach died?'

There is no way I should answer her question; it's too personal and I can't let this woman, about whom I know nothing and cannot trust, into my life in this way. But somehow I'm nodding.

'That's understandable, after everything you've been through.'

I'm relieved that she doesn't question me further. She's respecting a boundary; this is not a sign of diminished mental capacity. Once again, I don't know what to believe.

'Mia, that's it, I've told you everything now. From the short time I was there, I'm convinced that Zach wasn't about to take his own life.'

'But you don't know what happened after that. Things could have changed. Maybe when Josie came back she said something to tip him over the edge.'

'Mia, he was nowhere close to the edge.'

I let her words sink in, let it all consume me. I've got to be strong here, I can't fall apart now. 'What am I supposed to do with this information, Alison? Do you realise I could go to the police and tell them what you've told me? You kept information from them and you saw both Zach and Josie on that day.'

She nods. 'Yes, you could easily do that. But think about it, Mia. If I had done anything to either of them then why would I have told you any of this? I would want to be as far away from you as possible, wouldn't I? The reason I'm here, finally doing the right thing, is because I think Dominic had something to do with it. I just don't know what. And like I said before, I need your help to find something we can go to the police together with.'

Her words echo around the room, ramming into my skull, paralysing me.

'I… I need time to think. This is a lot to digest. I think you should go now, but I'll call you.'

There is no mistaking the disappointment on her face. I don't know what she expected me to do, but this is the best I can offer.

'Okay,' she says, when she eventually stands up. 'I understand. This is a hell of a lot to take in. Please just don't leave it too long. I can't be around that man much longer, Mia. I'm really afraid of him.'

She leaves my office and closes the door, and I can almost hear the time bomb she has set off, ticking louder and louder.

EIGHTEEN

Josie

'I need to speak to you. It's important.'

Zach sighs into the phone, but at least he's answered my call. 'Josie, I'm really sorry but you shouldn't be calling me. If you need to talk to me about uni work then of course I will, but you really have to see me after lectures. Or in my office.' His voice is too formal; he sounds nothing like the Zach I've come to know.

But I've been expecting him to say something like this so I'm fully prepared. 'It's not about uni, it's about my little brother. I think… I'm worried something might happen to him.' I tell him about Liv turning up in London and asking to see me. And that I've spent a restless night churning over her comments, and her veiled threat, and this morning I still don't know what to do.

Zach pauses for so long I think he might have cut me off, but then he finally speaks. His voice is warmer this time, but there is still a three-foot wall between us. 'Josie, I'm so sorry to hear that, but you really need to go to the police again. I just don't know what else I can do to help.'

He doesn't realise what it's taken for me to approach him with this. I hate the fact that I'm turning to him for help. Again. It's not me, but I'm desperate and I'll do what I have to for Kieren. 'I've spoken to the police already,' I tell him. 'But there's not much they can do. I just need to… talk it through with someone.' I don't need to explain this any further; Zach knows I can count the people I know in London on one hand, and none of them are anywhere close to being friends.

'Where are you?' he says, after another long pause.

'Outside the library, I've just parked up.' I'm about to ask him where he is but then a child cries out in the background, yelling something that sounds like *no*. He's at home. With his family. There is no way he can, or will, come to me.

'D'you know what? Just forget it. I shouldn't have called you.' I disconnect the call and throw my phone on the passenger seat of the car, not caring when it bounces and lands on the floor. I won't beg for Zach's friendship or anything else, I'll find a way to help Kieren by myself.

I roll down the window, reach into the glove compartment for my cigarettes and pull out the packet of Marlboro Lights, desperate for a nicotine fix to ease my anxiety. But as I take one out and lift it to my lips, I think of Liv last night, the lines around her mouth and the permanent smell of smoke she tries to mask with cheap perfume. I scrunch the packet and hurl it through the window into the bin that by chance is not too far from the car. My perfect aim is a small, meaningless victory.

My day of lectures passes slowly and I struggle to take anything in. I scribble down a few words but have no idea what they mean. All I can think of is my brother, and the monster he has to live with. Maybe she hasn't turned on him yet, but sooner or later she will. Hatred and bitterness are in her blood, the core of who she is.

At least now I know the name of the man who threatened me. Richard. The same person Kieren mentioned was taking him to McDonald's. I've already told the police officer I was dealing with, the one with the kind voice, so now at least they can speak to him. It shouldn't be too hard to find a cousin of Johnny's called Richard. Ha, I don't think Liv knew what she was giving away when she said his name, she was too busy revelling in her threats. She's such a fool.

It's a relief when my last lecture is finally over. I make my way to the car park, with no plan for what I'll do this evening. I don't have a shift at the coffee shop and somehow I'm up to date with my coursework, so there is nothing but an empty night looming ahead. But I won't drink a drop this evening; I need a clear head to work out how I will get Kieren away from Liv – sooner than I thought I'd have to.

I approach my car and see a woman standing by it. For a fleeting moment I think it must be Liv, come to have another go at persuading me, but I soon realise it's Alison.

'Can we talk?' she says, as I reach the car. She can barely bring herself to look at me, staring towards the library instead.

'What is it?' I can't help being abrupt –I don't trust this girl and she gives me the creeps – but I'm intrigued to know why she's waiting for me at my car.

'Um, will you be home tonight?' She drops her eyes to the ground.

'Why are you asking?'

'I… I think we need to talk. Properly this time, no arguing or anything.'

This is not what I expected her to say. 'What, you mean you'll actually listen to me? About Aaron? About everything?'

She nods and flicks her hair out of her face. 'Let's just clear the air, Josie. We're both stuck in that flat together until summer, and that's a long way off. So what do you think?'

I study her face, a poker face I have no chance of reading, and decide to trust her this once. There is too much going on in my life; I already have too many enemies to make another one out of the person I have to live with. And compared to Liv, Johnny and Richard, Alison is harmless.

'Okay, let's talk tonight.'

'I'll be home around seven,' she says, and flashes a thin smile before scurrying off.

She's like a mouse or some other little creature, I think as I watch her leave, her red hair flying away from her shoulders. Maybe I've been too hard on her.

I'm back in the car and starting up the engine when my phone beeps. Hoping it's Zach, I scoop it up and stare at the screen, but of course it's not him. It's a text from Liv: a photo of Kieren smiling into the camera, Liv's red nail-polished hand on his left shoulder.

The flat is freezing when I get home. At first I think the boiler must be broken but it seems to be fine when I check it. I check the radiators and find that all of them have been turned off – except Alison's. Unlike the rest of the flat, her room is cosy and warm. It doesn't take a genius to work out she's done this on purpose – but why? It's nothing to do with saving on heating bills as everything is included in our rent. And if she's trying to screw with me in this pathetic way then why did she insist on us having a chat this evening? Unless she did it before deciding to make peace with me. But I don't have time to dwell on her strange behaviour: there are more important things to worry about.

I turn all the radiators back on and, wrapping myself in my thickest, longest cardigan, I curl up on the sofa and stare at the picture of Kieren on my phone. He looks happy enough, but that witch's hand on his shoulder, like a claw, is sending a clear message: she doesn't care what happens to her son, it's more important to her that Johnny is out of prison.

Across the room I notice a full bottle of gin on the bookshelf. It's not mine; I never leave anything in communal places since my USB stick was taken, and I've never known Alison to drink. Confused, I decide to question her about it later.

My phone beeps again and this time I'm not so quick to check it, expecting it to be another picture of Kieren, or at least an abusive message from Liv.

But it's Zach. And he's telling me he's outside my flat.

'What are you doing here?' I ask, opening the door to him. Under any other circumstances I'd be pleased to see him – no, more than pleased – but not after the way he's been giving me the cold shoulder since he took me to the police station.

'Are you alone?' he says, peering behind me. He seems anxious; I've never seen him like this before.

'Yeah. Why? What's going on, Zach?' I check my watch. It's only ten to six, so there's at least an hour until Alison gets home for our chat.

Zach stands as still as a rock, both hands thrust into his pockets.

'Do you want to come in, then?' I move back to let him through, still not sure why he's turned up like this.

'I shouldn't be here, I really shouldn't. But I had to come. To… you know… check you're okay.'

'Then bloody come in, won't you?' I grab his arm and pull him inside. And once again we are no longer lecturer and student, but two people who like each other, despite the circumstances we're in.

He laughs and frees his hands from his pockets. 'I feel sorry for the man you end up marrying,' he says. But there is sadness in his smile.

'Why are you here, Zach? You've made it clear you don't want anything to do with me—'

'Of course I do. You're my student, Josie, and that comes first. Above any personal issues I might be struggling with.'

I keep hold of his arm and lead him to the sofa. 'Zach, you've got to stop talking in riddles. Tell me exactly what you mean.'

He sits down and shakes his head. 'I don't know, Josie. But I couldn't let you down. You needed me earlier and I turned my back on you. I'm sorry for that, it was inexcusable. None of this is your fault. You can't help… being you.'

'There you go again with those bloody riddles! Please, just stop. Start talking straight. I'm a big girl, I can handle it.'

He buries his head in his hands. 'I love my wife, Josie. I really do love her. She's this amazing, selfless woman who is just there for everyone and anyone. I really can't fault her. I mean, she's a huge perfectionist and it's a bit infuriating at times, but that's a small thing to live with. And she's a great mum to Freya. And Freya, well, she's just this amazing little thing that we both created. Yeah, sure, she's hard work, but I've said it before: there's no such thing as perfection.'

It should be hard for me to hear all this, but somehow it's not. It's giving me a glimpse of the private Zach. The man he doesn't want me to see. And it's hard to feel resentment when I know his wife came before me. Plus, there's a reason he's here with me now, and I can't help but feel excited by that. By him just being in my flat.

I sit on the floor and lean against the sofa. Once again the gin bottle catches my eye, but I ignore it. 'It sounds like you're really happy, Zach, so I don't understand why you seem so... I don't know. So something.'

'Ha, look at us! We're both writers and neither of us can find the word to sum me up.' Zach sinks to the floor so we're side by side. 'Sometimes when you say things out loud it brings them to life and makes them real. Things you've kept in your head. I mean, they're safe in your head, they can't hurt anyone, but once you've said them, well, that's it. Chaos. Destruction. People get hurt.'

I feel sorry for him in this moment. He was right when he said that I am free in a way he can never be. 'How about if I say it? Then you don't have to agree or disagree or anything, it's just out there.'

He stares at me, obviously finding it hard to claim responsibility for any of this. But I continue anyway because it needs to be said, and it doesn't matter who says it. 'You've got feelings for me. And you're a bit disgusted with yourself. You're a decent man and you don't ever want to cheat on your wife. But it's tearing you up a bit and I just won't go away. Even though you avoid me as much as possible, I'm still in your head and I'm not shifting. Am I right?'

Zach doesn't respond, of course he doesn't, but sadness darkens his eyes. He reaches over and takes my hand, giving it a brief squeeze before quickly letting go. 'So what's going on with your brother? I think you should tell me all about it.'

By the time I've finished, we've managed to move on from the conversation we had only moments ago – or at least we're both pretending we have. 'Do you really think she'd harm your brother?' Zach says.

I tell him that he'd only have to meet Liv for a few minutes to know there's evil inside her.

'Can you call social services?'

'They already know about her. Which is probably why she's been on her best behaviour lately. But they can't watch her all the time, can they? Anything could happen. She'll just wait until they lose interest in her.'

Zach takes my hand but quickly drops it again. 'I'm sorry,' he says, looking away.

There's no point making a big deal of his subconscious gesture. 'You're probably wondering why she would seem to be okay with Kieren when she couldn't stand the sight of me.'

Zach turns to me again, probably grateful I've not mentioned what just happened. 'Nothing in life surprises me,' he says. 'There are no limits to what people are capable of.'

'She had Kieren when she was older, more prepared for a baby perhaps. And he's a boy. I don't know, but I think that's the key thing. She can't be jealous of him for being younger, or smarter, or prettier. And she can't feel that he's ruined her life when according to her, I'd already done that.'

'Josie, you've told me before you don't know who your father was, but what about Kieren's?'

'Liv was actually seeing him for a while. He seemed okay at first and was all right to me. And when Kieren was first born he seemed happy to be a father. But then he left, like they all did when they realised what she was like, and he never once tried to see Kieren. Not then anyway, and I don't think he has in the last few years either. I heard he went to live in Spain, but I don't know how true that is. Other than my old neighbour, I'm just not connected to anyone in Brighton any more, thank God. Except for Kieren. And I can't leave him with her, Zach, I just can't.'

'Josie, you've got to be careful. Let's both have a think about this and see what we can come up with. There's got to be an answer.'

I don't tell him that I've done little else but think about it and so far have come up with nothing. 'Thanks, Zach,' I say instead. 'I know you're putting a lot on the line to help me.'

'I haven't done anything wrong, Josie.'

But it sounds as though he's trying to convince himself of that.

'But we're kind of involved on a personal level now, aren't we? Isn't that frowned upon by the uni?'

'Yes, probably. I can't say now that I'm just helping you with academic issues. That's one thing, but this… I don't know what this is. All I know is I can't turn my back on you.'

'You shouldn't risk your job for me.'

He shrugs and tries to laugh, but I can tell it's forced. 'Sod it. If that happened there'd be even more motivation for me to finish my book.'

From out in the hallway something clicks and I freeze. Alison must be home early, and the last thing we need is for her to find Zach here – she'll love exploiting that.

'What was that?' Zach whispers, jumping up and grabbing his coat. 'Well, I'm glad I could help,' he says, winking. 'Remember to hand it in on time.'

But when we head into the hallway there is no sign of Alison or anyone else. I check her room and it's empty, as are the kitchen and bathroom.

'Weird,' I mutter.

'Must have been the neighbours we heard,' Zach says.

But I know it wasn't. Alison was here, I'm sure of that. I don't mention this to Zach, though, as I see him out. He doesn't need anything more pushing him away. Though our connection is strong, our friendship is hanging by a thread.

After he leaves, I sit at the kitchen table with my laptop, researching everything I can about social services and whether or not I can push them to do anything about Liv. I'm so engrossed in the words that I barely come up for air.

And when I notice the time, it's eight fifteen, but there's still no sign of Alison.

NINETEEN

Mia

I'm standing at the door of Zach's parents' home, holding the hand of someone who is not Zach. Coming here with Will makes me yearn for Zach, for my past, but I need to fight this. He's gone. He betrayed me, and our daughter. Whatever Alison thinks did or didn't happen, there is no denying that he was in that girl's flat. Alone with her. That's all that matters.

Since I saw Alison yesterday I've done nothing but stew over her words. I can't decide what to do about it yet; it's better to do nothing for now than make the wrong choice. Alison clearly needs help; I just don't know in what way. So tonight is a welcome break from having to think of her and the mess caused by her world colliding with mine.

'Are you all right?' Will asks, squeezing my hand. I can tell from his words, and his eyes, that he's desperate for me to be okay. For me not to have changed my mind about us living together. But he doesn't need to worry. I am in this for keeps... just as I was supposed to be with Zach.

'More to the point, Will, are *you* okay? I know how weird this must be for you, too.'

'It is weird, definitely. But a good weird. A step in the right direction for us,' he says, still clasping my hand. 'Are we still going to tell them about us moving in together?'

'I don't see why not. Freya knows now so it's not fair to keep it from them. She's so excited about it she could easily blurt it out when she sees them next and that wouldn't be fair. They need to hear it from me.'

We all thought it best if Freya stayed at her friend Megan's house tonight, just so Graham and Pam could have a chance to get to know Will properly. Freya was only too happy to agree to an evening of pizza and chips, and probably ice cream, with her best friend.

'Right, let's do this,' Will says, taking a deep breath before he rings the bell.

Pam and Graham answer the door together, with huge smiles and tight hugs for both of us, and I can see Will is immediately put at ease. They are amazingly strong people to react in this way to what some might consider their son's replacement.

'We feel like we know you already.' Pam takes Will's arm and leads him through to the dining room. 'You've got a long drive home so dinner's practically ready. I just need a minute to get it served up.'

'Thank you,' Will says. 'Whatever it is smells delicious.'

Pam beams at his compliment and hurries off to the kitchen, and as Graham fills glasses with wine, Will winks at me, showing me that he will be okay tonight.

Even though it's a Wednesday night, Pam has made a huge roast dinner – enough to feed at least four more people. 'Better to have too much than too little,' she says, as she puts the heavily laden plates in front of us. 'Besides, it won't go to waste, Graham and I can have the rest tomorrow for lunch.'

Graham rolls his eyes. 'But we never do, do we? You always end up wanting to cook something else from scratch.' His tone is affectionate; this banter is the norm for these two. Zach used to admire the relationship the two of them have, how they can disagree about anything and everything but it never gets between them, never changes how they feel about each other. Solid, like a fortress, he used to say.

'Well, cooking keeps me busy,' Pam says. 'It's… good for me.' Her eyes glass over.

Over dinner, Pam fires questions at Will, even though I've already told her the answers to most of what she's asking. 'So you've never been married?'

Will doesn't seem to mind being asked such a personal question. 'Nope. Don't get me wrong, I'm not against it, and I've had a few long-term relationships, but it just never felt right.' His eyes flick to me, and I offer him an apologetic smile. 'I don't know, is it weird that at thirty-four I've never been married?'

Pam chuckles. 'Oh no, not at all – at least not these days. People are too busy with their careers, I suppose.'

'Guilty!' Will says, reaching for my hand. 'But I'm trying to change that.'

When we've all finished eating, both the men managing to clear their plates, Will glances at me and I know it's that time. I clear my throat. 'We've got something to tell you both.'

Pam's eyes widen, and I realise she might think this is a pregnancy announcement. I can't let her think that – it would break her heart, I'm sure, even though she would also be happy for me.

'Will and I are moving in together,' I say, as quickly as I can get the words out.

'Oh, that's wonderful!' Pam says, raising her glass.

We all follow suit, and I glance at Graham, just to check he's okay too, and I'm pleased to see a wide smile plastered on his face, as he toasts with one hand and pats Will on the arm with the other.

'Where will you live?' Pam asks.

'We'll sell both our properties and find somewhere new,' I say. 'It might take some time but it's quite exciting.'

'Well, we're thrilled for you,' Graham says, taking another sip of wine.

'I take it Freya knows?' Pam asks.

Will answers this time, and I'm glad he feels comfortable enough to answer questions about Freya. 'Yes, we told her earlier today and luckily she's really excited about it.'

Pam nods slowly. 'Of course she is.' Her eyes drop to her plate and she swirls food around with her fork. 'But then I suppose because she doesn't remember Zach it won't be strange or hard for her.' She looks at me and I'm surprised that the warmth has gone from her eyes. 'Oh, sorry, you two, just ignore me. It's all just very emotional. I really am pleased for you.'

'Of course it's emotional for you,' Will says, reaching over and placing his hand on her arm. 'But I will never pretend to be her father and she'll always know about Zach. We'll keep his memory alive for her, I promise. And I want you to know that I'm not trying to take his place in any way.'

But it will only ever be the good parts. Freya will only ever hear what a good father Zach was to her. I made that promise to myself when he died and I will never break it.

After we've all had coffee, Will helps Pam clear up while I stay with Graham. He's always been a quiet man, but tonight he's had a couple of glasses of wine so is more relaxed than normal. I stuck to fruit juice tonight because I wanted Will to be able to enjoy himself, so I am the designated driver.

'He's a nice fellow,' Graham says. 'Funny, but I reckon Zach would have liked him. I can almost see the two of them chatting, having a drink together.'

It's difficult when death means you end up in the arms of someone else. If I had known Zach and Will at the same time there is no doubt I would still have fallen for, and married, Zach. But strangely that doesn't make my feelings for Will any less than they were for Zach. Different, of course, very different, but fate has brought us together, determined that he is the one I should be with, not Zach.

'That's a serious face,' Graham says, and I realise I haven't responded to his comment.

'I think you're right,' I say. 'They probably would have got along.' They have something in common, after all – they both chose to be with me. 'Will's great. And he loves Freya. I'm just so blessed to have this second chance.'

'You'll all be fine,' Graham says. 'Life goes on, doesn't it, and you can't stop living it. Especially when you've got little Freya to think of. Thanks for bringing him here. And telling us. You didn't have to. By any account it's not really our business.'

I lean across and give him a hug. 'Freya is your business, Graham, and that means Will and I are too. Don't you forget that.'

He squeezes my shoulder. 'Well, he's a good man, like I said, and seems trustworthy, so you've both got my blessing. Not that you needed it.'

'Graham,' I say, slowly, 'how do you know when you can trust someone? Are we supposed to just give people the benefit of the doubt until something proves otherwise, or is it the other way around?'

He smiles wryly. 'You sound like Zach. Let me think about that for a second.' He takes a sip of wine. 'I think you have to trust your instincts. They never usually steer us wrong. Why, are you saying you're worried about Will? Because he doesn't—'

'No, it's not Will, just a client. I can't say anything more than that but I find her a bit strange – I just don't know what to make of her.'

'I would have thought you'd be used to difficult or unusual people in your line of work.'

'That's not exactly true. For the most part my clients are just everyday people who need a little help with something they're wrestling with. I'm not a psychiatrist so I don't see people with severe mental health difficulties. I'm not qualified for that.'

'No,' Graham says, 'but you must have met some people you just can't click with. Can't understand.'

His words echo through my head and now I know what I have to do. I don't understand Alison and what she's trying to achieve. And until I do, nothing will be laid to rest.

'They're lovely people,' Will says once we're in bed. 'Thanks for tonight, it must have been hard for you.'

'Actually it wasn't,' I say. 'And I feel good that we've told them. Now we can focus on the future. *Our* future.' I say these words to Will even though I know actually doing it will be impossible until I know the truth. Everything is clearer now. I've got to fight for my future, no matter what happens with Alison. I need to protect Freya and Will, so I will do what I have to. Just as I've always done.

Will kisses me and I can feel the happiness emanating from his body. I hate lying to him. Ultimately it was lies that resulted in Zach's death, and I can't bear any more. Would things have been different if Zach had been able to talk to me about how he was feeling? It would have been hard to accept or even understand his feelings for Josie Carpenter, but in my heart I know I would have tried. It's the lies that leave the bigger scar, that cause the mistrust. But I look at Will and know I can't destroy his happiness. At this point there is nothing I can tell him anyway.

'Don't get me wrong, I do miss Freya being here,' Will says, oblivious to my turmoil, 'but it's nice that I don't have to sleep in the spare room.'

And then he shows me how nice it is and I get lost in our passion, shutting out everyone but him. Afterwards, we cling to each other and I feel pleasure mixed with pain.

Will doesn't deserve someone with so much baggage – I've got to lay Zach to rest.

*

'Alison? It's me.' I say this as though she should know who I am, though I've called her from my mobile and she only has my office line.

'Mia. I'm glad you've called. So quickly too. Does this… does this mean you believe me?'

'I don't know what to believe, Alison, but I want to figure out the truth.'

I'm pacing my office, looking out at the park every time I pass the window, hoping it will keep me calm. It's raining this morning so it's not as busy out there as usual.

'Can you meet me at my house?' she says. 'Dominic's away on a course, so it's safe.'

I hesitate. Do I really want to do this? It feels like I'm about to jump off a cliff, free fall a thousand metres. 'Okay, I need a couple of hours, though. I've got a client this morning.'

Thankfully, Megan's mum is taking the girls to London Zoo this afternoon and then she'll drop Freya at home so I have a few hours clear. And Will has back-to-back meetings until six.

'Thanks,' Alison says. 'Thank you so much.'

Their house is pristine, cold and soulless. I don't like clutter but I could never live like this. There are no pictures on the clinical white walls and the dark wood flooring makes me feel claustrophobic. It doesn't feel like I'm in someone's home, more like I'm in a surgery or hospital, waiting for some sort of unpleasant procedure.

'Not my choice of decor,' Alison says as she takes my coat. 'Dominic's very particular about his surroundings. He hates mess of any kind.' She sighs. 'It's hard work, keeping this place up, but now I'm not working I suppose it gives me something to do.'

'You've given up work? Why?'

'I just need a bit of a break, some time to sort all this stuff out. It's easier this way. That's the beauty of temping.'

'Why do you stay with him?' I ask. It's not the first time I've put this to her, but she still hasn't given me a valid reason for putting herself through this. 'Especially if you think he hurt Josie.'

'Up until now, it's been because this is my life. Yes, it's messed up, but it's *my* mess and I can't imagine just walking away from it. What would I do?'

I want to tell her this is not the way to look at things but I don't get a chance.

'But all that's changed now since the picture. I want him to rot in hell. For what he did to Josie and for everything he's done to me. Come with me, I want to show you something.'

She heads down the hall and I follow her into the kitchen, my stomach churning. I'm alone with a woman I don't know if I can trust.

And then, just as I'm wondering what she wants to show me, she is pulling up her jumper, revealing a skinny torso covered in fresh, reddish-purple bruises. 'Dominic did this last night before he left. Something to remind me of him until he gets back, something to make sure I don't go anywhere.'

I rush to her and grab her hand. 'My God, Alison! You can't let him do this to you.'

'I don't know what to do, Mia. I've got no evidence to prove he did anything to Josie. I've searched the whole house, and his computer, several times – but there's nothing. Like I said before, I can't risk going to the police with just that photo because then he'll get away with it and I'll... I'll end up like her.'

'But that might happen anyway, Alison. Look at you.'

'No, it's no good. And I'm sorry I wasted your time with this. I just can't prove your husband didn't kill himself.'

I am not an impulsive or reckless person. Everything I do in my life is carefully considered, all the pros and cons meticulously weighed up, but Alison needs help and I can't afford to take my time over this. 'Pack some things, you're coming to stay with me.

We can sort out how to get you out of this mess once we've got you away from Dominic.'

Alison's jaw drops. She hasn't been expecting this from me. 'No… I can't let you do that. You don't even know me, it wouldn't be fair.'

'I'm not leaving you here, Alison. I can't make any promises but I can at least try and keep you safe for a couple of days until we manage to work something out.'

There is such a long silence that I think she's going to refuse again, but then she slowly nods. 'Maybe then. Just for a couple of days until I can work out what to do.'

While she heads upstairs to pack some clothes, I pace Alison's sterile kitchen and call Pam. 'I'm so sorry to do this, Pam, but I need to ask a huge favour. Could you have Freya with you for a few days? Just until the weekend?'

'Of course. Is everything okay, Mia?'

'Yes, sorry, everything's fine, but I think it would be good for her to spend some more time with you. I know you both get lonely there. And I've got lots of extra work to do so it would really help me out.'

Thankfully Pam doesn't ask what exactly I need to do that I couldn't fit into my normal working hours. 'Well, yes,' she says, 'we love the house being filled with Freya and her noise, but are you sure you're okay? You and Will are fine, aren't you?'

'We're great. He loved meeting you both last night, thank you for that. So is it okay if I drop her round this evening?'

'Oh, that soon? Um, yes, of course. I'll get her room ready straight away.'

Pam knows I'm keeping something from her; I have never been disorganised enough to have to spring something like this on them, but how can I tell her I'm letting one of my clients stay with me for a few days? She would never understand. But while I want to do my best to help Alison, and at the same time get to the truth of everything, I will not let her be around my daughter.

TWENTY

Josie

A loud noise wakes me and I shoot up, jumping out of bed before I realise it's Alison dropping something in the bathroom. I hear her humming to herself, something tuneless that sounds like it's coming from a child's mouth.

It's 8 a.m. and this is the first I've seen or heard of her since our conversation by my car at university. Fuming that she hasn't had the decency to explain herself, I rush to the bathroom, still in my pyjamas. I won't spare her the dignity of a knock – I'm going to unlock it from the outside, something I don't even think she knows is possible, otherwise I'm sure she would have asked the landlady to change the lock.

'What are you doing?' she squeals, when I burst in on her. She's not even in the shower but is about to start brushing her teeth.

'What the hell happened to you yesterday?'

She squeezes toothpaste onto her brush. 'I don't know what you're talking about.'

'Oh, come on! You told me you'd be home at seven and said you wanted to talk. What was the point if you weren't going to be home? What kind of stupid game are you playing here, Alison?'

She spins around. 'Josie, what are you talking about? I didn't even see you yesterday.'

This girl is bat-shit crazy. 'Why are you lying? You were waiting for me in the uni car park in the afternoon, you said you wanted to talk.'

'Oh, Josie, you must have had too much to drink or something. I wasn't even at uni yesterday. I didn't have any lectures so I spent the day and night with an old school friend.' She dabs her mouth with her towel. 'I really have no idea what you're talking about. Anyway, why would I wait for you in the uni car park when I can just catch up with you here?'

The smirk on her face warns me there's no point protesting. This is one of her weird games and there is nothing I can do. 'You're right,' I say. 'I must be mistaken.' I turn to walk out.

'I hope you enjoyed your evening, Josie.'

I don't even bother to respond.

'I think my flatmate knows about us.'

'Whoa, Josie, hold it right there! What do you mean *us*?' Zach looks around nervously before closing his office door.

'I mean that you were at my flat yesterday.'

'How do you know? Has she said something?'

'She hasn't said anything but I just know. She's been acting strangely. I mean, even stranger than usual. That noise we heard must have been her.'

Zach sits down at his desk and starts chewing his pen while he stares at me. 'Look, I know the two of you don't get on but maybe you should just try to make an effort with her. I could really do without gossip being spread around. That could be dangerous, Josie. You know that, don't you?'

He's right. It's not fair on him that he gets dragged into my fight with Alison, especially when he really hasn't done anything. 'I'll sort it, okay?'

But the frown remains on Zach's face. 'Please do. Look, I see you as a friend now, Josie, I think we share a lot of common ground and that's rare, but you do know—'

'I know, Zach.' I don't need him to spell out to me how we will never be anything more than that.

'Then please can you make your peace with her.'

'I have to go,' I say, and I turn quickly because I don't know whether I'm angry or upset.

Alison is curled up on the sofa reading a book when I get home. She sits up straighter when I come in – on guard, just as I am whenever we come into contact with each other.

'Can we talk?' I say, trying to make my voice soft. I know I can sound quite harsh sometimes – abrasive, even – and I don't want to put her on edge. I need to defuse this situation. Zach is right, he doesn't deserve malicious gossip to be spread about him when he's done nothing but try to help me.

'What is it?' she says, putting down her book and sliding her legs off the sofa.

There's something different about her. I was too caught up to notice it this morning but I'm sure it was there then too. She's more confident now. Not the passive quiet girl she has been since I've known her. And it's because she has something to hang over me, to suffocate me with whenever she wants.

I sit down next to her, forcing myself to see this through even though I can't find any part of her to like. 'Can we please try to sort things out? I don't know about you but I could really do without the arguing and tension between us. We've got enough to worry about with exams and assignments and stuff. If it's my fault then I'm sorry, but surely there's a way we can work things out?' I refrain from adding that this is exactly what she pretended to want as well. I must keep my anger under control.

She scrunches her nose and stares at me. 'And what's brought this on, Josie? You can't stand the sight of me usually so I'm surprised you're here, grovelling for my friendship.'

'Wait a minute, Alison, I said nothing about friendship. I'm just trying to make things… amicable. We don't have to be best buddies, but let's just try to be civil to each other.'

She ignores every word I've said. 'I've got friends, Josie. Plenty of them back home. I don't actually need any more. I'm sorry but friendship just doesn't work that way. You can't force it. We just don't like each other, do we? There's nothing we can do about that.'

I'm too shocked to speak. Shocked she's coming out with this, that she's being so assertive and sure of herself. So what's changed? *It's because she saw Zach here, it must be. She really has got one over on me now.*

'Anyway,' she continues, 'you seem to be doing a good job of making new friends yourself.'

'And what does that mean?' I can no longer keep the anger from my voice, even though this is exactly what she wants.

'I have to go,' she says, brushing past me on her way out.

The bar is noisy and crowded tonight and it's just what I need to drown everyone and everything out. My little brother isn't safe, Zach is practically washing his hands of me, and the girl I have to live with is borderline psychotic. I let out a raucous laugh because the only other option is to cry, and I won't let that happen.

'What's so funny?' Vanessa says. It's just the two of us at the moment but I'm sure others will join us through the evening. That's how it works with Vanessa. She just invites everyone out and whoever turns up, turns up. She doesn't really care who she drinks with, as long as she's out somewhere having fun. I don't even think she'd care if she was here alone.

'Life is what's funny,' I say, but she doesn't get it and stares at me blankly.

'Well, whatever it is, I think we need another drink. My round.' She trots off to the bar and leans right over it to order our drinks. It's obvious she fancies the barman but he clearly isn't interested. Vanessa's an attractive girl but she's way too needy, and a trainee alcoholic on top of that.

Isn't that a bit hypocritical coming from you, Josie? I shut that voice down and finish the remaining vodka in my glass. I won't be like Liv, I can take it or leave it. *Yeah, that's what they all believe.*

'That guy's staring at you,' Vanessa says, placing our drinks on the table.

This is the last thing I need, but I turn to see who she's talking about, just so I can be ready to shoot him down if he tries to approach me. But I know this guy. It's Aaron – the sleaze Alison is still hung up on. Why else would she still be holding what happened against me?

'Oh God, I know him. He's a piece of shit.' I crane to see who he's with, expecting it to be a girl, but there are two guys sitting with him.

'He looks all right to me,' Vanessa says, raising her glass at him and putting on a flirty smile that doesn't quite work.

'Stop it.' I pull her arm down and half her Malibu and Coke sloshes onto both of us and the back of her seat.

'Oops,' she says. 'I'd better get another one!'

'How about finishing what's in that one first? I'll get you another one later. It's still early, isn't it?'

She settles back down and stares at Aaron. 'So what's the deal with him? No good in bed?' She seems to find this hilarious and throws her head back against the chair, soaking her hair in the alcohol we've just spilt.

I can't deal with Vanessa's nonsense right now. It was a terrible idea to come here, and now Sleazy Aaron is staring at me, probably plotting some kind of payback, just as everyone else seems to be. 'Is anyone else meeting us tonight, Vanessa?' I need someone – anyone – to dilute her out.

She shrugs. 'Oh, probably, who knows,' she says, and swigs so much of her drink that half of it pours back out of her mouth.

And in her I see my reflection. This is me when I've had too much and no longer care. It's not attractive, but I keep ending up here anyway. I need to stop. As soon as someone else arrives to keep an eye on Vanessa, I'm out of here.

'Come on, girl, it's your round,' Vanessa says, finishing her drink and slamming it down on the table. 'You're a bit slow today.'

I'm relieved to escape to the bar, but the whole time I'm ordering our drinks I can feel Aaron watching me. I turn around and he's staring at me, scowling. I flash him a smile and turn back to get the drinks. Mine is just Coke this time.

Thankfully, when I get back to Vanessa, three of her friends are now crowded round the table. I've met them before but can only remember that one of the girls might be called Holly. But looking at her now, I'm sure I've got that wrong. I've had far too much to drink but I want to sober up now.

Just to prove you're not like Liv? Who are you kidding?

I hang around for a few minutes, and once they're all engrossed in conversation I make my getaway. None of them notice.

'Leaving already?' Aaron grabs my arm as I pass his table.

I yank my arm away. 'Get the hell off me!'

He holds his hands up. 'All right, calm down. Just being friendly.'

'Sure you are,' I say. 'We all know how good you are at being a *friend*.' I spit the last word at him.

I'm about to keep walking when I have an idea. Although Alison was weird before Aaron came on the scene, there's no doubt her true hatred of me springs from the way he left the flat that night, which she still thinks is my fault. Now is my chance to try to put that right.

Without explaining myself I sit next to Aaron, ignoring the sleazy smiles from his friends. 'So I'll tell you what I'll do, Aaron. I'll give you a chance to put something right, prove you do actually have a shred of decency in you.'

The smile disappears from his face and I take pleasure in how easily I've insulted him. 'And what would that be then? As if I didn't know.'

'Alison needs to know the truth. That evening you were at our flat I was only trying to stand up for her, to protect her. You know it, and I know it. In fact, she's the only person who doesn't. So I need you to tell her the truth. You said you were friends before so why would you treat her so badly?'

Aaron stares at me and grabs his bottle of beer. For a second I think he's going to smash it across my face and I flinch back. But he only takes a sip, and thankfully doesn't notice my reaction.

'Look, I can't be bothered with that shit. I'm done with Alison. She's… Let's just say she's not all there.'

Again, despite everything Alison's done, and her animosity towards me, I can't help but feel protective towards her. 'She's fine. And she trusted you, so don't be a piece of shit, Aaron.'

He doesn't answer for ages, and I can tell he's searching for something clever to say, glancing at his friends for inspiration or support – or anything, really – before finally speaking. 'Okay, whatever. I'll call her some time.'

That's it. He's given in. That was easier than I thought. I spring up, only too happy to get away from him and this place. 'Make it some time soon, Aaron.'

But as I walk to the bus stop I wonder if I've done the right thing after all. Or have I just made things a whole lot worse for myself?

TWENTY-ONE

Mia

After everything Zach did I know it's better to tell the truth wherever possible, no matter how difficult it might be; the only exception is when you need to protect people. This is why, so far, I haven't told Will about Alison. But even though I still can't tell him exactly who she is, or what she's said to me about Zach, that's as far as I want the lie to stretch.

So now, as I sit in the car outside Alison's house while she packs some things, I call Will and tell him what I can.

'I don't understand,' he says. 'This woman is a client of yours? And you're letting her stay in your house? That's just crazy, Mia. I think it's a huge mistake.'

I still can't completely trust Alison, but those bruises didn't look self-inflicted. And by keeping her close I will be able to observe her, try and figure out if she's telling the truth about what happened that night, or if she really is delusional.

'She's not exactly a stranger,' I say to Will. 'She used to know Zach. And she remembered I was a counsellor so she came to me for help. I can't tell you the details but I need to keep her safe from her partner. She's not ready to be on her own, Will, so this is the only option to get her away from him. Surely you can understand that?'

There is silence, followed by a heavy sigh. 'Not really. All I understand is that it's asking for trouble. I don't like this, Mia. It sounds… dangerous. You hardly know her, even if Zach did. And then there's her husband—'

'Partner. They're not married.'

'Well, either way, this is really not a good idea. Surely there's somewhere else she can go? She must have family. Friends. Or if not, can't she stay in a hotel or something?'

I tell him she hasn't mentioned anyone she could stay with and assure him I'm in no danger at all, but I know this won't put his mind at rest. 'I can't just dump her in a hotel, Will. And she's the one in danger, not me. I can't turn my back on her, can I?'

He sighs. 'No, I suppose you can't. That's not who you are. I do understand, I just hope you know what you're doing. Please be careful.'

'I will. Stop worrying. Everything will be fine.'

But he's not convinced. 'I'd feel better if I could meet her. Maybe I could come over after work tonight?'

'I don't know, Will. She might not be up to that. But I'll see. I've got to rush home and pack a few things for Freya before Megan's mum drops her home. Pam and Graham are coming to pick her up this evening so she can stay with them for a few days.'

'Oh,' says Will. 'I didn't realise that was happening.'

'It wasn't arranged until just now,' I say, but I don't elaborate on the reason. He'll worry even more if he hears me say I don't want Freya around Alison. 'It's best for everyone,' I add, when he doesn't respond.

'I really don't like this, Mia. Are you sure you know what you're doing?'

'She needs my help, Will. I've got no choice. If you knew what she'd been through…'

'Just be careful, okay?'

Before we say goodbye I promise to speak to Alison about him coming over this evening.

Just as I put my phone down there's a loud tap on the window. I haven't even noticed Alison appear so it's a shock to see her face staring back at me.

'Is it still okay?' she asks, as I open the door to help her with her bags. On the pavement are two large weekend bags and a small suitcase – far too much for a few nights. Despite the heat, my body shivers, but if feels as though I'm shaking on the inside. What am I doing?

'Of course. Come on, let's get going in case Dominic comes back.'

'It's funny being here like this,' Alison says, when we get to my house. 'I've imagined what the rest of your house might look like but it's not what I expected.'

Her words set me on edge but I try to give her the benefit of the doubt. She's just making small talk to fill the strange void between us. Neither of us spoke much in the car on the way here, but I told her not to mind my silence, that I just needed to focus on driving. But in the quiet I wondered if she'd changed her mind and was already planning how to tell me she wanted to go back to Dominic. To the life she claimed she was desperate to leave behind her.

'Are you okay? I know this is a big step for you.' I've got to do my best to put her at ease, to let her see she is safer here with me, even though I can't let her stay too long. But I can help her find her way forward, without the man who's abusing her.

'It's a bit weird. But thank you, Mia. This must be strange for you, too.'

'I can't lie about that. It's not something I ever thought I'd end up doing.'

'Well, Zach would say you're doing the right thing, wouldn't he? He seemed like a good man.'

The shock of her bringing up his name in this way renders me speechless. But I can't let myself forget that Zach is part of the reason I want her to stay.

'Oh, I'm sorry. I... That was a bit insensitive,' she says. 'I just meant that from the few minutes I spoke to him I really picked up a vibe that he was a decent man. He'd understand you wanting to help someone, wouldn't he?'

I nod, but inside I'm conflicted, wondering whether I've done the right thing, one minute convinced I haven't and the next certain I have no other choice. And then I remember the bruises all over her body and it reaffirms that I've got to see this through. Not only do I need to protect Alison – if she's telling the truth – but I also need to determine what she knows about Zach. If anything.

It's almost 8 p.m. by the time Pam and Graham collect Freya. She was a bit surprised when I told her she was going to spend a few extra days with them, but she soon got carried away with the excitement of being away from home. I'm sure being able to curl up with Socks all night was a big pull.

And now I am alone in my house with Alison.

'Your daughter seems a lovely girl,' she says, as soon as I've seen them all off.

I nod. 'I'm very blessed to have her.'

'She looks like Zach, doesn't she? She's got his light hair and eyes.'

'Yes, she's always looked more like him than me.' Something I found hard in the months following Zach's suicide, his mirror image constantly looking up at me.

Alison follows me into the kitchen. 'I can't imagine having children. I mean, I'd love to one day, but I can't see it for myself yet. I actually don't think I'd be a very good mum.'

'Well, that's understandable. You're still young. It's not unusual that at your age you can't see how a baby or child would fit into your life.'

She chuckles. 'Young. That's all relative, though, isn't it? I remember feeling old at twenty-one.'

Twenty-one. The age Josie Carpenter was when she met Zach. The age Alison was when the two girls lived together. I shudder.

'Well, believe me, Alison, you're not old. And even if you feel it at twenty-six, when you get to thirty, you'll wish you hadn't wasted time feeling that way.'

She stares at me for a moment. 'You are so right. That's the trouble with life, isn't it? It's so hard to get the right perspective on things.'

I turn away and begin searching for something to cook us for dinner. It feels odd talking to this woman – with twelve years and a whole lot more than age between us – as if we are close friends. She is still a stranger to me, even though Zach has bonded us together.

'That's true, but we need to try and stay positive,' I say. 'As much as we can.' I pull out a packet of pasta. 'Will this be okay for dinner? I can make Bolognese?'

'Oh, thanks, Mia, but I'm really not hungry. It's been a hard day.'

I study her thin frame and pale skin. 'You need to eat something, Alison.'

'I don't have a big appetite. The problem is I cook things for Dominic and he complains so much it ends up being wasted, and then I don't feel like eating mine. So I usually make myself a sandwich when he's gone to bed.'

'It's not going to be like that for you any more. Okay? We're going to have some food and then we need to talk about your next steps.'

'I know.' She sighs and looks around the house. 'It just feels so good to be here. Away from him, like I'm in a different world. I just want to take it all in.'

Her choice of words worries me. *Take it all in.* My house? My life? I've got to be careful here. Always on my guard, and one step ahead of her.

Despite saying she wasn't hungry, Alison wolfs down the food I place in front of her and hardly says a word in between mouthfuls. I barely touch mine because I'm still not comfortable with any of this. We are both avoiding mentioning Zach, and what led Alison to me in the first place. I know why I'm reluctant to talk about it, but I'm not sure why she is. It was only the other day she was begging me to help her prove Dominic harmed Josie.

'Do you know Dominic's ex-wife, Elaine?' I ask, my sudden question almost causing Alison to choke.

She stops eating and puts down her fork. 'I've met her a couple of times. Why?'

'I just wondered if you know what kind of person she is? What their marriage was like?'

'She seemed… very assertive. Like she knew exactly what she wanted. But it's hard to tell when you only have a few moments to make a judgement, isn't it? And as for their marriage, Dominic never talks about it. He refuses to. Says the past should be left in the past. What he probably means is that it's none of my business. Why do you ask, Mia? Do you know her?'

'No. But I'm just wondering if he abused her too.' I agree with Alison about Elaine. She didn't strike me as the type to be walked over – in fact, if anything, she appeared to be the kind of woman who would demand control, although outward confidence can mask many things.

Alison picks up her fork again and stares at a piece of pasta speared on the end of it. 'I don't think he did – Elaine was probably too controlling to let him. But he wouldn't tell me, would he? And people change, don't they? Maybe he wasn't always an abusive man. Or maybe… maybe I just brought it out of him.'

'Listen to me, Alison. It's never the fault of the person being abused. Never.'

'I know.' She puts down her fork. 'I just never thought I'd end up in an abusive relationship.'

'No one ever does. But now you know you're in one you can make some changes.'

Alison laughs. 'You just can't stop being a counsellor, can you? But you're right. Everything you say is always so... sensible. I can't fault any of it. Thank you again for everything you're doing for me. But...' She pauses. 'There's one thing I can't understand.'

'What's that?'

'Don't you want to know the truth about why your husband is dead?'

'Yes, but I need evidence. I've been through too much already for it all to come to nothing. I've spent five years believing Zach betrayed me, and worse, that he most likely murdered that girl, so unless there is proof to show me otherwise, I can't rake it all up again. I've just about come to terms with what happened and I don't want to get my hopes up for nothing. I can't do that to myself, or Freya.'

'But that photo on Dominic's computer. You even said yourself there was no way to explain it.'

'I meant I couldn't think of a way. That doesn't mean one doesn't exist. I need more than that, Alison. And I know you said you spoke to Zach and you trusted him from that short conversation, but I can't just go off your instincts. I hope you understand that. Just because Zach might have loved me doesn't mean he couldn't have hurt me. Or Josie Carpenter.'

There is a long silence as she takes in what I've said. I can sense her disappointment. I'm not saying what she wants to hear, and she can't understand why I'm not dropping everything to search for evidence. *Because I know what happened. I know it in my bones, in every inch of my skin. In every part of me. But she will never understand that.*

'Alison, if there's something – anything at all – that can prove Zach didn't do it, then I will be the happiest woman alive. And I will go straight to the police. But I just don't know how you think I can help find this evidence.'

Again, I sense the disappointment emanating from her. 'If you help me, I'm sure we can do it. I *know* Dominic is involved somehow, Mia.'

With her words, things are gradually becoming clearer. This isn't about Zach at all. Alison's so desperate for a way to get Dominic out of her life that she badly wants him to be guilty. So badly that the truth doesn't seem to matter, and it won't stop her.

'I think there's only one thing we can do, Alison. We need to go to the police with that photo at the same time as we report what Dominic's done to you. That's the only help I can offer.'

Minutes pass and I have no idea how she will respond to this. When it comes, her answer is a surprise. 'Okay, you're probably right. I do need to show that photo to the police. But are you ready for that? For everything it will bring up? They may very well reopen the investigation.'

I nod. I've thought of nothing else since she showed it to me. Since she came to that first appointment. 'We've got no choice, Alison. I think both of us need answers. But you've also got to be willing to tell them the truth about being there that night and talking to Zach. Are *you* ready for that?'

This silences her and I know her mind must be flashing through a hundred different scenarios. 'Yes,' she says eventually. 'I'll do whatever I have to do.'

Pleased that she seems to be making good progress, I ask if I can see the photo again. I was too stunned when she first showed it to me to take it all in, but looking at it again is something I need to do, even though I don't expect it to provide me with any answers.

Alison goes to the hall to get her bag. When she comes back she's already scrolling through the phone, but there's a frown on her face.

'What's the matter? Have you heard from Dominic? What's he saying?'

She shakes her head. 'No, it's not that. It's the video – it's gone. It's disappeared, Mia!'

TWENTY-TWO

Josie

Weeks pass and it's obvious Aaron hasn't spoken to Alison, hasn't bothered to do the decent thing and tell her I was defending her. I know this because nothing changes. If anything, her frostiness and bizarre behaviour escalates.

Things go missing from my room, but I ignore these petty incidents. I'm too busy worrying about Kieren, and Richard's threat, to devote any time to solving my issue with Alison. There's nothing personal I care about anyway, except a picture Kieren drew me before I left, to say goodbye. But I make sure that stays with me at all times. She'll never even set eyes on it. Though I'm at work, the café is quiet, so I pull the drawing out of my bag and smile at the two stick figures walking a dog we've never had. The one that's supposed to be me has long hair, before I cut it all off. We're both wearing huge misshapen smiles – something that rarely happened in that house. It's not a bad drawing for a five-year-old, but more important is what it represents: Kieren's dreams. He's always wanted a dog – it was one of his first words – and one day I will make sure I get him one.

I put the picture back in my bag. I'm supposed to keep all my things in the back office but Pierre's not here and I'll be closing up soon so I keep it on the floor by me.

I could easily retaliate and snoop through Alison's things, pay her back for invading my privacy, but I won't stoop to her level of craziness. And every day I pity her more than I hate her.

As for Zach, we are practically strangers now. His game of helping me one minute, claiming to be a friend, and then cutting me off the next was doing my head in. I've had enough; I'm done with him.

'Excuse me? A hot chocolate with extra cream, please.'

I've been so lost in my thoughts I haven't noticed anyone come into the coffee shop.

'Sorry. Anything else?' I smile at the customer, even though I'm exhausted and ready to go home. He looks familiar, maybe around my age, and he's dressed casually in jeans, trainers and a hooded top. Not the usual suited-up man we get in here at this time. I'm sure I know him but I can't place him.

'You're Josie, aren't you?'

Hearing my name puts me on alert and I edge away from him. My phone is in my bag by my feet, but by the time I've fumbled around for it anything could have happened.

'I'm Craig. I'm in your creative writing class.' He hands me a ten-pound note.

I relax a bit. 'Oh yeah.' But I don't recall him from any of the lectures. There are far too many students and I've had too much else going on to pay much attention to anyone.

'Don't worry, I don't really know too many people either so I'm not offended if you don't recognise me. Anyway, how are you finding it?' he asks, as I hand him his change and start making his drink.

I could tell him how much I enjoy it, that Zach has opened my eyes, made me see the world in a different way, but of course I won't tell him any of that clichéd shit. 'It's all right.'

Craig nods. 'To be honest, I'm struggling a bit with the assignments. I'm just not really that creative. I thought I was, before I started uni, but hey, I guess not. Actually, it's really stressing me out. I need to pass this year.'

I'm not sure why he's telling me all this when this is the first time we've spoken, but I find it refreshing. I'm so used to guys putting on an act, trying to make out they're so much more than they are, so it's nice to hear someone actually being human and admitting they're not perfect.

'Well, you should talk to Zach Hamilton,' I tell him. 'He's cool.'

'Yeah, I know. But he's already given me loads of extra help so I don't really want to hassle him again. The man's got a life outside uni!'

Hearing this shouldn't bother me but it does. I know Zach gives everything he's got to his students, and it shouldn't surprise me that I'm not the only person he's helped, but somehow I feel less... something. Special? God, I'm pathetic.

'Well, if it makes you feel better I don't exactly find this uni thing easy either. Most of it goes way above my head, to be honest. But d'you know what? I'm not going to let it beat me. I will finish this, and pass, if it kills me. There's always a way to achieve what you want.' I pause. 'Sorry if that's not very helpful.'

Craig smiles. 'No, it is. And you're right. Thanks. Maybe I just needed a kick up the arse. I need to stop thinking I can't do it and focus on... just doing it.'

'Here you go,' I say, handing him the hot chocolate. It makes me feel good to know I might have helped him find some motivation. 'Hope you can find somewhere to sit.'

He turns round, scans the empty room and laughs. 'Is it always this quiet? I've never been in here before.'

I lower my voice, even though there's nobody else in here. 'I call it the dead time. Most people are rushing home from work, and the students have long gone, so it's pointless us being open. But don't tell my manager that.'

He winks at me then thanks me for the drink, and I watch him head to a table in the corner. He seems okay. Perhaps I should make more effort to get to know the people on my course, instead of throwing all my focus onto Zach. But then I think of Alison and decide I'm better off keeping myself to myself.

By closing time Craig is still here, even though for the last ten minutes I've been hinting that we're closing soon. But I feel a bit sorry for him, sitting by himself with his lecture notes spread out in front of him and his pen poised over a piece of paper that's been blank for as long as he's been sitting there.

So I give him more time and start cleaning the tables.

'Can I help you with anything?' he asks, looking desperate for anything to do other than his assignment.

'No, Pierre will kill me. I'm the one he's paying so I should do it myself. He's probably watching the CCTV from home right now.' I'm not sure why I say this when we have no CCTV inside the shop, but it's dark outside and Craig's the only one in here, so perhaps it's my instincts protecting me after everything I've been through.

Craig nods. 'Makes sense. So, can I ask you a personal question?'

My heart sinks. Here it is. This guy is probably just as much a sleaze as Aaron, and all the others I've ever met, and has been waiting to ask me to go for a drink with him or something. His struggling student speech was just an act.

'What?' I say, letting my annoyance seep into my voice.

'Um… when I was talking to Zach, he, um, kind of said you'd be a great person to chat to about short stories. He said you'd got one of the highest marks he'd ever given. I just kind of need inspiration, I suppose. Like I said, I just don't think I'm creative.'

'Zach told you that?' I try not to smile, but there are annoying flutters in my stomach.

'Yeah. He's given up so much time for me and I think he's got a lot of stuff going on at home, but I could tell he was really impressed with you and thought you could help me.'

I'm so thrilled by Zach's compliment that I don't register much else of what Craig is saying. 'I really don't know how I could help.'

'Maybe just a chat or something some time, if you're ever free? I'll give you my number.' He rips a piece of paper from his pad and scribbles on it. 'I'd better go, got work in an hour. Late shift at the bookies.'

I watch him leave and realise I'm still smiling. Mostly because of what Zach said, but also because I actually think Craig might be quite a decent guy.

When I get home the flat is freezing, as usual. I've grown used to Alison's pathetic trick of turning all the radiators off except for her own, and usually I ignore it, but this evening I've reached the end of my rope.

I storm towards her door, but stop when I hear my name.

'I just can't stand her, she makes my skin crawl. I'm counting the days until the summer holiday.'

There is a pause and no one else speaks, so I realise she must be on the phone. I lean against the wall by her door and continue to listen.

'She's some kind of psycho or something. Always making things up. I can't trust her... But I know stuff about her and she has no idea. Stuff you wouldn't believe... No, not yet, but I will.'

She is walking around now. I can hear her feet shuffling on the carpet. 'I don't even know how she managed to get on a degree course. A fly's got more intelligence than she has, she's complete trash.'

It's time to walk away. I don't need to hear what she's saying; none of it is true and her comments say more about her than they do about me, but I can't help feeling as though I've been stung.

I think of the bottle of gin in the living room. It's calling my name but I won't listen; I won't be that person Alison and the rest of them want me to be. So I go straight to my room, with no idea how I'll spend the rest of the night.

Studying is the only thing I have left now, but I'm up to date with all my assignments. Desperate for something to quash the loneliness, I begin copying up lecture notes I've hastily scrawled at university. There's no need for me to do this, they're perfectly legible, but it will kill a couple of hours until I can sleep.

Vanessa texts and invites me to a party at her place but I delete her message without replying. And then I delete her phone number. Just in case I'm ever tempted.

I crawl into bed not long after this, with every inch of my body fighting tiredness and isolation. How can the absence of one person have left such a gap in my life when I've only known him such a short time?

But I can't let this weaken me, I've got to pick myself up.

Without thinking, I pick up my phone and begin texting.

Let's meet up some time.

Craig replies within seconds.

TWENTY-THREE

Mia

I couldn't sleep last night. Of course I couldn't. The video of Josie Carpenter's photo disappearing from Alison's phone was far too convenient, and she was insistent that it must have been Dominic who got rid of it.

'Does he know your passcode?' I had asked, expecting her to say yes. It made sense that someone so controlling would have access to his partner's phone, but Alison's answer had surprised me.

'Not that I know of – I've never given it to him. If I had then there's no way I would have kept that photo on there. No way. I would have transferred it somewhere safe. But I suppose he could have seen me typing it in and memorised it.'

'And when was the last time you looked at the video, or noticed it on there?' I had tried to catch her out, to find out if she could be trusted, but nothing she said has helped me decide either way.

'When I showed it to you,' was her reply. 'But that was only a couple of days ago. How could it have disappeared in that time?'

I'd told her to check properly and she spent some time doing this, but by the end of it there was still no video of the photo of Josie on the computer, and Alison was still insisting she had no clue how it could have happened.

'I know how this looks,' she'd said. 'But you saw it, didn't you? You know it was on my phone.'

'Yes, *I* saw it, Alison, but now we've got nothing to take to the police. We can't go in there and start accusing Dominic of anything without even that flimsy evidence, can we?'

She's done this on purpose, I'm sure of it. But why wouldn't she want to go to the police? Why show me the photo if she wasn't going to use it to get Dominic arrested? *To lure me in. To make me believe her. She wants to be in this house with me, it's been her plan all along.*

This terrifies me, but there's too much at stake here so I can't give in to my fear. Alison's here for a reason, and I need to know what that is.

It's only 5.30 a.m. but I get up to have a shower; I need to mentally prepare myself for the coming days and I want to be ready before Alison wakes up. But once I'm dressed and go downstairs, she's already there, sitting on the sofa. She's so busy looking at something on her phone that she doesn't hear me until I speak.

'Morning, Alison.'

She starts and almost drops her phone. 'Hi! I didn't hear you. Sorry, I was just… Dominic's been texting me since last night. Checking up on me. He's due back this afternoon… What's going to happen when he notices I've left?'

I cross to the sofa and sit beside her. 'You've got to stop worrying, Alison. Everything will be okay. We'll have breakfast and then go to the police together, okay? He won't be able to hurt you then.'

She visibly stiffens, and I find myself wondering if I've got this all wrong. But surely she wouldn't be able to fake her fear, her injuries? Unless there's another reason why she's scared and it involves talking to the police.

'I've already had a coffee and I don't think I can stomach any food right now,' Alison says. 'I hope you don't mind me helping myself, but it was so early I didn't want to wake you. '

I can't force her to eat; she's a grown woman who, despite how she comes across, is surprisingly wilful. 'Well, it's still quite early.

We can get something afterwards. I'm sure you'll feel a bit better then… Once you've made your statement.'

She nods and the screen of her phone lights up.

'Is that Dominic?'

'Yeah,' she says, as she scans the message. 'He says he'll be back at two o'clock and he'd better have heard from me by then.'

Hearing this makes my skin crawl. Even if there's a chance Dominic isn't one of them, there are men out there who treat women this way. Women they claim to love. 'You'll get through this,' I tell her.

'Thanks, Mia. I really don't know what I'd do without you. I'm sorry about the way we met, but I'm glad we have.'

But I don't feel the same way. She's opened up wounds I thought had finally healed and thrown my life into silent, suffocating turmoil. Instead, I say, 'I'll just get my jacket and then we can go.'

It's less than two minutes before I'm ready but in that time something has changed. Alison is pacing the living room, her arms folded against her chest. I can see she's having second thoughts.

'Mia… I've been thinking,' she says, still pacing the room. 'And I think I should go to the police station on my own.'

Although I half-expected this, I'm disappointed. Everything she's doing or saying has me questioning her honesty. But she's still a client – in some twisted way – so I will treat her as one.

'Are you sure? I'd really like to come with you. For support. You might find you need it once you're there and faced with sharing such personal things. Don't you think it would help you for me to be there with you?'

She shakes her head. 'I know it probably would help – I've thought about how difficult it's going to be – but I think it's better this way. I just… I'll be fine.'

There's nothing I can do but go along with her choice, but she's wrong if she thinks I can be fooled. There is too much at stake here. 'Okay, if you're sure. But call me if you change your mind.'

She looks relieved. Perhaps she expected more insistence from me. 'Thank you, Mia. Again. Will you be here when I get back?'

'Of course. I'll wait in for you. I know you don't have a key so don't worry.' And there's no way she will get one either. Letting her into my home when I'm here is about all I'm willing to risk.

At the front door she gives me a hug and my body tenses. She must notice it as she quickly steps back.

I close the door behind her then rush to the window. The police station is only a five-minute walk from here and she's heading in the right direction, through the park. But that's not enough to convince me she's actually going.

I'm still wearing my jacket and I check I've got my keys then rush outside. I can see her ahead of me, but I keep a far enough distance from her, just in case she turns around. It's possible she'd still notice me, but I have an excuse ready: I will tell her I need to give her Will's number just in case she can't get hold of me for any reason.

But by the time we are almost at the police station, she hasn't turned around once. She hasn't even stopped to pull her phone out of her bag or to look in any of the shops we pass.

And when she turns into the police station, I admit, once again, that I really don't know what to make of her. Truthful or deceitful? My mind flits between both of these and can't seem to settle on either.

Outside the building, Alison stops and lets a man walk in before her, but then she pushes straight through the doors and disappears inside.

I don't have a plan for how long I'll stay there, watching just to make sure she doesn't come out again within minutes, but after half an hour she still hasn't emerged.

I call Freya and her excited chatter distracts me from my surveillance, even though I keep my eyes on the doors. 'Can Megan come and stay here with me, Mum?'

'I don't think so, sweetheart. I think Grandma and Grandad just want to enjoy some time with you.'

'Oh. Okay.'

'But we can arrange for Megan to come and stay the night with us when you get back. How does that sound?'

She yelps down the phone and my heart swells. Everything I've had to go through, and will go through from now on, is worth it to hear and see my daughter happy.

When I've finished talking to Freya, I dial Will's number and deal with his disappointment that I didn't ask him to come for dinner last night. 'I'm so sorry but I just don't think she was up to it. This is a big deal for her – she's never had the strength to walk away from him before. I just think last night would have been too soon.'

'I do get that, Mia. I just hope you're not getting into something risky. But anyway, you already know how I feel about it and, well, I don't want to put pressure on you.'

I stare across at the police station, at the doors that seem to swallow people up. 'If it makes you feel better, we're at the police station right now. Alison's in there making a statement.'

'That's good. That's great. She's doing the right thing.' I can hear the tension leave Will's voice. 'So, I know she wasn't up to it yesterday, but how about I come over for dinner tonight? We can get a takeaway to save you cooking for a change.' Although his tone is casual I know how much he wants me to say yes. Will can't help being a protector, but he needs to know I don't need protecting.

I give in, even though I'm not sure what Alison's reaction will be. 'Okay, yes. That sounds like a good idea. I want you to meet her.' Even though Will doesn't know the full story, it will be good to get his opinion on Alison. My judgement is so clouded by Zach's death that I can't fully trust it, when normally I rely on instinct.

Will tells me he'll see me at seven then adds that he loves me before saying goodbye.

It's been almost an hour now since Alison went inside, so I decide to make my way home. For now, at least, it appears that she's telling the truth, but I know better than to put my complete trust in her.

I make the introductions but I can already sense that neither Will nor Alison feel comfortable in the other's presence. They are both polite enough, but Will is on edge, dropping Alison's hand almost before he's finished shaking it. I'm not used to seeing him like this.

I can understand his discomfort: he doesn't think Alison should be here, doesn't think I'm safe now I've let a stranger into my home. But Alison has no reason to be wary of Will.

'So, Alison, what do you do, then?' he asks, seconds after we've all sat down. The tone of his question makes me cringe, the accusation easy to detect – this really isn't like Will.

In spite of this, Alison doesn't appear to notice, or mind. 'Mostly admin work. But, well, I'm taking a break at the moment. To sort some things out.' She glances at me before turning back to Will.

Before he got here this evening, there were some things I had to get straight with Alison. I told her Will doesn't know everything she's told me, only that she used to know Zach and that she's staying here to get away from her partner.

'Why didn't you tell him?' she had asked, the stare she fixed on me accusing and judgemental. 'He's your partner, isn't he? Doesn't that mean you shouldn't keep secrets from him?'

'No, it means I need to do whatever I can to keep him from getting hurt. Will knows what he needs to know.'

'Okay, I'm sorry,' she'd said. 'I didn't mean to sound... I just wondered why.'

I had no choice but to be direct with her, despite how she might perceive it. 'Alison, that really isn't your business. All I'm trying to do is help you, and that doesn't mean you can question other parts of my life.'

'But you also want to know what happened with Zach, don't you? That's partly why I'm here, isn't it?'

'No. I know all I need to know. And there's no photo any more, Alison, so we both have to let this go.'

'Well, I'm not giving up on the truth,' she'd said. 'It always comes out in the end. I want Dominic to pay for what he's done. Not just to me but to Josie too.'

In the end, although she hadn't exactly agreed to keep things to herself, I have a feeling she won't say anything to Will. She needs my help so why would she do anything to jeopardise that? But one thing I'm learning is that Alison is unpredictable. She barely said a word when she came home from the police station, and gave me no details other than to say that they took her statement and were planning to question Dominic that night. I put her reticence down to being a bit shaken up by the experience, but now, watching her with Will, I see she has made a quick recovery.

Things don't get any better over dinner. Will bombards Alison with a stream of questions, and even my gentle kick under the table does nothing to stem the tide.

As soon as he gets up to go to the bathroom Alison turns to me, her voice a whisper. 'He doesn't like me, does he? Why? What have I done?'

I consider my answer carefully. 'It's not that Will doesn't like you, he's just a bit worried about this whole situation, that's all.'

'And by "this situation" you mean me staying here with you?'

'It just took him by surprise. He's used to me helping people whenever I can, but this is something quite different. It's not what you'd consider a normal scenario.'

Her eyes drop to the table. 'None of this is normal, is it? I mean, the whole thing with Dominic. How many people suspect their partners of this kind of thing?'

Alison seems to have forgotten to whom she's speaking. This is *exactly* what I've had to deal with, although Zach was already dead by the time he was labelled a murderer.

'Look, Mia, maybe Will would understand more if you told him everything?' she says. 'Maybe he could even help us.'

Everything I say to this woman seems to fall on deaf ears. I've already told her I'm trying to protect Will by keeping him out of this, so I don't know why she's pushing me to tell him.

'Alison, I can tell you right now what Will's words will be if I tell him everything. He'll say that you were in the flat that night and that you didn't tell the police. He'll force me to tell them and I know that's not what you want. He'll say I should be worried about this.' And the truth is, this *is* something I need to think about: Alison *was* there. She could very well have had something to do with it.

She stares at me, her eyes wide. 'But I had nothing to do with it. I wouldn't have come to you otherwise, would I? Surely he'd see that?'

I hear Will washing his hands in the downstairs toilet. 'We'll talk about this later, okay? Right now let's just focus on you. You've been to the police today so that's great. Next, we need to try and find you a new place to live.'

Alison stares at her plate, the timid girl again. All evidence of the defiant person she was just moments ago has gone. 'I haven't thought that far ahead, but I guess that's what I'll have to do. He'll never let me stay in the house, even though we both pay the mortgage. He put more money into it to begin with so I don't stand a chance.'

'I know it's scary but you can do this. I'll help you as much as I can. A fresh start will be good for you, Alison.' But as I say this I wonder if this is all it will take. She seems to have issues that go far beyond Dominic's abuse – I just need to get to them. And when I do, I will know exactly what happened that night at that flat.

When Will comes back in, Alison clams up. 'I might have an early night, if you don't mind, Mia. It's been a long day in so many ways.' She glances at Will. 'I'm sure you'd both like some time together, too, so I'll get out of your way.'

'You don't have to do that,' Will says, but his tone is still harsh.

Alison's eyes widen. 'Oh, no, that's fine. Thank you for the lovely food, Mia.' But she has barely touched hers.

Later in bed, I confront Will about his animosity towards Alison. I keep my voice low and speak right into his ear; she's only in the room next door and I can't risk her overhearing us.

'I don't like her,' Will says. 'There's something about her that isn't quite right – I noticed it straight away.'

'I know what you mean, but how should we expect her to be after what she's been through? She probably distrusts men now so it's not surprising she was a bit off with you.' Except she trusts Zach implicitly, even though she has no real evidence to suggest he wasn't guilty of anything.

Will turns to face me. 'No, it's more than that. But I do respect that you're helping her. In fact, I admire you for it. You're a better person than I am, Mia, because I certainly wouldn't let her stay in my house.'

'I'm not a better person than you. Perhaps I've just been tested more.' And if I was such a good person then wouldn't I immediately believe in Zach's innocence? I've wanted to over the years, but something within me wouldn't allow it.

'Just tell me it's only for a few days,' Will says.

'It will be. But however strange she can be, she needs a break in life.'

He doesn't say anything, and I try to distract him by pulling him towards me, my hands wandering across his body, even though it is hard to switch off from everything. But a few minutes later, when

Will is lost in the moment, and I'm trying to shut out destructive thoughts, I hear a noise at the bedroom door. I strain to see into the darkness, but I can just make out the shape of someone standing there before they disappear.

Alison.

How long has she been watching us?

TWENTY-FOUR

Josie

Spring is finally here and with it comes fresh hope for my future. I've heard nothing more from Liv or Richard, and have begun to think they might actually leave me alone now. Sinead still texts me regular updates on Kieren – the last one said he seems happy every time she sees him leaving the house with Liv, so my mind is put at rest, at least for now.

'What are you thinking about?' Craig says, rolling over so he's facing me. It's one of those rare April days when it's warm enough for short sleeves, so we're spending lunchtime in the park, lying on a blanket and staring up at the cloud-free sky.

'Nothing. Just living in the moment.' I haven't told him anything about my messed-up family. Not yet. This is the first time I've been able to just be *me*, without the stigma of what I've left behind.

Craig smiles. 'So, I was thinking… My parents are coming over this weekend. I know it's early days but maybe you could meet them? I know we're kind of just friends at the moment, but what do you reckon?'

Technically, Craig and I are a bit more than 'just friends', even though we haven't slept together. We spend most of our time with each other and I know he wants to be able to call me his girlfriend, but he respects my boundaries too much to push it. I've explained to him that I just don't want us to label anything, because as far as I can tell, that's when things go to shit.

'Yeah, why not?' I say. 'They'll probably hate me, but what the hell?'

'Are you kidding? They'll love you.'

'Just don't get your hopes up. And I'm not taking out my nose stud. I'm not going to try and pretend I'm someone or something else.'

Craig laughs. 'I wouldn't want you to – I want them to see who you really are. Look, they're really not judgemental at all, Josie. They're cool and I know you'll like them.'

He doesn't know my track record with parents, even my own. 'Well, I'll try to be on my best behaviour, just for you.'

I sit up so I can eat my sandwich and there, right in front of me, sitting on the bench opposite us, is Zach Hamilton. He's staring at us but looks away when he notices I've seen him. I don't know how long he's been there, but I'm sure that bench was empty when we sat down.

Despite everything, my stomach flips over. It's one thing seeing Zach in lectures, where I can prepare myself, but to suddenly catch sight of him like this messes me up. I thought he'd stopped coming to the park, just to avoid me, but clearly he must be over whatever he was wrestling with.

Beside me, Craig hasn't noticed Zach and continues eating his lunch. I'm glad he's not inside my head; knowing my thoughts would really hurt him. I try my best to ignore Zach being a few metres away from us, but when Craig's phone rings and he's distracted with the call, I can't help but watch Zach. He's jotting down notes and I wonder how close he is to finishing his book.

I don't even notice Craig is off his phone until he grabs the sandwich from my hand and shoves it into his mouth.

'Hey, I wanted that!' I push him gently and he fakes a backwards fall and lands on his elbows.

'That's abuse, that is!'

'Yeah? So is stealing someone's sandwich!'

We're both laughing, but I can feel Zach's eyes on us and when I steal a quick glance in his direction I see that I'm right.

'Shall we head back?' Craig says. 'I've got a tutorial in a few minutes.'

As we leave the park we walk straight past Zach's bench but I don't even acknowledge him. Craig does, of course, and nods to him before taking hold of my hand. And secretly I'm pleased that he has done this.

'I hope you don't think your boyfriend can stay over.'

I've only just stepped through the door when Alison launches her attack. It's as if she's been standing right here waiting for me to get home, even though she would have had no idea what time that would be. She's got worse over the last few weeks and takes every opportunity to demonstrate her hatred of me. Despite what I heard her saying about me on the phone, I've tried to make an effort, even stocking the kitchen cupboards with enough food for both of us when I can afford it, but nothing works with her.

'First, I assume you're talking about Craig, but you've got it wrong.' There's no way she means Zach, the two of us have barely spoken lately, which at least means she probably won't report him for anything now. 'He's not my boyfriend,' I continue, 'and second, if I want him to stay in my room then he can. Any time he likes.'

I expect her to shrink into herself now that I've put her in her place, but I'm forgetting that this is the new Alison, the one who actually stands up to people. But she's wrong if she thinks anything she says can get to me.

'I think you'll find we're not allowed to have people staying the night, Josie. Check your tenancy agreement. That's grounds for being chucked out.'

She's so smug as she says this that for the briefest second I want to slap the smile from her bony face. But then I remind myself to turn my anger to pity, because as difficult as my life has been, I would never trade places with Alison.

'I don't have time for this, Alison, and neither do you, I'm sure.'

'Oh, sorry, am I keeping you from valuable drinking time? I can imagine how hard it must be to have your problem.'

I won't rise to her bait. 'Actually, I haven't touched any alcohol for weeks now. Sorry to disappoint you.'

As I walk away I expect a reply, but there is only silence. And it only occurs to me much later to wonder how she knows anything about Craig when I've never mentioned him and he's never been to the flat when she's been at home.

I should have known better than to think things could go smoothly, that the peace I was feeling could last, and now, as I lock up the coffee shop and turn around to find Zach standing behind me, I know for sure there is trouble ahead.

'Can we talk?' he says. He looks stressed; there are dark circles around his eyes and it looks like he hasn't shaved for days. He's always been clean-cut, well groomed, so to see him like this is a shock.

'I thought we had nothing more to say to each other outside of uni?' I don't want to give him a hard time but I've had it up to here with his mind games. I know he's not doing anything on purpose, but he must realise what he's been doing to me.

'This is important, Josie. Shall we go for a drive? I'm in the car park over there.' He points across the road.

'No, I don't think so.' I put the keys in my bag. 'I've got to be somewhere.' This is a lie: Craig is working tonight and my only plans are to go home and crash out.

'How about a walk then?'

He sounds so desperate I can't help but give in. 'Okay. Five minutes.'

We cross the road and head away from the coffee shop. It's still light even though it's past 7 p.m. 'So are you and Craig together now?' Zach asks, trying to sound casual.

I focus on the pavement and try not to look at him. 'No. Yeah. Kind of, I suppose. Why?'

He shrugs. 'I've just seen you around together a lot. Is he treating you well?'

'What kind of question is that? He's a nice guy. What's this about, Zach? What are you doing here?' And now I do look at him, hoping to find clues in his face because his words are giving nothing away.

He shakes his head. 'I don't know, Josie, I just… I miss our chats, I guess. How have you been? I've been worried about you.'

We pass a bar I know well and I try to ignore the sudden urge to rush in and have a drink. 'Well, there's no need. I haven't heard from Liv or Richard and as far as I know, Kieren's okay. So I guess life's going well right now.' But I'm sure it will catch up with me soon. I've been avoiding thinking about Richard but he's not going to let his cousin rot in jail if he can do anything about it. But, again, I bury that thought.

Zach nods. 'Good, good. I'm glad to hear that. Maybe they came to their senses and realised how much trouble they could get into by threatening you.'

I stop walking and turn to face him. 'Zach, what's going on? You're acting really weird.' And then I laugh because I'm talking to my lecturer as if he's another student, or as if we are boyfriend and girlfriend.

Zach seems shocked. 'What's funny?' He must be confused, because there's really nothing funny going on here at all. It's all very sad.

'Nothing's funny, Zach. Just tell me why you wanted to talk to me.'

'I told you, I've been worried about you.' He looks around. 'Can we keep walking?'

'Yeah, when you start talking.'

But he doesn't, and after a few moments I head off anyway, knowing that soon enough he'll be by my side again. And here he is.

'How's your wife, Zach? And the little one?'

He smiles. 'Mia's great. And Freya, well, she's certainly got a lot of spirit.'

That's it. Nothing is ever going to change here. 'Well, it's great that we've had this chat, but I really need to go now. So, see you at uni.' I start to walk off, but he grabs my arm.

'I'm jealous, okay? I'm fucking jealous, Josie, and it's messing me up. Screwing with my head. I love my family, I really love my life, so why the fuck am I jealous of you being with Craig?'

His words stun me into silence, and he, too, seems shocked that he's said them. But they are out there now and can't be taken back. He can never unsay what he's just admitted to me.

'Oh, Josie, shit! I'm so sorry, I had no right to say that to you.' He clutches his head. 'Please, forget I said it.'

But I can't; I never will. Because he's just confirmed, finally, unequivocally, that what I've been feeling hasn't been futile. It hasn't just been some childish infatuation, this has been real. I am not some silly girl with a crush on her lecturer, I have felt this way about Zach because he has too.

A young couple holding hands walks past, so he lowers his voice. 'I know this is crazy, but I do really love my wife, and I'd never do anything to hurt her. But inside, I have all these... these feelings – and I just have to try and crush them. They're dangerous, Josie. For everyone. But I can do it, I can carry on and not act on anything because it's the right thing to do. Oh God, I'm so sorry.'

'Will you stop apologising? You practically told me all of this already, that night at my flat.'

He shakes his head. 'But I never said it out loud. Saying it brings it to life, makes it into something harmful, and I was trying not to do that. In all honesty, I didn't plan to tell you just now. I suppose I just wanted to know you're okay, and that Craig's being good to you.'

'I don't need protecting, Zach. I've done a pretty good job of looking after myself all these years.'

'Yeah, Little Miss Tough Nut, you certainly have.' He pats my arm to show me he's saying this affectionately. 'And I know you'll be okay, but that doesn't stop me worrying. Or caring.'

'Zach, you'd better go. Go home to your wife and your little girl. I think we've said all we need to say here. But I promise you, I'm doing okay. And Craig, he's a good guy.'

Seconds pass before Zach speaks again and in that time he studies my face, as if he's taking one last look at me, as if he'll never see me again. 'I'm glad to hear that, Josie. I just want you to be happy.'

'Goodbye, Zach.'

I watch him walk away, and feel as though my insides are being torn apart, shredded into a thousand tiny pieces.

TWENTY-FIVE

Mia

I don't tell Will that Alison was standing outside our bedroom door last night – it will only add to his bad feeling about her. And I can't just accuse her, in case I'm somehow mistaken; I don't know what she's up to, but I can't trust her and I can't let her leave before I find out why she's really here. Instead, I will deal with it my way.

She was in Josie's flat the night she disappeared, so there's every chance she knows something about what happened to her. And why is she so convinced it wasn't Zach, when the only evidence she has is a photo that's now disappeared? The only thing I'm sure of is that Alison is hiding something, but I have no idea how I'll find out what that is. I will just have to keep waiting and watching her. Sooner or later, if she knows something, she will slip up.

Once again Alison is awake and in the living room when I go downstairs, even though it's not yet 6 a.m. She's studying her phone, just as she was the last time I came down and found her here.

'I couldn't sleep,' she says, before I've even greeted her. 'Sorry you have to keep putting up with me being here when you come down in the morning. I just get a bit claustrophobic and can't stay in my room too long. It's nothing to do with your house, please don't think that, it's just me.'

But I barely hear her words; my mind is too busy picturing her shadow outside my bedroom door, how she must have heard

Will's heavy breathing, the words he spoke to me. This is not the first time she's made me shudder.

If Alison knows I saw her watching us then she certainly doesn't act like it.

'I heard you walking around last night. You couldn't have got much sleep at all,' I observe.

She doesn't flinch. 'Yeah, sorry if I kept you up, I was a bit restless. It's all this change, it's thrown me off course a bit.' She glances into the hall. 'Has Will gone home?'

'No, he's still asleep.' I keep my voice low. 'Weekends are his only chance to have a lie-in. Anyway, before he wakes up, can we have a quick chat?'

She smiles, but it's too forced, and when she speaks her voice is too loud. 'Of course. Is something wrong?'

How can she ask this, when we both know that everything's wrong? 'No, I just wanted to let you know I've been looking online and have found some flats you could rent. They're not in Ealing or Finchley, as I thought you probably didn't want to be that close to Dominic, and it might be good to distance yourself from the past.'

She looks at me, her face blank. 'Um, yeah, that's probably best. I hadn't really thought about what area I should live in. Ealing was home to me for a long time before we moved to East Finchley, and I don't really know the rest of London that well.' She stares at her nails. 'But you're right. It's probably a good idea not to stay around here.'

'Anyway, there are a couple of flats in Fulham and I looked at Hammersmith and Putney too. If you like any, I'll come with you to view them. We could make some calls today. I think you'll find at least one you like, Alison.'

She shrugs. 'There's no point putting it off, I suppose. Okay, can you email me the links? I know you'll have found me some decent places to look at.'

I get straight on my phone and send her all the property information I've gathered, waiting to hear her phone ping with an email alert. But after a few seconds there's nothing but silence. I stare at the phone in her hand.

'Oh, I must have it on silent,' she says. 'I keep doing that by accident.' She taps her phone a few times. 'There, got it. Thanks. I'll have a look in a bit.'

'Have you heard from Dominic again?' I ask, wondering exactly what she was doing on her phone.

'No, not since yesterday morning. It's a bit weird actually – his silence makes me feel even more on edge.'

'Maybe he's actually listening to the police and leaving you alone?'

'Hmmm, maybe. But that's not his style. He doesn't like being told what to do... By anyone.'

'But I'm sure he doesn't want to end up in prison, Alison.'

'No. No, he wouldn't, would he? Even if it's where he belongs.'

I ignore what she's just said because it will only lead to another conversation about me helping her find proof of Dominic's guilt. 'Well, you should think about changing your mobile number. That reminds me, there's another thing I wanted to talk to you about. There's a support group that meets every Wednesday and I think it might really help you if you went along. You don't have to book in or anything – just turn up. I'll even come with you if you like. They're really nice people who run it, Alison, and everyone who goes is in the same situation as you. They know what you're going through, and they can help you, probably more than I can.'

There are tears in her eyes as she answers. 'I doubt anyone can help me more than you, but thank you, Mia. You're being so good to me, I really don't know how I'll ever be able to thank you enough.'

Her words seem so heartfelt that I want desperately to believe her. But I won't allow myself to be misled. 'The only thanks I want is for you to keep up the strength to stay away from Dominic. And to get your life back on track. I don't need anything more than that.'

'I won't let you down,' Alison says. She studies my face for a moment and I can tell she's thinking carefully about what she'll say next. 'You're such a selfless person, Mia. It's not easy to always put other people first. It almost makes me ashamed of myself.'

I am struck by her choice of word. 'Ashamed? Why?'

She hesitates for a moment. 'Because of the way I treated Josie.' Her eyes flick to the ceiling. 'Don't get me wrong, I was hardly a bully – and believe me, Josie wasn't the type to take any shit from anyone – but I just wasn't nice to her. Ever. And, I don't know, maybe things would have turned out differently if I'd just been a bit kinder.'

Although I'm surprised she's opening up like this, it's a good sign. She's being more talkative now and that's bound to reveal something she might not want to, sooner or later. 'I don't think it would have made any difference,' I say. 'Josie still would have met Zach and…'

'Like I said before, I really believed what he said to me. I'm not sure anything ever happened between them.'

I think carefully about whether to probe further but decide I've got nothing to lose. 'Did you ever see them together?'

'Mia, are you sure you want to talk about this? I thought you wanted to leave the past where it is.'

'I do, but there are just so many gaps in the information I have, it's helpful to have them filled in. It helps to lay things to rest.'

Alison seems to consider this carefully before answering. 'Okay. If you're sure. He was at the flat another time. I mean, there could have been more times, but I only saw him there once, in addition to the night that, you know… Anyway, neither of them knew I was there.'

The familiar bubble of nausea grows inside me. 'What were they doing?'

'Oh, nothing unusual. Just talking. But I have to admit that at the time I thought it was a bit dodgy. There weren't many lecturers who made house calls, but then again quite a few were on friendly terms with the students. It's a bit different when you're all adults, isn't it? And Zach wasn't exactly old.'

'Thirty-five,' I say. But it was still inappropriate. Josie was Zach's student and he had a duty to keep his distance from her. *Why, Zach? Why did you risk everything for this girl?* I've spent so many sleepless nights wrestling with this question but I've never been able to come close to an answer. As far as I can see he had everything he could need and more. But it's never that simple, is it? Yes, she was attractive, but Zach was above superficiality. So what was it about her he found so fascinating? This is what I need to find out from Alison, and I have limited time to do it.

'What was she like?' I ask. 'I know you didn't like her, but what kind of person was she?'

Again Alison gives me that look: the one that says she doesn't know how much to tell me. 'She was… strong, I guess. Nothing got to her; it was as if everything that happened just bounced straight off her. I know she'd been through a lot with her family, but it must have just made her even tougher. She was stubborn, a fighter.' She looks at the floor. 'All the things I wish I'd been. Still wish I was.'

I don't answer.

'I know what you're thinking. Of course Zach must have been attracted to her when she was such a strong person, and beautiful too.'

'I… I don't know what I'm thinking.' I stand up and walk to the window, turning my back on Alison, doing all I can, other than leaving the room, to avoid picturing the girl my husband fell for.

'But she was also deeply flawed,' Alison continues. 'She drank like a fish and despite fooling the world into thinking she was okay with her hideous mother, it must have torn her apart inside.'

I turn round again. 'Alison, what do you think happened to her?'

She sighs. 'I wish I knew. I know she must be dead but I don't think it was your husband, I really don't. Surely you believe that? You knew him better than anyone.'

But how well do we ever know anyone? 'Sometimes we just can't see what people are truly capable of, Alison.'

'So what do you think happened then?'

I've had a long time to think about this. 'I think Zach got caught up in something and regretted it in the end. Maybe Josie was threatening to tell me and he... he lost control. He realised what he was about to lose.'

'That's possible. But it doesn't explain the photo of Josie on Dominic's computer. I'm telling you, Mia, he did something to her. I know it.' She begins chewing her nail, something I've never noticed her doing before. 'I need to go back to the house. When he's not there. To check his computer again.'

There are so many reasons why this is a terrible idea, but I know before I speak it will be hard to convince her not to do it. 'You can't, Alison. It's too risky. He knows you've been to the police now, so if he finds you there imagine how he might react. Also, think about this: he could claim that you put the photo there and then the police will start looking at you. And isn't that the main reason you've not come forward about being in the flat that night?'

She stares at me and I swell up with guilt. I don't mean to frighten her, but she needs to stay away from that man and I've got to do what I can to help her do that.

'I could never have hurt Josie,' she says, but her words are flat. 'You believe me, don't you?'

But do I? I don't know what she is or isn't capable of, even though I intend to find out. 'Alison, all that matters right now is keeping you safe and finding you somewhere to live.'

'You think I'm lying about Zach, don't you? That's why you're not desperate to pursue anything. You just don't believe a word I'm saying!' She's raising her voice now, loud enough to wake Will.

'Please keep your voice down – I don't want Will dragged into this.' I lower my voice so that hopefully she'll do the same. And then I find myself explaining once again why I need firm evidence before I will allow myself to get my hopes up. But it seems she will never understand that I've spent too long believing Zach was guilty, that I've come to terms with it, that it will only be self-destructive to believe otherwise, unless there is proof. 'It will be the police who find it, if there ever is anything to find, Alison. Not us.'

She stares at me for so long I feel as if her eyes are burning into me. Even though none of this should be a shock to her when I've said it all before. Then finally she responds. 'I suppose it's the counsellor in you that makes you feel this way,' she says. 'You're not reacting with your heart, are you? You're just letting your brain dictate how you feel.'

I force myself to remain calm – Alison is extremely troubled, so I can't tip her over the edge. 'You're probably right. But my priorities are Freya and Will, and they come before anything else. I'm not going to do anything that could hurt them.'

'Hurt who?' Will's voice echoes into the room as he appears in the doorway.

'We were just talking about my partner... Dominic. Sorry if we woke you,' says Alison, jumping in before I've even formed an excuse to offer him.

'I did hear voices, but don't worry, I needed to get up anyway.' His wink assures me that he couldn't have heard what we were talking about. 'I'm starving. Have you both had breakfast?'

Alison shakes her head. 'It's too early for me.'

'No, I won't yet,' I say. 'I've got some paperwork I want to catch up on first.'

Will frowns but doesn't question me, and when he heads off to the kitchen I turn to Alison. 'Promise me you won't go to your house?'

She nods. 'He'll be at home today. He never leaves the house on Saturdays, all he does is sit in front of the football.'

'Just stay here and relax. You could sit outside in the back garden and have some peace. Have a look at those flats I sent you and we can go and see some this afternoon.'

'Okay,' she says, already flicking through her phone. 'Hope you have a productive morning.'

Will comes to find me in my office before lunch. I've been so engrossed in my work that I don't realise how hungry I am until he places a sandwich on my desk. 'I know you didn't have breakfast so thought you might need this,' he says. 'And don't worry, I even offered to make Alison one, but she refused it. She's just sitting in the garden. Don't say I didn't try.'

'Is she okay? What's she been doing all morning?'

'Reading in the sun every time I've checked. She seems... relaxed? It's hard to believe she's an abused woman.'

'I know. But I've seen the bruises, and they were definitely real.'

'Hmmm. Well, I guess we all have different ways of dealing with things. Look, I'm trying to make an effort with her – but the truth is, I just don't trust her. I don't know what it is but there's something about her that... I don't know, I can't even explain it.'

'Will, I do know what you mean. It's like she plans what she's saying too carefully, as if she's scared she'll trip herself up.'

'Yes! That's exactly it.'

'But I've got to help her.'

He lets out a heavy sigh. 'I know that. I just don't like you being here alone with her, and I have to pop out for a bit, get some things done. Will you be okay?'

I assure him I will and let him know we'll be flat hunting this afternoon.

'Good. Well, I'll be back this evening. I'm not leaving you alone with her all night.'

I grab his hand. 'Thank you. Even though I can take care of myself.'

'I know you can,' he says. 'But do you know what? It's not a bad thing to let other people help you once in a while, Mia.'

Once Will's gone, I try to organise my thoughts. I need a plan for what to do about Alison. If I'm ever to find out what she's really doing in my house, and in my life, then I need to take drastic action.

TWENTY-SIX

Josie

Craig and I sit in his bedroom, huddled under his duvet because it's so cold in here. I'm wearing my coat too, but he doesn't seem to be offended.

'Bloody heating,' he says, putting his arm around me. 'It takes forever to kick in. Sorry.'

But he has nothing to apologise for; I would much rather be here in his flat, no matter how cold it is, than at home, wondering what Alison will say or do next. Nobody has ever put me on edge like she does, not even Johnny. It's the silent people you have to watch out for – not the mouthy, full-of-shit people like Johnny and Richard.

Craig's parents have just left. His mum cooked us the nicest home-cooked meal I've ever had, and despite my initial reservations, I actually enjoyed myself.

'You were right about your parents,' I tell him, burying myself further into the crook of his arm. 'They actually *are* cool. I had a lot of fun this afternoon.'

'Mum loved you, I could tell. Dad too. And that's a first because they've never liked any girls I've introduced them to before. Seriously. Never.'

'Oh well, there's still plenty of time for them to hate me.' I'm only half-joking.

Craig pulls me round to face him and kisses me, and for once I give in and let him. I'm so used to pushing people away at this point but I don't want to do that now. I want to make a go of it with him. But the further we go, the harder I find it to focus. My head is all over the place and I'm everywhere except present with Craig.

He stops and pulls back. 'Are you okay, Josie? Is something wrong?'

I tell him I'm fine and force myself to kiss him harder, more urgently, to prove that I'm okay. To feel *something*. But with my eyes closed, it's Zach I see, Zach I want to be with, Zach my whole body aches for.

I freeze up and push Craig away.

'I'm sorry, I can't do this. I have to go. I'm sorry.'

'Why? Josie, what's wrong? Have I done something?'

But I don't stop to answer because there's nothing I can tell him that will make sense or make him feel any better. Hating myself more than I ever have in my life, I rush from his room without looking back.

Walking home does nothing to clear my head and it doesn't help that Craig keeps calling and texting me. I should never have started anything with him when my heart's not in it. But I can never have Zach, so where does that leave me?

I'm about to turn off my phone when it rings again, but this time it's Sinead. My heart almost stops. She's only ever texted me before; it's usually me calling her if I need more detailed information about how Kieren is doing.

'Sinead? What is it? Has something happened?'

'Sorry, Josie, I don't want to panic you but, well, I haven't actually seen Kieren for a few days. And it's term time, so Liv should be taking him to school every morning, but she's been leaving the house without him.'

I struggle to take in what she's saying. 'So you think she's leaving him at home alone?' This wouldn't surprise me. And actually, if that's what she's doing then I finally have a chance to get Kieren out of there. There is no way social services will allow a five-year-old to be left at home alone.

'I don't know. I just know I haven't seen him for ages but Liv's still been going out. Maybe not in time for the school run, but probably a bit later. Around ten-ish.'

'Sinead, can you remember when you last saw him? What day was it?'

There's a long pause. 'I'm not sure. Probably when I texted you last week. Friday, was it? I saw Liv bringing him back from school, but haven't seen him since then. I haven't even heard him and usually he's out in the back garden at some point, even if it's freezing or raining.'

Now I'm starting to panic. 'Can you go and knock on the door? See if he's there?'

'Oh, Josie, what would I say? I can't tell her I'm checking if Kieren's there, can I? And she can't stand me so what other reason would I have to be knocking on her door?'

'I don't know! Say anything!' I'm yelling now, even though Sinead doesn't deserve that – she's only ever looked out for me. 'This is important, Sinead!'

'Look, Josie, if you're that worried then why don't you call the police? I can't just go round there with no reason. No way. Sorry, love. I've been happy helping you all this time because I know what a bitch Liv is, but I can't get involved in this. Just call the police.'

'Sinead, please—'

But she's cut me off.

For a few seconds I stare at my phone in disbelief, but then fear for Kieren forces me to act.

*

It's late evening by the time I get to Brighton and make my way to Liv's house. I walk past Sinead's and try not to feel angry with her. After all, I can't blame her for fearing the repercussions of crossing Liv. Sinead has seen what she's capable of doing to her own daughter, so she knows Liv wouldn't give a second thought to causing her neighbour harm if she felt it was deserved.

There's a light on in the hallway of Liv's house so I take a deep breath and head up the path, banging on the door when I reach it. There's no point pretending this is a polite social call.

Within seconds she is flinging open the door, ready to curse whoever's making such a racket, but when she sees it's me she seems to forget what she was about to say.

'What the hell are you doing here? I hope it's to tell me you're going to the police.'

'Let me in,' I say. I don't set her straight, because I need to get in the house, need to see that Kieren is okay, without her realising that's why I'm here.

'If you're fucking me around, Josie, I swear, I'll—'

'Just let me in, Liv, or I'm going straight home.'

She looks behind her for a second before moving aside, and I step forward, my heart threatening to burst from my chest. I haven't set foot in this place since the attack.

'Go in the front room,' she says. But she doesn't follow me; instead, she takes her time closing the front door and then makes a show of sorting out the shoes that are piled up there. I don't know what game she's playing – Liv never tidies up anything.

Even before I open the front-room door, I know for sure it's a trap, but I go in anyway, because I need to know Kieren is okay and his safety comes before my own.

He's slouched on the sofa, staring at the TV, one of his legs casually crossed over the other as if he feels at home here. *Richard*. He doesn't even flinch when he sees me and barely glances in my direction.

'You'd better be here to tell me you're putting things right,' he says, wiping his nose with his sleeve, his eyes still fixed on the TV.

I stay in the doorway and Liv barges past me, plonking herself on the sofa next to Richard. They are too cosy, too comfortable with each other; I sense it immediately.

'Where's Kieren?' I ask, unable to keep the anger from my voice. Something isn't right here; they are too smug.

Liv snorts. 'What's it to you? None of your bloody business!'

'He's my brother, and I'm more of a mother to him than you've been since the second he was born, so it *is* my business. Where is he?'

Richard leans forward and rests his arm on Liv's knee. 'You don't just get to come in here and ask all sorts of sodding questions. Now, what are you doing about the police? Because the way I see it, you've now got two things to tell them you were wrong about.' He's too calm and I don't like it. Too in control. They know something I don't.

'What are you talking about? What's the second thing?'

He leans further forward. 'I don't appreciate the police knocking on my door in the middle of the bloody night, asking whether I was in London that night months ago. Prying into my business. I already told you, bitch, that I have an airtight alibi. But you still thought you'd try, didn't you?'

So they did chase it up after all. That's something, at least. 'Yeah, I'm not letting you get away with that, or your pathetic threats. I'm still here, aren't I, Richard? So I guess you were full of shit.' My words mask the fear I'm feeling inside. After all, I don't know this man, and if he's anything like his cousin he won't think twice about hurting me. And what have they done with Kieren?

'You think you're such a tough bitch, don't you?' He laughs, and beside him Liv joins in. She's being exactly how she was with Johnny and that can only mean one thing: there's something going on with these two. 'Well, you weren't so tough when Johnny was beating you half to death, were you? A bit of a mess, by his account. You're not as hard as you think you are, Josie.' A smile spreads across his face. That night in the car I didn't notice the thick scar under his eye, but now I see it clearly. This man is no stranger to fighting.

Ignoring my fear, and Richard's statement, I turn to face the woman who will never be my mother. 'Just tell me where Kieren is.' I try to keep my voice calm, even though my panic is rising.

Liv scrunches her whole face and suddenly she looks twenty years older. 'Who do you think you are? If you're not going to help Johnny then you can get the fuck out. I've tried to warn you, but whatever happens to you now is your own fault. Just get out of my house, Josie.' She hisses her words at me.

'Okay,' I say. 'That's fine with me.' And when they both turn back to the television I walk away and shut the door. Then I run to the stairs and climb them two at a time. I've got to know if Kieren is here, and I'll deal with whatever those two do to me after I've checked.

Within seconds I hear heavy footsteps following me, and Richard shouting at me to get downstairs. But I don't listen. I fling open Kieren's bedroom door – preparing myself to expect the worst – and I'm shocked to find him here, asleep in his bed. The commotion makes him stir and he slowly sits up, squinting into the light from the hall. 'JoJo?' he murmurs, his voice thick with sleep. 'You're here!'

But before I can ask if he's okay, Richard grabs me by my hair and drags me backwards, throwing me towards the stairs, my head crashing into the wall. But I ignore the pain. 'Why is Kieren in bed already? Why hasn't he been at school?'

Liv is on the stairs now, her eyes almost popping out of her head, wild with all the hatred she has for me. 'He's ill, you stupid cow! Now get out of here – or this time it'll be me calling the bloody police.'

'I'll see her out,' says Richard, grabbing my arm and pulling me up.

And then I hear Kieren's voice again and turn to see him standing behind his bedroom door, his face the only part of him visible. 'JoJo,' he says, his eyes filling with tears. 'Don't go.'

'It's okay, Kieren,' I say, shrugging out of Richard's grasp. 'I'll see you soon. Don't you worry about anything, I'll be back.'

'No, you won't,' Richard says once we're downstairs. He shoves me towards the front door, then leans down and whispers in my ear, his sticky breath hot against my skin. 'I'll kill you, Josie. Do you understand? Johnny should have done it in the first place, but don't worry, I'll make sure it happens. I won't even have to get my hands dirty.'

And then he gives one final shove and I'm outside, the heels of my palms scraping against the pavement as I break my fall.

TWENTY-SEVEN

Mia

Alison does everything I ask of her; we visit several flats and she puts down a deposit on one in Hammersmith. It's currently empty so is available immediately, but the letting agent tells us they need to check references and get paperwork sorted from the landlord, so it will be at least Thursday before she can move in.

It's only Monday now, but Freya is happy to stay with Pam and Graham until then, and the extra days buy me more time.

I watch Alison whenever I can, studying her carefully, and with each passing day she seems to become more confident, moving further away from the timid woman who walked into my office on that first day we met. As far as I know, she's had no contact with Dominic, and she's spending less and less time on her phone, so, on the surface, at least, it appears that she's making an effort to start her new life. But it is almost too perfect, too staged, and if it hadn't been for her watching Will and me in bed the other night, I might have begun to trust her.

I've told Alison I'm going on a course today, because now I have everything in place to catch her out with her lie.

Dominic has agreed to meet me and I've made sure it's somewhere public. I don't want to be alone with him in his house and I can't risk him finding out Alison has been staying with me. So now I'm in a coffee shop, close to where Zach used to work, and Dominic is late. I've considered the possibility that he might not turn up at all, but I'm willing to bet he's so desperate for information on Alison that he'll make sure he gets here.

Twenty minutes later he rushes through the door, scanning the room until he spots me. 'Mia, I'm so sorry.' He pulls out a chair and sits down. 'I had a meeting that overran and then had to get back to Ealing. Thanks for waiting. And thanks for calling. You said you'd heard from Alison?'

'Yes, that's right. But there's no way I'm telling you where she is.' I hold my breath and wait for his reaction.

'What? Why? What do you mean?'

'I've seen her bruises, Dominic. First-hand. The bruises that you left all over her body.'

He leans forward and bangs his knuckles on the table. 'Whoa, hold on! If you're talking about that small bruise on her arm, that was an accident. She was hysterical and I was trying to calm her down. Maybe I grabbed her a bit too hard and it… it left a mark. But there's no way I'd hurt her deliberately.'

'A mark is not how I'd describe it. But I'm sure the police have already talked to you about that. Anyway, that's not the only reason I'm here.'

'Wait, Mia, what are you talking about? What police?'

'Oh, come on, Dominic. I know Alison's been to the police and that they've spoken to you. There's no point denying anything any more.'

His mouth hangs open and he stumbles on his words. 'Alison's been to the police? What about?'

'About the physical abuse she's suffered at your hands. Probably mental abuse too. All of it. They know everything, Dominic.'

'Wait, physical abuse? Are you saying I've hurt Alison? Is that what she's told you?'

'She's my client. I can't discuss that with you.'

'Mia, listen, I've told you before that Alison's not in her right frame of mind. She needs help, she's disturbed.'

'So you keep saying. But of course you would say that, wouldn't you? Especially when she's not around to defend herself. That's just what men like you do, isn't it?'

'You've got this all wrong. And the police haven't spoken to me about anything. Surely you can check that? I would never hurt Alison – or any woman.'

His words are so confident, so adamant, that I find myself doubting what I'm doing. What if I've got this all wrong? I start to feel short of breath. It won't be long until panic overwhelms me again, unless I can calm myself down and think rationally. I've got to salvage this before it's too late.

'Prove it to me. Prove you haven't done anything to Alison, and that she's as troubled as you say she is.'

'I can't. How can I prove it? It's my word against hers, isn't it?' He lets out a deep breath and his head flops back against his chair. 'Wait. Maybe there is something.' He leans forward again and pulls his phone from his pocket. 'This is a text she sent me on Thursday.'

He holds the phone out and I tentatively take it, unsure what I'll find on the screen. It's definitely a text from Alison, but the words almost stop my breath.

I've got to go away for a few days to be by myself. I'm sorry, I just need some time to get myself straight. But I love you. Never forget that.

I read it again, hoping the words will say something different this time around, something that proves Alison has been telling the truth, because even though I've doubted her at times, her lying to me throws everything into question. I wanted to believe her claims about Dominic; that they stemmed from the confused mind of an unstable woman in an abusive relationship. But whether or not she truly knows anything about Zach, she has fabricated this story about her own partner. But why?

Dominic gives me some time then reaches for his phone. 'From the look on your face I can tell that's done something in my favour. What exactly did she tell you?'

I don't mention that Alison's been staying with me for the last few days, but I tell Dominic I've seen her and that she went to the police station; supposedly to report his abuse.

'But what did she say to them? I swear, they haven't called me or come round or anything.'

That's when it dawns on me that I don't actually know what she was doing in there. I was outside, and didn't even wait to see her come out. Shooting pains cut through my stomach. When I manage to speak my voice is almost a whisper. 'I don't know what she said. Or if she even actually spoke to them.'

Dominic shakes his head. 'This is what she does, Mia. I tried to tell you. She makes things up, tells lies to cover her tracks and then that leads to even more lies.' He checks his watch. 'Look, will you come somewhere with me? There's someone I want you to meet. It might help you understand a bit more.'

I stare at him but don't know how to reply.

'You can drive if that makes you feel more comfortable? It's only in Hayes, so not far.'

Alison's parents must only be in their fifties, yet they look at least twenty years older than that. They live in a tiny ground-floor flat, but inside it's neat and well maintained.

Dominic has already filled me in on the way here, and there was sadness in his voice as he told me they used to own a large house in Milton Keynes but had to sell it to move to London to be closer to Alison. This was all they could afford and they even had to throw in over half their savings to buy it.

'I hadn't met her at that point,' Dominic had explained. 'It wasn't long after, you know, what happened with Zach and Josie and everything. It just really affected Alison and she lost it a bit. Had some sort of breakdown. But they can tell you more about it.'

So now I stand in their cramped kitchen, not sure where this will lead or what I will find out, what it will mean for the future.

'I'm so sorry for your loss,' Camilla Frances says. It was no surprise to find out from Dominic that Cummings isn't Alison's real name. That might explain why I found no trace of her on the Internet when I first looked her up.

'Why Cummings?' I'd asked Dominic.

But he had no idea. 'She probably just picked a name at random from the credits of a TV programme or something like that. Things are not always clearly thought out with Alison. A lot of the time what she does is just random.'

The loss Camilla refers to must be Zach, but to me it could also mean what I'm about to lose: everything I've believed in. 'Thank you,' I say.

'It must be so awful for you. I hope people are leaving you alone now.'

I nod and try not to show my discomfort. If I tread carefully I will leave here with a much better insight into Alison, so I can't afford to make an enemy of Camilla and Anthony. 'It's been a long road but nobody seems to bother me any more. I did get a lot of abuse about Zach in the beginning. Well, for over a year at least, but people seem to have short memories.'

She takes my hand. 'Well, I'm glad they're leaving you alone now.' She turns to Dominic. 'Please tell me you've found her?'

'Yes, well, sort of. She's not at home but I have heard from her this time. And she's okay, so there's really no need to worry.'

Camilla sinks back against the worktop. 'I do nothing but worry about her, though. You know that, Dominic.'

He moves across to her and takes her hand. I'm not easily fooled by people but it's getting harder to believe that this is an abusive man, although I know from experience that they can be extremely charming with other people. But still, Alison's text seems to refute everything she's said so far.

But she is tied up in what happened to Zach and Josie, I know it.

'Well, I thought it might be good for you to speak to Mia. She's a counsellor, too, so I think it will help us all actually.' He turns to me and offers an apologetic smile.

Camilla nods, but a frown appears on her husband's face. 'All this talking,' says Anthony. 'It hasn't done Alison any good so far, has it? And it's been years. We've never cared about money and we'll pay anything we need to in order to help her, but we really have very little left now.'

I shouldn't be surprised to hear Alison had been seeing someone before she came to me. 'I won't take any of your money,' I say to Anthony. 'I just want to help Alison.'

'I, um, thank you. That's very kind of you.'

'I really think Mia's the best person to help us,' Dominic says. 'Especially as it seems finding Mia has heightened Alison's obsession, for some reason.'

'Don't call it that,' Anthony says. 'It's not an obsession. She just needs help, that's all.'

This isn't the first time I've felt out of my depth since Alison stepped into my life, and I hate feeling out of control. 'Just what exactly is going on?' I say to all of them.

'Let's go and sit in the garden,' Camilla says. 'It's too crowded in here.'

We all trudge outside and I'm grateful to breathe in the fresh air. The garden is quite large, given the size of the flat, and it's freshly mown and as neat as the inside.

As soon as we've sat down, Camilla begins speaking. 'My daughter's not a bad person, Mia. She's not. She just… well, what happened to Josie hit her really hard.'

She must see the doubt scrawled on my face because she quickly adds to her statement. 'I know they weren't close, but they did live together all those months, so Alison felt a part of Josie's life, I suppose.'

I tell her that's understandable, but from everything Alison's said about Josie I wonder just how true this is. She disliked her intensely, so why would she care about never seeing Josie again? Alison claimed that Dominic is somehow connected to Josie's disappearance, but now that doesn't seem likely. So why is she doing all this?

No matter how much I think about it, or find out, I still don't know who to trust.

'She fell apart after it happened,' Anthony says. 'Didn't even finish her degree and never tried to go back. It was the beginning of the trouble for her. She just seemed to have no direction. No purpose any more.'

'I think she's made Josie her purpose,' adds Dominic. 'It gives her something to do, especially now she's having a break from work.' He shakes his head. 'I've tried to help her, Mia, I really have, but nothing works. And now she's made up this stuff about me abusing her. Why would she do that?'

'Because she's sick and she needs help. Medication or something.' Anthony answers before I can even think of how to respond to this question.

'I'll do whatever I can to help her,' I say. 'But I need a lot more information first. What was she like before she met Josie?'

'She was always a clever child,' Camilla says, 'but she never found it easy to make friends. Socialising just wasn't her strong point. But we weren't worried about it because she was doing so well academically. We had no concerns about her future.'

'Until she met Josie.' Anthony reaches for his wife's hand. 'That was the start of it, I think. She just had so much hatred for that girl, though as far as we could see Josie hadn't done anything other than be a totally different person from Alison.'

It's a struggle to get this next question out. 'I know this may be hard to hear, but do you think she may have been jealous of Josie?'

Camilla is quick to disagree. 'No, I don't think it was that, I really don't. Alison's a pretty girl, why would she be jealous of anyone?'

I have to set her straight. 'Jealousy isn't just about looks, Camilla. It can be about any aspect of someone. Anything in their life.'

'But that girl had nothing. Her mother's boyfriend almost beat her to death and her mum did nothing. Alison couldn't have been loved more. So why would she be jealous of that girl?'

'I don't know.' If I did know, then I'd understand exactly what Alison is playing at, but I'm still none the wiser.

I turn to Dominic. 'Alison only just found me and it's been five years since it happened. Why now?'

He shrugs. 'Only she can answer that. I've tried to find out but I have no idea.'

The photo. It's got to be linked to that.

For the next half hour I listen while Camilla and Anthony paint me a picture of their daughter, but at the end of it I still have no clue what she's doing, or who to believe.

'We'd better get going,' Dominic says. 'I've got a lot of things to prepare for my classes tomorrow.'

In the car, Dominic directs me to Finchley. 'So now do you believe me?'

'I might, but there's one thing I need to check first. When I drop you off, can I come in for a minute?'

Dominic frowns. 'Okay – but why? I'm not hiding her there, if that's what you're thinking.'

'If you want to help Alison, please just humour me.'

It's so different being in Alison's house this time. My perspective has shifted, even though I'm still not sure what I believe.

'I'd offer you a drink,' Dominic says, 'but I'm sure you don't want one. So are you going to tell me why you wanted to come here?'

I feel braver than I thought I would, being here, but that's because I've got everything at stake. Freya. Will. And I'll do whatever I can to protect them. 'I need to see your computer, Dominic. I'm sorry, I know it's intrusive, but, well, when I tell you why, I hope you'll understand.'

He frowns and stares at me, probably shocked by my audacity.

'But why would you need to see my computer? What's it got to do with Alison? She has her own laptop, she never uses mine.'

I make a split-second decision, hoping I don't regret it, and tell him everything Alison has told me, about the picture she found on his computer, and her suspicions that Dominic was involved in Josie's death. I've got nothing to lose now; at least one of them is lying to me and this is the only way to find out who it is.

Dominic sits down and buries his head in his hands. 'I can't believe she'd say something like that. She can't really think I had anything to do with Josie... Why would she tell you all this?'

'She said the photo was on your computer, Dominic. And that it was probably downloaded from your phone. The video I saw actually showed her finding it.'

'So that's why you want to see it?' He jumps up. 'Come on. I'll even let you switch it on just so you know I'm not getting rid of anything on there.'

Upstairs in his study he stays true to his word and I turn on his computer while he keeps his distance, hovering in the doorway. 'I don't have a password on it,' he says. 'Never thought there was any need – it's only me and Alison living here. And I thought I could trust her.' He sighs. 'Anyway, you should probably take a seat – it might take you a while to check everywhere for that photo.'

I retrace the steps Alison filmed herself taking, and browse Dominic's photos, but there is no sign of Josie. I even see the photos it was jammed between, and this convinces me even more the photo was planted. There's no way Dominic could have known I would come here and ask to check his computer, and why would he delete it now after keeping it for all these years? It must have been Alison. She put it there and tried to make him look guilty – but why?

For the next half hour I thoroughly scan the rest of Dominic's computer, just to make sure the photo isn't anywhere else. There are plenty of lesson plans and other work documents, but nothing remotely personal.

'I don't use it for anything other than work,' he explains, as if he knows exactly what I'm thinking. He's sitting on the small sofa in the corner of the study, watching everything I do. 'The truth is I'm not very good with technology. Alison always sorts out the computer stuff in the house. She's quite the expert, actually.'

'Well, the photo's not here,' I say. 'Not anywhere I can find it at least.'

'So now will you finally believe me?'

'If I'm going to help you, and help Alison, I need to know everything you know about what happened that night with my husband and Josie.'

'Well, that's not much. Anyway, how's this going to help Alison?'

'You said yourself she's fixated on what happened to Josie, so I believe that's why she's come to me. I think she's crying out for help.'

'So why accuse me of harming Josie? And all the abuse stuff?'

'Because she needed me to listen to her, and that certainly got my attention.'

'You're a counsellor, though. You would have helped her anyway, even if she hadn't said all that.'

I shake my head. 'Actually, if the situation wasn't so desperate I probably would have told her I was too close to this to be able to help her. I would have referred her to someone else.'

He considers my words for a moment. 'I suppose that makes sense. Nothing else does, though.'

But it's all starting to become clear to me now.

Alison knows exactly what happened to Josie.

TWENTY-EIGHT

Josie

I'm shattered when I get home from Brighton. All I want to do is crawl into bed and pretend the world doesn't exist. My whole body aches but it doesn't feel like a physical pain. It's emotional. Maybe it's fear that I'll never see Kieren again. He's too young to tell anyone he wants to come and live with me, and I've tried everything with social services, so, other than kidnapping him, there's nothing I can do, and that cuts like a knife wound; the worst pain I've ever felt. But in my usual style, I do the only thing I can: I block it out. Make it go away. Don't think about anything or anyone.

I almost scream when I open my bedroom door and Alison is there, sitting on my bed in total darkness, except for the glow coming from my laptop screen. I don't remember leaving it on. I'm sure I didn't.

'What are you doing in here? Get out, Alison.' I don't care if I sound rude, or nasty or anything else. I've had enough of this girl.

'I thought we could start again,' she says, her voice too jolly. I've never heard her like this before so it takes me a moment to work out that she's drunk. 'Here, I've poured us some wine.'

There are two glasses on the floor: one of them almost empty and the other full. 'I've been saving it for you, Josie. Waiting for you to get home. I'm sure you like rosé.' She picks up the full glass.

I wouldn't believe this if it wasn't right in front of me: pure, innocent Alison is sloshed. I bet she's so unused to alcohol she only needed a sip for it to go straight to her head.

'I know I shouldn't be in here,' she says. 'Sorry. But let's have a drink together. It's something we should have done a long time ago.' She waves her glass around and wine spills onto my duvet. 'Make peace.'

I join her on my bed. 'I don't drink any more, Alison. You know that.'

'Oh, really?' She takes a swig of wine, far too much in one go. 'And why's that, then?'

'Well, you're the one who told me I had a drink problem.' I shouldn't be engaging in this conversation with her but I'm too exhausted to fight too hard.

She chuckles. 'Did I really say that? Oh yeah. Well, you do, actually. Sorry, but it's true.'

But she looks far from sorry. I should have known her so-called 'making peace' wouldn't last two seconds. 'Okay, Alison, I think you should go now. Your room is right next door.'

She doesn't move. 'Hang on. I'm sorry, okay? I shouldn't have said that. Look, I'll put my drink down so neither of us has any.' She leans over and fumbles to put her glass down on the floor. I quickly grab it from her before the whole thing ends up all over the carpet. The flat's already shabby but when it's time to leave I'm not losing my deposit because of Alison.

'Let's talk about something else,' she continues.

For the first time in my life I give in. 'Fine, but it's late and I need to get some sleep soon. I've got an early shift in the coffee shop tomorrow.'

She smiles, and I'm not sure why this is making her so happy. It's as if the alcohol has transformed her personality, rather than just making her lose her inhibitions. 'Okay. So, something interesting happened today, Josie. Craig was round here when I got home. Knocking on the door. Actually, make that *pounding* on the door.'

I stiffen. 'What did he say? Did you let him in?'

'Of course I let him in. He's your boyfriend, isn't he? Well, he *was* your boyfriend. He told me you two had pretty much broken up but he had no idea why.'

It makes me uncomfortable that Alison is prying into my business when for months we've barely said more than a few sentences to each other. And most of those were insults. 'What did you say to that?'

'I told him I didn't even know you two were together. He seemed a bit upset by that, but I told him not to take it personally, that these things happen. You know, all the platitudes. But he was very upset.'

But I did the right thing for him. It's better to be cruel to him now than get further involved before realising it isn't right. That would cut him up even more.

Alison reaches for her glass. 'He's really got it bad for you, hasn't he? Poor guy. Still, I'm sure you'll find someone else soon. People like you always do.'

'What the hell is that supposed to mean, Alison?'

She holds up her hands. 'I meant it as a compliment. You're an attractive girl.' Her words are forced, unnatural, so now I know for sure she's playing some kind of sick game.

'I need to get some sleep now. Goodnight, Alison.' I pick up the bottle of wine lying on my bed and thrust it towards her. 'Here you go.'

She pulls herself up and staggers to her feet. 'Well, it's been nice having this chat. We must do it again soon. How come you never have family here?'

Her sudden question stuns me into silence, so it takes me a moment before I can speak. 'Goodnight, Alison.'

As soon as she's gone I pull out my phone. I ignored it all the way home from Brighton because I didn't want to think about Craig. About anything. But now I know he was here, I need to talk to him.

He picks up immediately. 'Josie, thank God! I've been trying to call you all day.'

'I know. I'm sorry, I just wasn't ready to talk. Did you come to my flat?'

'Yeah, didn't you get any of my voicemails?'

'I haven't checked them. Sorry.'

'Josie, your flatmate is a freak. She... Look, can we meet and talk about this?'

'It's been a long day and I need to go to bed, Craig, I'm really knackered. But you're right about Alison being a bit strange. I thought I'd told you that.'

'You did. But, seriously, this was something else. *She's* something else. She told me all this crazy stuff. I mean, *really* crazy stuff. What is up with her?'

His words hit me like a fist. 'What... what exactly did she say? Tell me everything.'

'She made up all this stuff about you and I know it's all bull.'

'Just tell me!' He doesn't deserve it, but it's an effort not to scream at him.

'She said your mum's boyfriend tried to kill you and left you for dead.'

My blood freezes. Alison must have found out about it on the Internet. Since moving to London I've kept this from everyone but Zach and it feels like a violation for anyone to be bringing it up. I can't speak.

'Josie? Are you there?'

Eventually I find some words. 'I'm here.'

'Why would she say that?'

'Because she hates me, Craig. And she's crazy.'

'I'm so sorry, Josie, she almost had me believing her. I mean, she seemed so convincing. But then she told me some other stuff that I know isn't true.'

The first thing I think is that Alison probably told him I did something with Aaron; that I deliberately came between them. I prepare myself for this. But what Craig says next shocks me to my core.

'She said you've been sleeping with Zach Hamilton.'

'What sick game are you playing?' I throw my phone at Alison and it smacks against her arm. I'm not usually a violent person but my anger is uncontrollable. She's really crossed a line this time.

'Let me guess. You've spoken to Craig and he told you what I said. Well, it's all true, isn't it?'

It's a struggle to be calm but I can't lose control here. 'You know I could get you in a lot of trouble for spreading malicious lies about me?'

'Yes, you could. *If* they were lies. But everything I said is true. So go ahead and report whatever you want to whoever you want. Actually, an investigation into your sick affair would be a good thing.'

Alison has won. All along she's wanted to screw with me and now she's finally found something that will. Even though Zach has done nothing wrong, even a hint of anything like this would destroy his career. I can't let that happen, not after everything he's done for me.

Anger explodes within me and now I am out of control, witnessing my body doing something I never thought I could: rushing to Alison's bed and grabbing her by the throat. Even the voice coming from me doesn't sound like my own. 'Go ahead, but if you do anything to hurt Zach in any way I will make it my mission in life to destroy your miserable existence. So make a choice, Alison, because if you spread these lies around, I will never let this go.' And then I walk away, hearing her gulps as she tries to recover herself.

In my room I sink onto my bed and cover my face with my pillow to drown out my tears. I am no better than Johnny or Richard; Liv was right about me.

TWENTY-NINE

Mia

I didn't tell Dominic that Alison's been staying with me; I want to speak to her first, to give her a chance to explain herself. I'm sure she will have prepared for every eventuality, but everyone deserves a chance to defend themselves. That's something Zach never had. Despite this, now I know how disturbed she is, it scares me to think her lies are symptomatic of something dangerous.

But when I get home, prepared for a difficult conversation, prepared for anything to happen, the house is empty. I call Alison's name but only silence follows my words. I do a quick search of each room and am not too concerned; it's possible she needed to get out of the house for some fresh air. But then I notice her bags are missing from the spare room. In fact, everything she brought with her has gone and the bed is neatly made, as if she was never here.

Panic begins to consume me; Alison was dangerous enough in my house – I know that now – but missing, she is even more of a risk. To me, to Dominic, maybe even to herself.

Even though I know she won't answer, I try her mobile, leaving a message when her voicemail kicks in. 'Alison, please call me. Whatever's happened, we can talk about this. I'm on your side, just call me.'

Next, I try Will, relieved to hear his voice when he answers. 'Is there any chance you've seen or heard from Alison?'

'Um, no. Why? What's happened?'

'I went out this morning and when I got back just now she was gone. I mean, all her things have gone. Everything.'

'Well, that's a good thing, isn't it? I was getting worried she'd never leave.'

'No, it's not a good thing. She's… very unstable. More than I thought.' But I can't expect Will to understand this.

'What exactly does that mean? Has she done something?'

I tell him I don't have time to explain it right now but promise I will as soon as I can.

But, of course, he won't let it go so easily. 'Are you sure she hasn't just moved out? You said she'd found a place.'

'She has, but it's not ready until Thursday. And she would have said goodbye if that were the case.'

'I don't like this, Mia. I'm coming over. I've got a meeting in half an hour but I'll cancel it.'

'There's no need. I'm fine. She's not here, is she?'

'No, but I think you've got a lot to tell me, haven't you?'

It's funny how things can suddenly take a sharp turn. How carefully laid plans and ideas can quickly go awry when you're thrown a curveball. Although I always intended to eventually be honest with Will about Alison, it wasn't supposed to be like this. But he needs to know and I won't keep it from him any longer.

We're sitting outside in the garden, but the pleasant heat and bright sunlight do nothing to make what I have to tell him any easier.

'I don't understand,' he says, once I've explained everything. His confusion is no surprise when it is only now that I'm starting to get any idea about who Alison really is myself. 'Are you saying you think she killed Josie? That it wasn't Zach after all?'

Now that the words are out there and no longer just in my head, they seem to make even more sense. 'I don't know for sure, Will, but I really think so.'

'But why would she come to you for help then? Why would she insist Zach is innocent?'

This is the question that's been plaguing me. 'I think that was just to get my attention. There's no way I would have listened to her otherwise. But she's really disturbed, Will. Maybe she's so out of touch with reality that she doesn't even remember doing anything. It's possible that she might actually believe Dominic is guilty.'

Will is silent for such a long time that I can almost hear his brain ticking. Calculating. Trying to make sense of what seems impossible. 'And you believe this Dominic? Are you sure he can be trusted? What if *he's* the one lying about Alison?'

I tell him that I wasn't sure to start with, but after speaking to Alison's parents and checking Dominic's computer, I'm now convinced he hasn't hurt her.

'Okay, well, we need to go to the police. They'll find Alison and hopefully get the truth out of her. There's no other way to know, is there? Even if she walked through that door now I doubt she'd tell you what really happened.' His sigh comes out as a whistle. 'I *knew* there was something not right here, I just knew. I wish you'd told me before.'

'But do you see why I couldn't? I don't turn my back on people, Will. I was only trying to help her. And find out the truth about Zach. I thought I knew it all, but then Alison turns up and it's like a bomb's exploded.'

He reaches across the table to take my hand. 'Whatever the truth is with Zach, it doesn't change anything in your life now. You've still got Freya, and you've still got me. Knowing about what Zach did never affected my feelings towards you. It had nothing to do with you. And if he's innocent, well, then I'm happy for you and Freya. And I'll still be here.'

I squeeze his hand because I'm too choked up to speak.

'It still doesn't make sense that she's made up all these lies about her partner. She must have known you could have checked it out.'

'The only way I can explain that is with how advanced her mental illness must be. Her bruises looked real, Will. What more evidence would I need? But now I think about it, they could have been carefully applied make-up. I was too shocked to stare at them and turned away pretty quickly.'

'Come on,' he says, 'the sooner we go to the police the better.'

'I need to get Freya first, Will. I can't be away from her when I don't know why Alison is so fixated on me, and we could be ages at the police station.'

He stares towards the back of the garden for a moment.

'Tell you what. I'll pick Freya up. You need to do this and I don't think it should wait.'

'Mummy! I thought I wasn't coming home yet,' Freya says, rushing through the door and into my arms.

I scoop her up and breathe in the smell of her shampoo. She is safe. We're all here together, and everything will be fine. 'Well, I missed you so much I asked Will to bring you home.'

'I'm glad,' she says. 'But I think Grandma and Grandad were a bit sad.'

I tell her we'll go and see them again soon and, appeased by this news, Freya rushes off to play in the garden.

As soon as she's out of earshot, Will asks me what happened with the police.

'They assured me they're taking it seriously and that they're look into everything, but I could tell the officer I spoke to wasn't too convinced.'

'I suppose they need to be careful until they've got evidence,' Will says. 'Just try to put it out of your mind. She could have done anything while she was here but she's gone now and I really don't think she'll come back. Maybe she found out you'd gone to see Dominic and got spooked. That could be why she disappeared.'

I hope he's right. After five years, I need this to end now.

'Don't worry, Mia. And don't let it play on your mind. The police are looking for her now. You did everything you could to help her but if she won't help herself then there's nothing more you could have done.'

So for the second time in my life, I will try to block out everything that's happened and focus on what's important, the family I have right in front of me. It works for a while, but when I go to bed and close my eyes, it's Alison's face I see. Will fell asleep on the sofa a couple of hours ago and I didn't want to wake him so I left him to rest, but now I wish he was here. With everything else I had to explain to him, I forgot to tell him about Alison watching us that night, but now I wish I had, because she was there for a reason. She was there for me.

My phone starts to vibrate on the bedside table and I know without looking that it's her, as if my thoughts have summoned her.

I don't say anything but listen to her speak. 'I know you're there, Mia. We need to talk and there's no one else I can turn to. Will you meet me?'

Every bone in my body screams out *no*, but somehow my words say the opposite. 'Where?'

'South Ealing station.'

'Alison, you should know I've been to the police. You need help.'

She ignores what this means. 'I thought *you* were helping me?'

'I was… I am. But you've got to start telling the truth. You do realise you won't get better unless you do this?'

There's a long pause before she answers. 'I know. But just come – alone, please. Don't tell them where I'll be. They'll find me eventually, won't they? I just want to talk to you first.'

When I don't answer she makes another attempt to convince me. 'You'll never know what happened with Zach and Josie otherwise, will you? Because I won't tell the police and they can't make me talk. Whatever they do, they can't make me talk.'

Alison is disturbed enough to mean this, so I have little choice. I tell her I'll be there in ten minutes. Before I leave, I check on Freya and Will, watching them both for a few minutes, peaceful in their sleep. I try to tell myself I'm not doing this because I'm worried something will happen to me, that I'm soaking up their images to give me more courage.

'I'm sorry,' I whisper into the air. 'But I need answers. I need to know, for Zach's sake.'

Alison is already at the station when I head towards it. I didn't want to wake Will by starting the car so I've walked here. She's wearing a denim jacket, black leggings and bright white trainers that seem to glow in the dark. Her hair looks freshly washed, and I wonder where she's been staying.

It's past midnight now so the station is closed, but I'm relieved to see a group of young men across the road, perched on a wall with beers in their hands.

I don't bother with pleasantries when I reach her. This woman has lied to me from the second I met her. 'Start talking, Alison. What's this all about?'

But she shakes her head. 'Not here. I need to show you something.'

I take a step back. 'There's no way I'm going anywhere. We can talk right here or not at all.'

'It's not far from here, I promise. If you don't want to come then that's your choice. But like I said, I won't be talking to the police. Though what does that matter? You've spent this long not

really knowing the truth, so I suppose it makes no difference.'
She turns to walk away.

My mind is in turmoil and I grip my phone in my pocket. I
should call the police now, it's the safest thing to do. But then I
will never know, because I don't doubt that Alison will take this
to the grave with her if I don't give in to her request.

But before I can even make a decision, my feet are moving
forward and I am following Alison Cummings, or Alison Frances,
or whatever her name is, into a deserted street. The whole time
I follow her she doesn't turn around, but she knows I'm behind
her. My shoes are flat but click against the pavement, the sound
echoing into the night.

After a few more roads I know where she's going. She's taking
me to the flat she used to share with Josie Carpenter. The flat
where Zach died. The shortness of breath comes quickly, forcing
me to stop and double over.

'Are you okay?' she asks. 'I guess you know where we are, then.'
She takes hold of my arm and eases me up. 'You'll be okay. But
we need to go inside.'

'I… I can't go in there.'

'Yes, you can. You want answers, don't you?' Her voice is
strangely gentle and soothing, as if she is the therapist and I the
patient. But I can't be fooled by her again. She has wanted to get
me here all along.

'No,' I say again, but she's leading me forward. Gently, but also
determined and forceful.

'How can we even get in there? Who lives there now?'

She pulls out a set of keys from her pocket. 'Nobody. Do you
believe in coincidences, Alison? Because I never used to. But when
you were helping me look for flats I found this one available to
rent. You wouldn't have noticed it because it was two bedrooms
and in Ealing, but I couldn't believe it when I saw the listing. So
I had to rent it. It's as if it was meant to be.'

Again, I am lost for words, lost for a solution to this problem. If I go in there I am putting myself at risk, but if I don't then I will never have the answers I need.

'Are you coming then?' she asks, already heading up the narrow path to the front door.

Trying to suppress the panic bubbling inside me, I follow her and step into the flat where Zach died.

The first thing I notice is the musty smell. It's been masked with some air freshener but it's still there, underneath, like a reminder of what happened here.

A ghost that won't go away.

'Just ignore the smell,' Alison says. 'The landlady's found it hard to rent this place in the last five years so it's been empty most of the time. She couldn't believe her luck when I said I'd take it. So, anyway, it's mine for six months at least. More if I want it.'

'But why would you want to stay here, Alison? It's not... it's not good for you.'

'Probably harder for you than it is for me,' she says. 'I didn't lose someone I loved in here.' Her words send a shiver up my spine. I shouldn't have come in; I need to get out before it's too late.

'Come and sit down,' she says. 'The living room's just here.' She points to a closed door and once again I follow her.

The room is a surprise. It looks freshly decorated and the furniture appears to be brand new.

'D'you like it?' Alison says. 'I thought I'd make an effort. Cost me a lot of money to do up, but it's worth it. And the landlady said I could do whatever I want in here.'

'Why have you done this? What's it all for, Alison?'

She sits on the sofa and crosses her legs. 'That's a funny question to ask, when there must be so many other things you want to know. But I'll answer. This is my home now – of course I want it to look nice. You should have seen it before. It was a typical student place, cheap carpets and boring magnolia walls. But I suppose neither of us cared. It was never meant to be forever.' She stares at me and her eyes feel like lasers cutting through me. 'Although, I suppose for Josie it *was* forever, wasn't it? *Her* forever.'

Staying where I am in the doorway, I try not to let fear show in my voice. I need to keep calm and not do anything to set Alison off. If I can do this right, there's a good chance I will make it out of here safely.

'Alison, I really want to help you, so I think you should tell me what happened to Josie. What exactly did you do to her?'

THIRTY

Josie

Alison has gone. Moved out, leaving no trace that she was ever here. I should feel happy – this is what I've wanted for months – but instead I feel empty, and more alone than I've ever felt in my life. There's also the guilt. Because I must have driven her away, mustn't I? I threatened her like a thug who uses fear to get what they want. And the way my anger consumed me, it's a miracle I didn't do her any harm.

She didn't tell me she was leaving, but she'd gone the day after our argument and I didn't even notice she'd left until I got home from my shift at the coffee shop. I didn't even have a chance to apologise, and I like to think I would have. That maybe it took me almost losing control to make me see that things had gone way too far. But I guess it doesn't matter; she just wanted to get as far away from me as possible, as quickly as she could.

What does that make me?

That was two months ago and every day since I've wanted to tell her I'm sorry for threatening her, even though I know she won't listen. Every day I am ready to deal with the consequences. If she reports Zach for something he hasn't even done then at least we have the truth on our side. I try calling her mobile every few days, but of course she doesn't answer.

Summer is nearly here, and with it, the end of my first year. I've nearly made it. Done what no one thought I ever could. But nothing takes away the emptiness.

Craig still texts me and, although it's a bit awkward, we meet up occasionally, but there is nothing between us any more. He probably thinks he had a lucky escape after I admitted to him what Alison said about my family was true. Of course he offered tons of supportive words, but something had changed: I wasn't the strong person he'd always thought me to be.

And then there's Zach. I've done well to stay away from him, even though I know how he feels about me. If I was a different person, feeling the way I do about him, I would have pursued him, regardless of his personal circumstances. I know there's a strong possibility he would have cracked eventually, if I'd been relentless enough. But I couldn't do that to him. I already saw how much I have torn him apart, and that's without us doing a thing.

We don't have much to say to each other any more, but he always has a smile for me whenever we pass in the corridor, and I make do with this. Eventually I'm sure the pain I feel in the pit of my stomach whenever I see him will pass.

I've worked all day today – pulling a double shift because Pierre was desperate when Lucia called in sick and no one else could cover – so now I slump on the sofa, exhausted, and curl up in a ball. I close my eyes and, like a child, hope it will all go away when I open them again, but no, I'm still here in this dump of a flat, with my life falling down around me. And I'm still Josie Carpenter – the girl who brings trouble wherever she goes.

With these thoughts consuming me, I spot the bottle of gin on the bookshelf. Alison never did move it and neither did I, feeling proud of myself every time I walked past it without giving in. But now it's calling my name. Daring me to have just one sip. Just one glass. An adult's way to make the world disappear.

I give in and grab the bottle, taking it back to the sofa and cradling it in my hands. And the funny thing is, I don't care. It tastes awful sliding down my throat, like sharp knives, but I carry on anyway.

I'm feeling better by the time I've finished the bottle, and I rummage through the cupboards in search of more, even though I know I won't find any. It's been months since I touched any alcohol, so there's no chance of finding anything still lying around.

To distract myself I pick up my phone and scroll through my contacts until I see her name. Liv Carpenter. I don't really have a plan, I only know I want to mess with her head, just like she's tried to do to me all these years. It's amazing how inspiration can strike when you've had a few.

'And what the hell do *you* want?' she says when she answers.

I laugh before I speak. 'To tell you I've won, Liv. I've finally won. You're not going to do anything to me. Not you. And not Richard.'

'Oh really? And why is that?'

'Let's just say that if you, Richard or anyone else comes anywhere near me to try and harm me in any way then I'm going straight to the prison to have a chat with Johnny.'

She grunts down the phone. 'Ha! A chat with Johnny? And why would you want to do that? I'm sure he'll be really pleased to see you.'

'Oh, he will when I tell him what you've been doing.'

Silence. She knows exactly where I'm going with this.

'What's the matter, Liv? Lost your voice for once?'

'Just what exactly are you saying, Josie? Get to the sodding point.'

'I know all about you and Richard.' I don't, not for sure anyway, but Liv will never know that.

'I don't know what the hell you're talking about.'

'I know what the two of you are doing, behind Johnny's back. I'm sure he'd love to know you're shacked up with his cousin.'

Silence again. For longer this time. I thought she might at least deny it.

'Listen, you little bitch, if you ever say anything to him, I'll—'

'But you won't do anything, will you, Liv? Because you'll probably be dead in some gutter somewhere before you even have a chance to get to me. Johnny won't stand for his woman screwing around with his cousin, will he? Apart from anything else, you've both made a fool out of him and I know he won't stand for that. And I guarantee that whatever he does to you will be a million times worse than what he did to me.'

'It's your word against ours, though, Josie, and who d'you think he'll believe? The woman he loves or the little whore who put him in prison?'

I'm ready for this. 'Maybe. But then all I have to do is show him the photo I took of you two from outside your window and, well, I'm sure that will convince him.'

And then, when she begins cursing and screaming down the phone, I cut her off. I should feel good after this – it's the first time I've actually been able to wipe the nasty smirk off her face – but somehow I feel more empty, and more alone than ever.

For a while I stay put, telling myself I don't need any more, that I've had enough to take the edge off, but then I get scared that what I've already had will wear off and I'll be back to my reality. I can't deal with that right now.

Without thinking, I grab my jacket and keys and head to the corner shop, trying my best to appear sober. But the man behind the counter doesn't care that I'm blatantly pissed, and he doesn't bat an eyelid when I plonk a bottle of gin down on the counter. I'd prefer something else – anything else – but I'm not stupid enough to mix my drinks.

I hand him a twenty-pound note and accidentally scatter the change all over the floor when he gives it to me. 'Keep it,' I say, because I just don't care any more. He tuts and curses under his breath that I've given him extra work to do, but I don't care.

Back at home I make a start on the second bottle and everything becomes a blur. Somehow hours pass and I only notice the time because someone is pounding on the door.

For some reason I think it must be Alison, and I rush to answer, almost falling flat on my face as I trip over my phone charger. I don't even remember leaving it on the floor.

But when I fling the door open, it's not Alison standing there.

THIRTY-ONE

Mia

'Josie was her own worst enemy,' Alison says.

She walks to the window and stares through the blinds before pulling them shut. 'I mean, she tried to be strong and keep things together, but in the end she was just... weak. But she couldn't see it. Oh no, she thought she was invincible, made of titanium.'

I have always found it difficult to hear anything about Josie, but now I silently beg Alison to keep talking. I need to know everything that happened. Yes, she's telling me all this for a reason, and I have no doubt she's planned it all, right down to the smallest detail, but I'll deal with whatever comes. Right now, my desperation for the truth overshadows everything else.

From my seat on the sofa, I look around the room. There doesn't appear to be anything she could use to harm me, there are no pockets on any of her clothes, and I'm convinced I'm physically stronger than her. If it comes to that.

'Were you jealous of her?' I turn to Alison, no longer caring if my words offend her. It doesn't matter any more.

She considers my question for a moment. 'Maybe.'

I expected a denial, but finally Alison is telling me something that may actually hold a grain of truth. 'Why? As far as I can see you had a whole lot more than she ever did. Your parents love you, for starters. Josie never had that.' I want to stand up but I'm too afraid to move. Alison, still standing by the window, has the position of power.

'You didn't let me finish. I think I was a bit jealous of her *to start with*. Until I got to know her. Before that all I saw was this beautiful, confident girl who would never have any problems getting any man to fall for her. She was just so different to me. I'd barely even had a boyfriend.'

I stare at Alison's face as she talks. She's an attractive girl, so any problems she had with men must have been because of who she is, what's inside of her.

'I really did want to like her, though,' she continues. 'I tried to give her a chance, but everything about her just rubbed me up the wrong way. I suppose I did that to her too, though. Anyway, none of that matters now, does it? Like I was saying, she was the kind of girl who could have just about anyone she wanted, even a university lecturer. I mean, how many people could say that they had someone risk their career to be with them?'

The ground seems to fall away beneath my feet. 'I knew you were lying when you said you believed Zach didn't do anything with her. Everything you've said to me since the day I laid eyes on you has been fabricated, hasn't it, Alison?'

She comes closer towards me. 'We'll get to the part about my lies, Mia, but to answer your first question, the truth is, I wasn't there in the room with them. I can't tell you whether or not he slept with her, but that doesn't mean he didn't want to, that he wasn't tempted.'

Alison's words are like bricks crashing against my head. 'You didn't talk to him that night, did you?' I say.

'Yes, I did, Mia, but you're jumping way ahead.' She flicks her wrist and checks the time on an old-looking gold watch. I didn't think people her age even bothered with watches any more, but then Alison isn't typical of a twenty-six-year-old. 'If I'm going to do this, I'm doing it at my own pace. We've got all night, haven't we? You're not going anywhere, are you?'

I don't answer, but once again comfort myself by clasping the cold, hard metal of my phone, still in my pocket.

'The trouble is I have a big problem with all this, Alison. With everything you say. You've lied to me so many times before, so why should I believe anything you say now?'

'That's your choice. And actually it doesn't matter what you believe. It only matters what *I* believe.'

This woman is crazy, and I've been foolish to come here, thinking I could get any sense out of her. Given her track record, how could I expect her to be honest now? 'Dominic never abused you, did he? And you put that photo of Josie on his computer, didn't you?'

'Well, I suppose that one wasn't hard to work out. Yes, that was a photo of Josie I had on my phone.'

'But where did you get it? It looked like a selfie, so she must have sent it to you.'

'She did – by mistake. I don't know who it was intended for, but I don't think it was for me. Unless she just wanted to say a big "fuck you" to me. That's what it looks like she's thinking in it.'

'And did she send it the night she died?'

Alison nods and sits on the sofa next to me. It's all I can do not to jump up and move as far away from her as possible.

'Yes,' she says. 'That's part of the reason why I came over here. I hadn't seen her for months, not even at uni. Well, I'd spotted her there a few times but always hid so she never saw me. But I was so angry with her. All those months of living together, messing with each other, took their toll on me and I just wanted... I don't know, closure? That night I was studying in the library at uni when she sent me the photo. It was late and I assumed she was probably drunk – as usual. I was so mad I just wanted to rip into her. I'd tried to before, many times, but it never quite came out right. I always ended up seeming weak. That's what Josie did to me, Mia, she *weakened* me. Made me feel like I was completely useless, though in reality I had far more going for me academically than she did.'

I take in her words, commit them to my memory for when I have to repeat what she's told me as evidence.

'So you lied to Zach when you told him you'd come here to look for your bracelet? The one your mum supposedly gave you.'

'Yes, that was a lie. There's no bracelet. It was the easiest thing to tell Zach at the time. But that's not important, Mia.'

She's right – that's just a small lie in a forest of hundreds. 'Why did you move out in the end, Alison? What had happened between you two that was worse than the fights you'd already had?'

'I told her I was going to report her relationship with Zach. Well, of course she didn't like that and threatened me. A nasty threat. And I guess it spooked me, because I knew by then what kind of family she came from and what had already happened to her, so there was no telling what she was capable of.' She pauses and turns to me. 'I'm not proud of my threat to her. Especially when I had no evidence that she and Zach had ever done anything together, but, well, that's how fuelled with rage I was. I like that phrase, don't you? Fuelled with rage.'

I grip my phone a little tighter. I don't know how much longer I can wait, but she hasn't told me what she did yet and I've come too far now to sacrifice finally knowing the truth.

How ironic that Alison actually feared Josie, given what she did. I shake my head. 'So that's why you killed her? To stop her harming you? You're going to try and say it was some sort of self-defence?'

Alison stands up, towering over me; I can't help but reel back. 'Oh no, I'm not going to say that at all. Because I didn't kill her.'

THIRTY-TWO

Josie

I stare at Zach. 'What... what are you doing here?'

He frowns. 'What do you mean? You called me. About a thousand times. Why didn't you answer when I called back? I've been worried sick about you, Josie. What's going on?'

This must be a dream; I never called Zach. He can't really be standing at my door. I grope around in my pocket for my phone and check my call history. Sure enough, there are six calls to Zach and three missed calls from him, as well as two text messages asking if I'm okay.

'Oops!' I say. 'Sorry, I must have drunk-dialled you.'

His face falls, disappointment sketched all over it. He thought I was better than this, above this kind of juvenile behaviour. 'Josie, I thought you'd stopped drinking, that you were making a fresh start.'

'What's the point?' I say. If Zach thinks I'm a stupid little girl then why not live up to his idea of me?

He hasn't made any move to come in so I'm not surprised when he tells me this probably isn't the best time to talk. 'You need to get some rest, Josie. Let's catch up tomorrow.'

But there won't be any catching up or chatting or anything else tomorrow. Tomorrow I will just be pushed aside again, into a neat little compartment in his head. Somewhere safe, where he won't let me out. I can't let him go. I grab his arm and pull him inside, expecting resistance but it doesn't come. He sighs but lets me drag him in and shut the front door.

'I shouldn't be here,' he says, 'especially if you've been drinking.' But he doesn't stop me guiding him into the living room.

'That's all you ever say, Zach.' I slump onto the sofa and pat the seat next to me. 'Just sit and keep me company, that's all. Come on.'

He checks his watch. 'Maybe for a little while. But it's pretty late and I'll need to get back home soon.' Finally, he sits down, but he chooses the seat at the other end of the sofa. 'So where's your flatmate? Alison, isn't it?'

'She moved out. Couldn't bear to be around me any more.' I laugh, even though there's nothing funny at all. That's the beauty of gin.

Zach ignores it and tries his best to pretend I'm sober. 'Well, that's a good thing, isn't it? You two didn't get along, did you? At least this is one less thing for you to stress about.'

But he's wrong. 'At least she was someone. Someone always here when I came home. Now there's just silence. And no food.' I start to giggle again, and even though I'm angry with myself for doing it, I can't seem to stop. And the serious expression on Zach's face sets me off even more.

He ignores it. 'But what about Craig? I bet he's here all the time.'

I throw my head back against the sofa. 'Let's just say things didn't exactly work out there.'

There's a pause, and even in my drunken state I wonder if Zach's happy to hear this, deep down in that part of him he's trying to suppress. 'I'm sorry to hear that,' he says, and I long to tell him it's because of him. Because he's the only man I want.

'Ask me why, Zach.'

Again a pause, longer this time. 'I don't think I should, Josie. It's not my business, it's between you and Craig.'

But it *is* Zach's business. I almost tell him this but stop myself just in time – I'm not that much of an arsehole. 'Drink?' I hold up my bottle of gin.

He shakes his head. 'Ha! No, thanks. And I think you've had enough for both of us.'

I take a long swig from the bottle. 'I'm only just getting started, believe me.'

'Josie, slow down. Why are you feeling so sorry for yourself? This isn't you.' He makes a swipe for the bottle but even in my state I'm too fast and pull it away.

'What's brought you to this?' he adds, when I don't answer. 'Has something happened with your mum? Is your brother okay?'

'Don't call her that – she's no mother to me, you know that. Or to Kieren, even though she's pretending she's a good one to him. Oh, God, how can I let him be in that house with her? With *them*.'

'What do you mean *them*? Please don't tell me that man's out of prison?'

'No. No, it's not him, but I think she's shacking up with his cousin – Richard. He's the one who came all the way to London to threaten me into withdrawing my statement to the police about Johnny.'

'That's just… crazy.'

'I know. It's like something off *Jeremy Kyle*, isn't it? You couldn't make this shit up. But, I'm really worried, Zach. Kieren might be all young and cute now but he'll grow up soon enough. I've got to get him out of there. I can't stand by and let something happen to him. It could be tomorrow, or years down the line, but I've got to do something.'

Zach moves closer to me and places his hand on my arm. 'You have to stay calm, Josie. Look, you've already reported everything to the police and social services – I think you have to let them deal with it now.'

'But eventually they'll stop thinking about her, they'll give up because she's putting on this motherly act, and that's when it will happen. And this time it could be worse than what happened to me!' I sound hysterical, and Zach keeps his hand on my arm. But he should let go of me. He really should.

'Listen to me, Josie. You've got to be strong. Like I know you are. Things will work out in the end, they always do. Trust me. Think of what you've already been through and survived.'

And looking at Zach now, I do trust him. Even through my lens of alcohol, I can see he has never meant me any harm, has only ever looked out for me.

I don't know I'm making the biggest mistake of my life until I'm actually doing it, but suddenly I'm moving closer to Zach, leaning into him and pushing my mouth against his, desperate to taste him, to draw him into me, to never let him go.

It must only last a second, maybe even less than that, and then he's shoving me away, his face creased with panic. 'Josie, you shouldn't have done that. We can't... I love my wife. More than love her, she's my whole world.'

Suddenly I feel sober, hearing Zach's words filled with so much anguish and pain. I'm so ashamed of myself that I run from the flat.

THIRTY-THREE

Mia

Hearing Alison's denial, there is no doubt in my mind what I have to do now. She is not going to give me any answers, so I have to accept that I'll never know exactly what happened that night.

'I could do with some water,' I say, trying to make my voice sound hoarse, although I know she won't believe me. She can't possibly think that I will let her get away with what she's done.

But as usual, she is full of surprises. 'Fine,' she says. 'I'll be right back.'

I'm stunned that she's leaving me in the room alone when she knows I must have my mobile on me, but perhaps this is an oversight. What I'm sure of now, though, is that the front door is locked, and there is no way for me to get out. That's the only thing that would explain her confidence.

But I still don't know what she wants from me.

Keeping my eye on the living-room door, I quickly pull out my phone and dial Will's number, hoping he'll answer and that it won't go to his voicemail. When he picks up, his voice is thick with tiredness and without a word I toggle down the volume and slip the phone back in my pocket, still connected, and shout out to Alison.

'I'm here,' she says, appearing in the doorway with a glass of water. She puts it on the carpet by my feet, but she must know there is no way I will touch a single drop.

'What am I doing here, Alison? You're claiming you didn't harm Josie, so what do you want from me?'

She joins me on the sofa. 'Well, it's like I said before: I wanted you to know the truth about Zach. That he didn't sleep with Josie. It's important to me that you know that.'

Alison's psychosis must run deeper than I imagined; her words are a huge contradiction to what she said earlier about not being able to know. But of course she has an answer when I question her about this.

'I said I wasn't in the room with them, so I have no real evidence, but like I told you before, I spoke to Zach and I believe every word he said. Every single word. He really loved you. And Freya. You must have been his whole world.' She begins biting her nails.

But we weren't, were we? I tell Alison that nothing she is saying makes sense, but she doesn't reply. I need to tread carefully; I don't want her to clam up now.

'Tell me this, at least: why did you need me to know all this?'

'Because I want justice for Josie.'

And now it's all becoming clearer. Somehow, in her deranged mind, and despite what she's saying, Alison must think Zach killed Josie. Just like everyone else. Her claim that Dominic was involved must have just been to get me to listen; she wouldn't have known whether or not I thought Zach was guilty. It's possible she's blocked out any memory of what she herself did, and is now focusing it on Zach. With him dead, I'm the one who must take the blame for what happened to Josie.

I need to keep her talking so Will has long enough to call the police. He will have heard our conversation and I hope it's enough for him to realise something is very wrong. And once he's called them, they should be able to find our location from my mobile phone – at least, I hope so. It is too risky to mention the address now with Alison in the room with me. As much as it hurts me to do this, I need to go along with whatever she already believes.

'You know, I've blamed myself all these years, Alison. For all of it. What happened to Zach and what happened to Josie.'

'Is that right?'

I look her directly in the eye: it's the best way to convince someone you are telling the truth. 'Yes. The truth is, if I'd been a better wife then maybe none of it would have happened. He wouldn't have had space in his life for Josie. Whether or not anything physical happened between them, there's no disputing he had feelings for her. And that's what I blame myself for.'

Alison stares at me. 'Well, this is interesting. Carry on.'

My heart pounds heavily in my chest. 'I probably expected too much from him. From our life. I always strove for perfection but that must have been exhausting for him. I mean, I know it was. He said as much. Not in a nasty way, but still. It was there between us.'

With the words catching in my throat, I tell Alison how I pushed Zach to have a baby when he probably wasn't quite ready. 'He was trying to write his novel and I just thought he'd be able to do it easily, even with a newborn in the house. It never occurred to me that he'd struggle, because *I* didn't. I just got on with it.'

Alison utters a contemptuous laugh. 'Well, of course Little Miss Perfect can cope with anything.'

'No, you've got me wrong. I don't think I'm perfect. Clearly I'm not. Because I lost my husband, my little girl's father. She was only two at the time, Alison.'

She nods, and just for a second it's easy to forget the situation we're in. We could just be two friends discussing my grief. 'Poor thing. That must have been hard for you, but I'm sure you coped. You always do, don't you?'

It's becoming clear that Alison's not going to make this easy for me. She's determined to force the blame on someone, even if the pieces of the jigsaw don't fit. Could never fit.

'I just did the best I could in a bad situation. That's what I always try to do, Alison.'

'Well, it's not always that easy for other people, Mia. We're not all as perfect as you. I'm not. Josie certainly wasn't.'

I ignore her jibe. 'Why do you want justice for Josie? You hated the girl. Why have you spent five years obsessing over this?' Nothing I'm saying is what any counsellor should say, but we're beyond that now.

'Ha! Obsession? Is that what you think this is? Well, if that's what you want to label it then it doesn't matter. But this is not about obsession, Mia. Like I said, this is about putting things right. I spent so much time hating her when I should have been there for her. She wasn't a bad person, and I should have taken the time to get to know her. Well, I left it too late then, but now she's gone I have to try and make amends.'

Make amends for killing her. Anxiety is overwhelming me now. The longer I sit here, the more I know Alison's not going to let me leave this flat in anything but a body bag. I can only pray that Will has heard every word and called the police. But time seems to have slowed down, and it's an effort to keep her talking. She will see through me soon enough, I'm sure.

'Alison, you said earlier you didn't think there was anything going on between them, so what do you think he was doing in the flat that night? It was late, wasn't it? Way past ten o'clock.' I need to catch her out, get her to say something that will incriminate her.

'Everyone thinks she must have been blackmailing him. Threatening to report their affair and tell you about it. Zach's family and his job were both important to him, weren't they, Mia? Important enough that he'd do anything to protect those things.'

This is exactly how the media reported it. That Zach must have carefully planned to kill Josie, initially with the drugs he used on himself, but somehow that didn't work and so he stabbed her instead, and hid her body somewhere. Afterwards he panicked and took his own life with the poison he'd intended to use on her.

'Where do you think her body is, Alison? What would Zach have done with it?'

'I have no idea, Mia. And I don't know why he came back here afterwards to end his own life. Maybe he came back to clean things up but then it all got too much for him. Because he wasn't an evil man, was he, Mia? Despite it all.'

There are tears in my eyes now but I force them back.

But not before Alison notices. 'Who are those tears for, Mia? For Zach? For Josie? For yourself?'

'For all of us, Alison. Because it was all just a terrible mess. But you don't need to keep living like this, you can be free of it all.'

'Free of what? And what am I living like?'

'Out for revenge – on me, because Zach's not here for you to take things out on. Five years is a long time to have lived your life for this… cause.'

'Are you trying to counsel me, Mia? I think it's a bit too late for that so maybe you should save your breath.' She stands up and leans over me. 'Actually, before you shut up you can—'

A loud crash silences us both and it takes me a moment to realise it's the front door being forced open. The police have come. I am safe, and they will take Alison away and lock her up.

Two officers appear in the doorway, and I'm surprised to see they're both armed. They must have wondered what they would be walking into. I don't even hear what they say – I'm too numb, the fear I've kept at bay since I stepped inside this flat suddenly paralysing me, even though I'm safe now.

All I know is that they're talking to Alison, and then she is screaming at them. 'Wait, you've got it all wrong!' She squirms and wriggles, trying to break free from the officer who has gripped her arm, but she has no chance against him.

'Tell them, Mia, tell them the truth—'

They haul her out of the flat before she can say any more.

That's all I hear before I sink to the floor and let out the flood of tears I've been holding back.

'Are you okay, miss?' the other officer asks.

'I will be,' I manage to say. 'I think I will be now.'

THIRTY-FOUR

Josie

I'm in a bar and I have no idea where it is. I only know I must have walked here. But who cares? It's so crowded there's barely even any standing room. But this suits me fine. I don't want to be noticed, I don't want any dirty old men perving over me, offering to buy me drinks with smug smiles on their faces because they'll think it entitles them to something else.

All I need is more drink. But as I walk to the bar something doesn't feel right and I can't think what it is. All I know is that everything in my life is wrong. And I've done something terrible. I just don't know what.

'What can I get you?' one of the bartenders asks. He doesn't even apologise for me having to wait so long to be served, and he barely looks at me. To him I'm just another irrelevant face.

'A Bloody Mary,' I say, trying not to slur my words.

He heads off to make it and I lean on the bar to wait. When he comes back he places my drink in front of me and mumbles something I assume is the price. I reach for my bag then realise I don't have it. I check my pockets but there's no money, only my mobile, which from the blank screen I assume has a dead battery.

'Oh, sorry. Left my purse. Be back in a sec.' I rush from the bar and get swallowed up by the crowd. I don't even care if the barman sees me leave through the front door and thinks I'm some lowlife. Maybe that's exactly what I am.

When I get outside I realise I haven't walked that far after all. I'm on Ealing Broadway, only about half an hour from the flat – I just need to get home. It only occurs to me when I'm standing outside my front door that I don't have my keys. I must have dropped them somewhere. 'Damn it!' I scream into the night. 'Shit!'

I fall back against the door, preparing myself to sleep on the doorstep until I can call the landlord in the morning, but instead of it catching my fall, I am toppling into the flat. I must have left it open, which is no surprise given the state I'm in, but thank God I did.

Inside, I debate whether to grab my purse and go back to the bar, but I can't even remember where I left it. I stumble into the front room and somehow Zach is there, lying asleep on the sofa. What is he doing here? He must have come to see me and fallen asleep waiting because I've taken so long to get home.

I crouch down beside him, nestling my head against him. He doesn't move. 'Hey, Zach,' I say. 'I'm back. What are you doing here?' I shake him and he still doesn't move.

That's when I peer closely at his face and start to scream even before I fully register what's happening. Zach is not asleep. He's dead.

What have I done? What the fuck have I done?

THIRTY-FIVE

Two months later

Mia

I sit on the balcony and watch Freya and Will playing football on the beach below. Her sun hat is too large for her and keeps falling off, but each time it does, Will picks it up again and places it back on her head.

This place is a paradise, and it's impossible to feel anything other than calm here, with miles of sandy beaches stretching in both directions, and the sea clean and warm. We couldn't be further from London, physically and metaphorically.

It was Will's idea to come to the Maldives. We needed to get away, he'd said. Far away. He knew exactly what I needed: distance from Alison and everything that went before. So now I sit here with a cocktail in my hand and my feet up on the opposite chair, warming my skin in the sun.

For years I couldn't let myself think about the night Zach died; it was too painful, and reliving it would only cause even more of me to crumble away, to die inside, but now, in this beautiful place, I will allow myself to think of it. This will be a final goodbye to Zach, before I start my new life with Will.

Zach and I had always been close. He used to tell me I completed him, that he couldn't imagine existing without me, and then we'd laugh about it because it sounded like something from a soppy romance novel. But he meant it, and I felt the same way. I let myself go with Zach in a way that I never had with anyone else. In my previous relationships I had always kept people at a distance. Not because I'd been badly hurt before, but because I didn't believe in them. But then Zach appeared and I fell hard. He might not have realised how hard, of course, because I'm too controlled to let emotions get the better of me, but I knew I was in deep.

And that was fine. For a long time, everything was perfect.

But then something changed. It wasn't noticeable at first, so I can't pinpoint exactly when it happened, but slowly Zach became more distant. I assumed it was because he was struggling with his novel, but he'd been working on it as long as I'd known him, so I wasn't completely convinced it was that. Then I thought it must be because of Freya; Zach adored her but he couldn't quite juggle parenthood and the rest of his life the way I could.

He never said this to me but I could tell he was simply going through the motions on autopilot, just trying to get through each day. I tried to make things easier for him; I made sure I took Freya out for hours every day so that he would have time to himself, time to harness his creativity. I did all the cooking and housework, but it made little difference. Zach continued slipping away from me.

I'd never been a jealous or insecure person. I always believed that if someone doesn't love you any more then you have to let them go, let them be free. At least that's what I thought I believed, until I convinced myself that Zach was having an affair. Then suddenly there was everything to fight for. And I'm nothing if not a fighter. I couldn't let Freya lose her dad, not when I knew in my heart he still loved me; I had to find out what was going on.

The first time I saw Josie she was sitting in the park with him. I'd decided to surprise him and turned up unexpectedly at the university with something nice for his lunch. I convinced myself I was doing this as a thoughtful gesture, but the truth was I wanted to check up on him. *Be careful what you wish for.* They weren't doing anything, or even sitting too closely together on that bench, but I knew something wasn't right.

It wasn't the way she was staring at him, her eyes full of adulation – I was used to Zach's students idolising him. It was the expression on *his* face that gave it away. I hadn't seen him look that calm, that at peace, for a long time. It reminded me of when we first met, how I was his whole world and nothing else seemed to exist.

This terrified me as much as if the two of them had been kissing. I don't remember exactly how long I watched them for, but when I headed back home I felt dead inside. But I didn't have the proof I'd need to confront him, and I wasn't about to hysterically accuse him, like an out-of-control, irrational woman – I was stronger than that. I would get my evidence.

It was all I could think about while I sat trying to entertain Freya, to give my little girl the attention she needed and deserved. But I was so numb that I just couldn't be mentally present in the room with her.

For days I checked Zach's phone. But there was never anything that looked suspicious. Of course there wasn't – he was too clever to leave a trail. This made me feel even worse, as if he was betraying me even more by hiding his tracks so well.

And then, weeks later, there was a text message from someone called Josie. I still remember the words. *Finished now. Just wondering where you are?* Yes, those two sentences could have been harmless, but Zach had never mentioned anyone called Josie before and I was sure he didn't normally keep any students' numbers in his phone.

So I did some investigating. I went through all Zach's paperwork and found class lists of all his students with photos below their names. There were hundreds of them, and it took me ages to find her, but suddenly there she was, staring at me with a confident, pretty smile on her face. Josie Carpenter. The girl I had seen in the park.

But this still wasn't enough evidence, so I started following him, whenever I had a free moment. I was lucky that Graham and Pam always watched Freya, and they never asked too many questions. They were only too happy to spend time with their granddaughter.

I thought I couldn't feel any worse – and then I saw Zach go into her flat. He wasn't there for long, but it was long enough for what I knew they must be doing in there. Of course I couldn't see, but that just made things worse. My imagination conjured up the two of them together, Josie's hands all over my husband.

I threw up all over the pavement. And then I left. I couldn't risk him seeing me. Although this was all the evidence I needed, I no longer wanted to confront him. I couldn't. He was Freya's dad and leaving him would have far-reaching consequences for the rest of her life. I couldn't do that to her, I had to keep our family together.

So weeks passed and I said nothing. It wasn't because I was being weak, accepting what Zach was up to – it definitely wasn't that. But my focus turned to Josie and I couldn't get her out of my mind. She was barely into adulthood and it sickened me that Zach could find anything attractive in, anything in common with, someone so much younger than him.

But I knew there had to be something about her. Zach would never have been interested only in someone's body; it was minds that attracted him. And this made me loathe her even more. This cut me even deeper.

I investigated that girl's life. Googled her at every opportunity. She didn't have a Facebook or Twitter account, but I did find an interesting article about an attack that had happened when she was eighteen. I should have felt sorry for her but instead I was even angrier. Here was a young woman who'd been through hell, so why was she now inflicting a different hell on someone else? Her family sounded awful; dysfunctional didn't even come close to describing it, so she must have known what breaking up Zach's marriage would do to Freya.

But she didn't care. She continued to pursue my husband, weaken him, because I was sure he would have put up a fight – at least initially. Zach is not a nasty man. I've never doubted that he loved me and Freya.

What I didn't bargain on, when I decided not to confront him, was that my whole life would fall apart. He became increasingly distant and I found it harder to cope. I'd never been depressed before but now I found myself sinking deeper and deeper into a bottomless hole.

How would I ever free myself? How would I ever get Josie Carpenter out of my head? She haunted my dreams, sabotaged every waking moment of the day so that I, too, was just going through the motions with Freya. Feeding her, keeping her clean, making sure she had enough exercise and play, but never really being present with her.

That's what did it: the thought that I was losing time I'd never get back with my daughter. Josie Carpenter had now stolen my whole family.

It is surreal now to recall what happened next, as if it wasn't me at all. I'm watching someone else take the steps I took. It's not me I see stepping into that Internet café, researching drugs, checking whether or not they would leave a trace once they're dissolved in water.

I smiled when I came across a suitable one: Ketamine, a horse tranquilizer. It would guarantee death almost instantly. Better that way. Kinder. I wasn't a monster, after all – I had a heart. It proved difficult to get hold of any, but eventually I managed to find a dealer who could point me in the right direction.

The night I went to her flat was warm. I remember I didn't need a jacket. Zach had taken Freya to his parents' house and was planning on staying there. To give me a break, he'd said. 'Because despite being superwoman, you look exhausted.' He didn't know the half of it.

Once again I was numb when I knocked on her door, observing myself from above, not part of any of this. Perhaps I wouldn't have used the ketamine, maybe I needed it for reassurance, just in case, but when the door opened and it was Zach standing there, something inside me snapped.

His mouth hung open and he stumbled to get any words out. 'Mia, what? What are you doing here?'

I didn't answer but stormed past him, not even noticing my surroundings. I searched every room but there was no sign of Josie.

'Mia, I can explain.' Zach looked distraught, following me around, and this made me even angrier. If his being there had been innocent then he wouldn't have been so anxious, would he? He would have already explained what he was doing in one of his students' flats.

He grabbed my arm and led me into the living room. It was bare and ugly, with only a dirty cream sofa and a sideboard in it. Zach didn't belong here. Neither of us did. Although we'd both lived in far worse places, we had long ago put our student days behind us.

Zach guided me to the sofa and then sat beside me. I let him because I was still numb – I still wasn't me. We stared at each other for what seemed like minutes, but must have only been seconds, before he finally began to talk.

'Mia, I'm not sure how you came to be here, but I promise you this is nothing weird. One of my students, Josie Carpenter, lives here and I've just been helping her out. She's... she's been having a really tough time this year and has been through a lot. I know what this might look like – oh God, I really do – but I am *not* involved with her. You have to believe that.'

I stared at him, somehow able to control my rage. 'Where is she, Zach? Why are you here and she's not?'

He took a deep breath. 'Basically she got upset about something and stormed out. She left her keys so I was just waiting for her to come back. She won't be able to get in if I go so I've had no choice but to stay here.' His words seemed to merge together and I didn't really hear any of them.

'What was she upset about?'

My question hovered in the air between us. It was make or break time for Zach. He was either going to lie to me or tell me the truth.

'This is really hard to tell you but she... she tried to kiss me. I'm so sorry, Mia, I should have known she was falling for me. I should have kept away from her. I'll never forgive myself for letting it get that far. But I swear to you, I never touched her. Not once.'

And with that lie, Zach sealed his fate.

'Okay,' I said. 'I'm going to go home now. We can talk about this later. Can I use the bathroom?'

Zach's eyes widened. 'Um, yeah. It's the door past the kitchen on the left.'

I expected him to follow me, to not let me loose in his girl-friend's house, but he stayed where he was, perched on the sofa with his hands resting on his knees. That was his next mistake.

The kitchen was bare, but clean in comparison to the rest of the place, and I silently searched through cupboards, looking for the right thing. When I spotted a small bottle of Evian in the fridge it almost felt too easy, like it was meant to be. Fate. There was nothing else there to drink, so she was bound to get to it eventually. It didn't matter to me whether it was that night or the following week, as long as she drank it.

Reaching in my bag I pulled out the ketamine and poured it into the bottle, shaking it, even though it was colourless and odourless, so there would be no sign of it in the water. Then, feeling nothing in my heart and nothing in my head, I placed the bottle back where I'd found it.

Then I went to the bathroom, just to flush the toilet so Zach wouldn't think I'd had time to go in the kitchen.

I walked right past him on my way out and glanced at him but didn't stop to say anything. That's what hurts the most now. I had no idea that would be the last time I'd catch sight of him. How could I have foreseen that he'd drink Josie's bottle of water?

I just wanted Josie dead. Not Zach. Never Zach.

But that's just what I'll have to live with. That is my punishment. I'll also never know what really happened to Josie, who disposed of her body and why.

Alison denies it, of course, and she's had a complete breakdown now, which isn't surprising after everything that's happened, so she's not fit to stand trial for anything. Besides, there's no real evidence, is there? And that's what it always comes down to.

There is a chance Zach didn't drink the water until much later, so maybe Josie did come back and they had a huge fight. He would have known he'd lost me at that point, and maybe his pain turned into anger. But I cannot comprehend that it was Zach who did that to her; he was always so calm, never angry with anyone. But then again, who knows what's really within us? I would never have thought myself capable of taking someone's life either.

I've thought long and hard about what Alison meant when she begged me to tell the police the truth. She knows I was there that night, she must have seen me. One thing I can't understand is why it took her five years to track me down, but then the workings of an unstable mind are never easy to fathom. It's possible she didn't know who I was until she came across my website – perhaps when she was looking for a new counsellor – and saw my picture. Then maybe it all clicked into place in her head.

Of course, she won't have any evidence that I'm responsible for Zach's death, but it doesn't look good that I never came forward. But then neither did she.

This certainly helps explain the real reason for her tracking me down. When she told me she was there that night, of course I wondered if she might have seen me, but I had to bide my time.

I had to wait to see what she would do, and always ensure I was one step ahead of her.

She wanted justice for Josie, and I was the one who had to pay. Perhaps she hoped I would confess, but her mental illness really obscured her judgement because she didn't bargain on me pointing the blame at her.

It's Dominic I feel sorry for. He knew she was troubled, but had no idea to what extent. It's just sad that half of everything Alison said was actually true, and the rest she said only to catch me out. That's why she initially tried to make out that Dominic was abusive, that he had something to do with Josie's death. Everything she said, and did, was to set a trap for me. I'm still not quite sure what she hoped to achieve by claiming Dominic had something to do with Josie's death, but it must have been an attempt to throw me off the scent. She didn't want me to think she suspected me of anything. Not until she was ready to confront me.

What a tangled web we have woven. But at least now I have my closure. No more panic attacks. I am safe.

THIRTY-SIX

Josie

It's my birthday today but nobody knows that. They don't even know how old I really am because I've added on two extra years, just to make sure nobody can track me down. So now I'm twenty-eight, not twenty-six. But time no longer matters. Every day is the same, every minute identical to the one that's gone before, and this is the way it will be for me forever. Josie Carpenter is dead, and now I am someone else, someone without the past she had. I've made sure of that.

Over five years it's become easier to remember I'm no longer Josie, easier to say *Joanne* instead. Or Jo, just in case I start to slip up. I had to pick something similar to Josie – it's too easy to get caught off guard.

But no matter what I do, I will always be waiting for that knock on the door. The one that will tell me it's all over. My time is up.

I'm not sure why I chose Cornwall to be my home – perhaps, after being in Brighton for so long, I needed to be near the sea again. There's something about it that makes me feel free, as if I could just dive into the water and keep on swimming at any moment. The sea can take me anywhere I want to go.

'Hey, Jo!' Someone on the other side of the road calls my name. My head flicks up, but it's only Alfie, the elderly man who lives further down my street. He's out for his usual morning walk with his dog, just as I am, and he crosses over to greet us, a huge smile on his face. He has no idea how such a small thing can do so much to lift my spirits.

'How's she doing today?' He leans down to give Pepper a stroke.

'Hot, I think. She's got too much fur.'

He laughs even though what I've said isn't really funny. But maybe that's just me – it's hard to find anything funny any more.

Pepper starts to jump up and begins excitedly sniffing Boxer. I pull her away and apologise, even though it's the same every time the two of us bump into each other when we're walking our dogs.

Pepper is good company for me, but I really got her for Kieren. I got him the dog he always wanted. I still live in hope that one day I'll see my little brother again, even though I know the chances of that are slim.

He'll be ten now. Ten years old and I have no idea what he looks like. What his favourite colour is, or whether he can ride a bike. I have no idea what Liv is like with him as he grows older, but I pray he at least has the courage to stand up to her, just like he will have seen me doing.

But one day I'll know all about him. I can't let Zach's death be for nothing. Something good has to come out of something so terrible.

'Are you okay, Jo?' Alfie says. 'You've gone a bit pale.'

I snap to attention. 'Oh, yeah, just a bit dehydrated, I think. This heat! It's too much, isn't it?' I have always preferred the icy-cold sharpness of winter.

'Yep, it sure is. Hey, listen to us – we moan when we don't get any sun then when we do actually get some we complain about how we can't take it! No pleasing us, is there?' He chuckles and I almost want to reach out and hug him. He is a kind man, proof that good, decent people do actually exist in this world. People like Zach.

We say our goodbyes and Alfie crosses back over the road, heading towards his house.

I watch him walk away and it doesn't feel real. Nothing I see or do these days ever does. But that's because *I'm* no longer real.

As I head off in the direction of the beach, with Pepper marching in front of me, I think about Zach, as I do every day, and once again I tell him I'm sorry. There are so many things I have to apologise to him for: being unable to hide my feelings for him, drawing him into my life, leaving him in my flat while I ran away. Not to mention the worst one of all: making it look as though I'd been killed, spilling my blood everywhere so that it was more convincing.

I had to disappear, Zach, I'm sorry.

On the beach I let Pepper off the lead and sit down, pulling my notebook and pen from my bag. I scribble some notes for my next chapter while my only companion hurtles across the sand, chasing after her ball.

Every word I write is for Zach, to prove that he wasn't wrong about me; that I can make something of myself. I didn't get to finish university, but one day I will take up my studies again. Finish what I started. And in the meantime, when my book's finished, I plan to get it published. At least this is what I tell myself. But the reality is that I can never admit to anyone who I really am, or go public with what happened, because I committed an awful crime.

Tears splatter onto my notebook, blurring the words I've just written. Perhaps today nothing more will come. No more inspiration. I have days like that. But then I just move on to the next.

I pull out my phone instead and Google my name, just as I do every day, to check whether anything new has been discovered. I tried not to do this at first, five years ago, but it ate me up inside that I didn't know what was happening in the outside world, what Josie Carpenter's presumed fate was. So I gave in and checked, and now every day it is my morning ritual, along with this walk to the beach with Pepper.

There's been nothing new for so long that for a second I think my mind is playing tricks on me when I see the article. Alison Frances has been arrested and held for questioning. I read every word, my body heating up, feeling like I will explode any moment.

Police have arrested Alison in connection with my disappearance. Apparently she was stalking Zach's wife, and they now think Alison is the one who killed me and hid my body.

I feel sick to my stomach but carry on reading. Apparently Alison has suffered some sort of breakdown, so they haven't been able to get anything out of her, other than her claims that it was Zach's wife who killed him – not suicide, as they'd originally suspected.

My pulse races and it's a struggle to stay calm. What does this mean? Why would Alison think Zach's wife had anything to do with it? I've never believed that Zach committed suicide; I have always thought it was me who did that to him. But is there any chance I've been wrong all this time?

I have never been able to come to terms with doing that to him. I was a hardcore drinker in those days, but I never once blacked out to the point where I didn't remember what I'd done. And surely doing something so dreadful as killing someone would have to come back to you, even in stages? My excitement grows as I consider the possibility that I may have been wrong. That I may be innocent.

I know how unstable Alison was, even all those years ago, so can't imagine what state she's in now, but if there's any chance I can help her, and free myself at the same time, then I've got to grab it.

At the bottom of the page is a link to an interview with Josie Carpenter's mother. Anger burns inside me as I read how 'distraught' Liv Carpenter has not only lost her beloved daughter, but now she's had to let her son, ten-year-old Kieren, live with his father in Spain. According to Liv, she has fallen apart so much that she feels it best to let Kieren's father bring him up, even though she will visit him as much as she can. 'For his sake,' she says, apparently with tears rolling down her cheeks.

But I know the truth of it will be very different from this. Liv will have reached her breaking point with Kieren, probably because she just wants to be alone with Richard, and will have been only too happy to get rid of him.

Despite seething with rage at her actions, I'm glad he is free of her. Glad that he will never have to go through what I did. I only hope his father is doing right by him. Whoever he is, I doubt he is anywhere close to the monster she is. I wonder how she tracked him down, and how she convinced him to take Kieren.

From across the beach, Pepper runs back to me, kicking up a spray of sand as she goes and dropping the ball in front of me. I throw it back out. 'Last time,' I say. 'We have to get going in a minute.'

I gather up my things and place them back in my bag. I feel lighter than I ever have, as if this is the first day of the rest of my life.

Perhaps I always knew that Josie would have to be resurrected one day. But I'm ready. I need to help Alison; I cannot let her take the blame for something she had nothing to do with. She was never a bad person, she just got lost in her life, and I know how easily that can happen. I will finally get to apologise to her. And I don't know how or why Zach's wife is tied up in this, but I will make sure the whole truth is finally set free.

Standing, I scoop up my bag and whistle to Pepper, who comes flying towards me with her ball in her mouth. 'Come on, girl,' I say. 'We need to go home and pack. Then we're going on a trip to London.'

A LETTER FROM KATHRYN

Thank you so much for taking the time to read my sixth psychological thriller, *Silent Lies* – I really hope you got involved with the characters and were taken by surprise at the end! If you did enjoy it, and want to keep up-to-date with all my latest releases, just sign up at the following link. Your email address will never be shared and you can unsubscribe at any time.

www.bookouture.com/kathryn-croft

I always thoroughly enjoy plotting and writing my books and I hope you enjoyed the ride this one took you on.

Whether you've just discovered my books or have enjoyed any of my previous novels, I'm extremely grateful for your support. Reviews are so important to authors, so if you did enjoy it then I'd be extremely grateful if you could spare a moment to post a quick review to let others know your thoughts. As always, any recommendations to family and friends would also be greatly appreciated!

It's always wonderful to hear from readers so please feel free to contact me via Twitter, my Facebook page or directly through my website.

authorkathryncroft

twitter.com/katcroft

www.kathryncroft.com

Thank you again for all your support!

Kathryn x

ACKNOWLEDGEMENTS

As always I must thank the hugely talented and hard-working team of people who have made this book possible: Keshini Naidoo, I'm truly blessed to have you as my editor – thank you for all your help and advice. Madeleine Milburn – thank you for all you and your fantastic team at the Madeleine Milburn Literary, TV & Film Agency do for me. Olly Rhodes and the whole Bookouture team – I'm so grateful and proud to be one of your authors! Thank you also to Julie Fergusson for an insightful copyedit, and Jane Donovan for her thorough proofreading skills.

Thank you to everyone who has picked up a copy of my book, whatever the format, and taken a chance on my writing. You may be a long-term fan of my work or maybe you've only just discovered me by accident, maybe you'll read my next one or maybe you won't, but whatever the case, thank you for giving me a read!

A huge thank you to book reviewers and bloggers; your time and effort is very much appreciated.

And finally, my family and friends, who never cease to amaze me with all your praise, encouragement and support. To my wonderful little son, everything I do, I do for you now and I hope one day you'll be proud of Mummy (even though you're not allowed to read any of my books until you're eighteen... actually make that thirty!)